EVERY SON'S FEAR

JOANNA WARRINGTON

2021 Joanna Warrington

All rights reserved

Disclaimer and Background to the story

Every Son's Fear is the standalone sequel to *Every Mother's Fear* and *Every Father's Fear*. It is a fictional story based on the thalidomide disaster; one of the blackest episodes in medical history, which had devastating consequences for thousands of families across the world. Thalidomide was used to treat a range of medical conditions. It was thought to be safe for pregnant women, who took it to alleviate morning sickness. Thalidomide caused thousands of children worldwide to be born with malformed limbs, and the drug was taken off the market late in 1961.

There is also mention in this book of other medical scandals which weave into this story and are used in a fictional way. The story is set in 1976. The events are loosely based on events of that year. However, the scandal concerning the use of hospital incinerators rather than crematoria to dispose of aborted and miscarried babies and the stillborn was a more recent scandal and was reported in the news in 2014. Nevertheless, it was a practice that could have been happening in our hospitals for many years before that date and could have applied to the disposal of deformed babies in the 1950s and 1960s.

I would like to thank the following people for their help with this project: Lorraine Mercer MBE, Lisa Rodriques CBE, Margaret French, Karen Braysher, Facebook group, '1970's Memory Lane' and my wonderful writers' critique group in Eastbourne, whose comments and advice were invaluable.

The characters in this story are fictitious. Any resemblance to actual persons, living or dead, is coincidental. The story reflects the situations and experiences that families and thalidomide survivors might have faced, draws on real events and real experiences and has been thoroughly researched.

St Bede's is loosely based on Chailey Heritage School in East Sussex, the first purpose-built school for disabled children in the UK. It was founded in 1903 and is where many of the British thalidomide survivors were cared for and educated. There are various schools around the UK called St. Bede's. The name is coincidental and bears no relation to any of these schools.

I have used the word 'handicap' and 'handicapped' in this book because this was the terminology used at the time, rather than the modern term, 'disabled' or 'disability.'

❀ Created with Vellum

PROLOGUE

June 1976

THE CAFÉ WASN'T much of anything, but it offered certain constants: a mug of strong tea, a pasty and privacy. Stepping inside, Vince joined the queue. The clink of china, low hum of conversation and a track by Elton John filled the air. After paying for his food, he headed to the back of the café to sit in his favourite booth, in the corner away from other diners. Approaching, he saw the booth was occupied. Two men, opposite each other drinking coffee.

'He's my son.' The words were spoken in a forceful, threatening tone. The man who'd spoken turned around, looking straight at Vince, as if embarrassed at being overheard. Vince had seen him somewhere before.

Vince wandered over to the opposite side of the café where he spied a vacant table. Lifting his mug to his mouth, he glanced over to the booth in the corner to see the two men get up to leave.

He realised now who the man was.

Jasper.

The journalist who worked with his brother. But who was the scruffy oik with him? He didn't look the type he'd imagine a talented journalist would mix with.

Vince was good at recalling faces and recognised Jasper from his picture at the top of his regular newspaper column, and from his interview in a television documentary about the thalidomide scandal.

He wished he had the guts to go over, speak to him, ask him for an interview. But now was not the time. Jasper was embroiled in something.

If anyone was going to tell his story, he wanted it to be Jasper. He just had to pluck up the courage to make that call.

Vince closed his eyes. The images were always there. There was no escape. The blood haunted Vince, splattering his skin, soaking into his clothing, leaving him smelling like an abattoir. That metallic aroma filling his nostrils. He could see it, a flash of scarlet when he closed his eyes at night. Blood, once flowing scarlet through tiny veins.

And the flesh—a tangled mess, ruins of a child, a monster, hard to tell. Those images replaying in his head in a never-ending loop of horror. And the faces of the mothers. Their agonising screams, as if their dreams had bled out right there onto the floor, everything those women had longed for, all the love they'd hoped to bring into the world. He remembered the doctor's instructions to those women.

Go home and have another.

Nine months after dishing out the sweeties—that wonder drug.

Thalidomide.

All those years stuck in that basement, what it had done to him. It was those memories that spurred him on. He wanted his story to be heard and it wasn't too late. But had he the guts to bare his soul, tell the world?

Pondering that thought, he traced the top of the mug with a finger in endless circles, a habit he realised started way back when he worked at the hospital.

Leaving the café, he saw the men still chatting on the other side of the road. He wandered along the pavement, half an eye on them. They parted, saying their goodbyes.

A blonde woman waved to Jasper, who joined her and kissed her on the cheek.

On a whim, Vince crossed the road and followed the scruffy man. At the end of the road the man called out to a boy standing outside Woolworth's.

'Toby, come on then, time for football. Did you buy any sweets in there?'

Was this the boy that Jasper had been referring to when he'd said, *he's my son?*

Vince liked a mystery. It kept his mind occupied. And if he could find out as much as he could about Jasper's life before approaching him for an interview, it would help.

1

August 1976

ANY OTHER YEAR, Sandy would have appreciated this glorious endless summer they were experiencing. But thirty weeks' pregnant, feeling like a blob, every fibre of her body was uncomfortable and swollen. Her floral dress clung to her legs as she arrived at the doctor's surgery for her regular antenatal appointment. She dreaded the thought of a long wait in an airless, windowless room heaving with sweaty bodies, restless, noisy children. This appointment was going to be hard. She wanted to ask the doctor something important and that was all she could focus on.

Sandy pushed through the double doors, checked in at reception and plonked herself down on a plastic chair. She stared at the posters on the wall. It had been tough embarking on another pregnancy. Was she doing it for the right reasons? In the end, age had been the deciding factor. Thirty-six, her body clock ticking faster. It was now or never.

The midwife popped her head round the corner of the waiting room and called Sandy in.

'Almost at the finish line now, Mrs Cooper,' the midwife said cheerily over her shoulder as Sandy followed her into the consulting room.

Sandy climbed onto the couch while the midwife washed her hands vigorously at a sink in the corner of the room, drying them with several paper towels. 'Is baby moving a lot?'

'Yes, if it's a boy he'll be a goalie or a girl, she'll be a ballerina. It goes mad when I'm in the bath.' Sandy laughed. There were different shapes that pressed from inside her stomach. A fist, a foot?

'I'm going to check your weight, blood pressure and baby's size and position. Then if you can pop to the loo, we need to do a urine test to check for protein. Your blood test for anaemia came back fine.'

After completing her checks, the midwife asked, 'do you have any questions?'

'Yes, I do. Nearly sixteen years ago I had a baby. A boy. He died soon after he was born. I never got to say goodbye. To this day, I still don't know what happened to his body. I was too scared to ask. But now that I'm pregnant again, it's playing on my mind. My mum told me not to dwell on it, to forget him and I thought that was for the best. All I was told was that he had no arms. When I asked the doctor who helped deliver him, he said it was a one-off, a freak of nature. I took those tablets, Distaval, for morning sickness. It was only months later that I read about thalidomide in the newspapers. And my husband was working for a medical journal and knew a lot about it. I've always assumed he was a thalidomide baby, but nobody's ever told me for certain. I know that none of this is relevant to this pregnancy and all this time later, but it's been bothering me.'

The midwife looked at her with compassion. 'Can I ask you to wait outside? I'm going to speak to your doctor, and we'll have a look at your notes. I agree with you. You need answers and you've waited long enough.'

Sandy returned to the waiting room, anxious about what her medical records would throw up.

Until her pregnancy she'd been involved at St Bede's, the nearby school and residential home for handicapped children, mainly helping with fund-raising, where she'd talked to some of the parents of thalidomide children. One poor mother hadn't found out until ten years after the birth of her child that the medication her GP had prescribed was Distaval.

A short while later she was asked to return to the consulting room where her doctor and midwife were waiting.

'Was my baby a thalidomide?' Sandy blurted out as soon as the door was closed.

'We can't say for certain, but it's probable, given you were prescribed Distaval.'

'Why didn't my doctor get in touch with me?' Sandy asked. Tears were rolling down her cheeks. She thought she'd come to terms with the past. Every emotion hit her at once. *Why? All this time later?*

She wasn't alone. She knew that. So many thalidomide families had never been given answers. In a small way this was comforting. But that didn't make it any easier. Her baby was damaged. Damaged by the tablets she'd swallowed.

The doctor folded his hands in his lap and looked embarrassed. 'I can only guess that he thought it was for the best you didn't know. Or he could have been as much in the dark as you were.'

She'd never been able to mourn. That was the fact of it. 'It's unforgiveable. I shouldn't have had to put two and two together based on what I read in the newspapers.'

'I'm sorry, Mrs Cooper. You've been through a dreadful experience.' The doctor swivelled his chair back and forth then gave a polite cough as if indicating the conversation was over.

Why couldn't they just admit they'd been in the wrong?

They were supposed to be professionals. She felt her blood rising.

'What happened to him? What happened to my baby? Where is his grave?' The questions were fired like bullets as anger took hold.

The midwife and the doctor exchanged glances. 'Your baby was cremated.'

'They didn't ask me if I wanted the ashes.'

THAT EVENING OVER DINNER, Sandy told Jasper about her antenatal appointment. She wanted to tell him how she'd been feeling lately, the questions that had been running through her head, the conversation at the surgery.

They were tucking into steak and chips. Jasper sagged back into his chair, put his knife and fork down and reached out to touch her hand. 'That's good. Nothing's going to go wrong this time.'

This was Jasper. His calm, kind voice, trying his best to reassure her. She wondered how he coped, how he could spend so much time hanging out with Toby. The boy was a constant reminder. Didn't it bring it back to him?

She stared at her plate of food; her appetite gone. It was different for him. It had been her journey, not his. But every time she saw Toby, it was a reminder of what she went through.

2

Toby peered into the hamster's cage. Eek, what had happened to Elvis? He'd lost half of his fur and there was a bright red spot on his back. Elvis was struggling to climb the walkway to the upper level of his cage. As he watched, the poor little creature took a tumble. It broke Toby's heart to watch him suffer like this. Toby opened the cage and picked him up. His belly was covered in one big dark brown patch. His fur was now patchy and thin, and his skin looked like the eczema on the back of Toby's legs. It was a pitiful sight. Poor little Elvis. Toby was dreading him dying.

Toby thought they should take the hamster to the vet. Maybe there was something the vet could do to put him out of his misery. It wasn't right to leave him like this.

Bill put his hand on Toby's shoulder. 'He's not long for this world, son, he'll slip away in his sleep any day now. He's done well. He's two years old.'

After putting the hamster back in the cage, Toby tried to feed him—a slice of cucumber, a piece of strawberry—but he wasn't interested in food, not even a slice of banana. He had to drink. Water would keep him alive, for now. Toby carefully put him down while he filled an eggcup with water, then offered it to Elvis who managed a sip.

'I think he's got cancer,' Bill whispered from behind Toby.

Cancer was a killer. That was how his mum had gone when Toby was twelve. He hadn't been allowed to visit her in the hospice.

'Did Mum suffer like this?' He wanted to ask his dad if she'd had giant blood spots on her tummy and gashes on her face, sticky eyes, and shaky legs she couldn't stand on. Like Elvis. He tried not to think about it, but it was hard not to.

'No, she was out of it, on morphine.'

IT WAS the middle of the night. Toby crept down the stairs, avoiding the creaky step where there was a worn patch of carpet, careful not to wake his dad. Glancing up the stairwell he heard his dad's thunderous snoring coming from the front bedroom, sounding like a lawnmower in full throttle.

As he tiptoed into the kitchen, Toby's nose wrinkled. The smell was worse. It was sweet but also like rotting meat. Before reaching the corner of the kitchen, he held his breath and strained to listen. When he heard nothing, he wondered, could this be it? How long could it go on for, this waiting? If Toby was going to catch him eating, drinking or playing, now was the time, because Elvis was nocturnal. Toby waited for the familiar scratching sounds he desperately wanted to hear. When there was still no sound, he nudged the light switch on with his chin and inched towards the cage, terrified he was going to find his beloved hamster, Elvis, dead. His eyes darted around the cage. Where was he? Elvis was curled up in a ball at the bottom of the cage. He was alive. But in pain. He guessed that much. He looked like a doughnut with a heartbeat. Toby wondered why he wasn't sleeping in his snug cotton wool-filled bed at the end of the plastic tubing and then he remembered how he'd struggled to climb the walkway to the upper level of the cage.

It wasn't right to leave him like this. Surely there was something the vet could do.

Toby leaned towards the bars, watching his back rise and fall, wondering how big his little heart was. He imagined a pea-sized heart beating away, but it couldn't be that big. The size of a lentil, those horrible things that Sandy always put in stews to—in her words—bulk out the meal and make it go further. How could that lentil carry on beating, pumping blood around his frail body?

∽

'I THINK we'd better take him to the vet,' Bill said solemnly over breakfast. 'I thought he would have slipped away peacefully in his sleep by now.'

Toby stopped eating his cornflakes and looked sad. Bill's heart went out to him. The last time he'd seen his son this broken was when Rona, Bill's wife, had died. It had been hard supporting his son through such a difficult time, but he'd had to get on with things as best he could. It hadn't been easy. He'd been a self-employed builder at the time and keeping the business afloat had been imperative. Bill deeply regretted the way he'd handled things, taking solace in whisky, drowning selfishly in his own sorrow, disregarding his son's grief for the woman Toby thought had been his mother.

Elvis was only a hamster, but Bill was determined to be understanding. He had to be extra sensitive about everything that happened to Toby because life wasn't easy for the lad. Toby was born with a deformity called phocomelia. He had normal legs, unlike many of the thalidomide-damaged children, but he didn't have arms. His flipper-like hands were attached to his shoulders. Growing up he'd become proficient at using his feet for everyday tasks, including now, holding his spoon between his toes to feed himself.

'I'm going to really miss Elvis, Dad.'

'So am I, son,' Bill said while still dwelling on the past. He looked directly at Toby to show the lad he had his dad's full attention. 'The way he always scuttled out of his bed when he heard me at the worktop chopping up veg. It won't be the same without the little fella.'

'And watching him eat a nut between his paws.'

'We better get it over with. No point in letting the little critter suffer any longer. It's a shame you can't do the same when people get really sick, have them put down. Would be more humane.'

'Are you thinking of Mum? You never talk about her.'

'Yeah, guess I am,' Bill said, staring into his mug of tea.

'Was she in a lot of pain before she died?' Toby whispered, as if scared to ask the question.

'I like to think she wasn't,' Bill said, getting up and slinging his empty mug into the sink.

'Can we bury him in the garden?'

'Of course. I'll ring the vet and we can take him over there after your football course.'

∽

ENGROSSED IN THINKING ABOUT ELVIS, Toby had forgotten about football. He'd always loved football, which is why his dad had signed him on to the three-day holiday programme. Courses like this one kept him busy during the long school holidays and meant that he was mixing with children who lived in the nearby town of Haslemere and who attended the local comprehensive school. Toby knew deep down that he had to get used to mixing with able-bodied children. He had to get over his fears, otherwise he'd spend the rest of his life feeling self-conscious, aware of being different. He longed to fit in to what he called the 'normal world' outside the handicapped environment of St Bede's.

'I'm not in the mood for football,' Toby grumbled.

'It'll do you good,' Bill said. 'Will broaden your horizon.' Toby wasn't so sure. He knew he was right, but the memories of being bullied when they'd lived in Blackpool, Toby a pupil at the comprehensive, were still vivid. His hand burned with a cigarette, chained up in a wood and threatened with a butcher's cleaver—it was still fresh in his mind and made him wary of what he called 'normal kids.' Coming down to Haslemere to attend St Bede's, a residential and day school for handicapped children, had been an enormous relief. Toby felt at home, as if he belonged, being around children like himself. They all had something wrong with them and he'd no longer felt the odd one out. Jasper, Sandy's husband, and Bill's closest friend who Toby looked up to and admired, would agree with Bill. Jasper often told Toby, 'You need to integrate.' For a while he'd hadn't known what the word meant. It seemed like a new-fangled word he'd made up, but Toby understood what Jasper meant and agreed with him. He needed to integrate into the wider community because the day would come when he'd have to leave St Bede's and brave it out into the big wide world. He dreaded the thought of that day. With just one year left at St. Bede's, Toby would take his O levels the following summer. He had no idea what would happen after that and where he would go next. He was both scared thinking about it, but also excited, not knowing what opportunities the future would hold.

3

'Come on then, upstairs, get your stuff,' Bill coaxed.

Toby looked at him. 'Can't you, do it? Would be quicker.'

That wasn't going to happen. His mum had taught him how to be independent and had insisted he try to do things for himself.

'It won't do him any good if we're constantly running around after him. That's what your mum used to tell me and she's right. I do enough around here as it is.'

He could still hear her voice in his head. After she'd died, his dad had been tough with him, repeating all the things his mum used to say to chivvy him along. Even though over the years he'd moaned and complained and at times been stubborn and lazy, he knew their approach had paid off. He'd got into a pattern, a way of doing things. He could cope and was proud of that. Many of the other thalidomide-damaged children at St. Bede's couldn't, but they were much worse than him. Some had neither arms nor legs.

Toby ran upstairs and into his bedroom. Life wasn't easy for him, but he found alternate ways to do things. He picked up his stick with a hook on the end of it and grabbed the clothes he needed, holding the stick in his mouth, and putting the items into his kit bag.

Gripping the strings of his kit bag between his teeth, he headed downstairs. The course was about developing football skills: passing, shooting, heading, agility, balance. Yesterday had been the first day of the course and he hadn't enjoyed it. He'd attended holiday courses like this one before: swimming, skateboarding, and sailing and loved them, but the boys on this course unnerved him.

'How many boys are on the course?' Bill asked when he was back downstairs.

'Eleven. There was something about the way they looked at me yesterday—not all of them—just a few.'

He didn't want to elaborate. It was the same look he'd seen in the eyes of the three bullies at his old school. Were they sizing him up, about to enter a boxing ring? It made him feel scared and he wasn't looking forward to the day ahead. But what was going to happen? Nothing. He was being stupid. It was the memory of the brutal attack he'd suffered three years ago that still played in his mind.

'I'll drop you off at the clubhouse,' Bill said, slipping sandwiches and an apple into Toby's bag.

'It's not far, I'd rather walk.'

'Okay, suit yourself. I'll ring the vet and we can take him early this evening.'

'I feel sad.' Toby frowned and looked towards the cage.

'Me too.' Trying to be cheerful, Bill ruffled Toby's mop of strawberry curls and suggested getting another hamster.

'I don't want another one,' Toby said, aware that he was sounding stroppy and ungrateful. 'Elvis was a legend, the best hamster ever. It won't be the same.'

. . .

FROM THE COTTAGE where they lived in the grounds of St. Bede's, Toby followed the bracken-flanked footpath to the main road and on towards the village. It was a baking hot day and the tarmac felt sticky under his flip-flops. The sun was beaming down, there wasn't a single cloud in the sky, the heat was intense and already he was starting to sweat. His fingers itched, but he couldn't scratch them. It had been an exceptionally hot summer according to the news and Toby couldn't remember when he'd last seen a drop of rain. He'd assumed the weather would break eventually, but it wasn't showing any signs of that happening. It was horrible having a five-inch-deep bath and sharing that bath with his dad, and his clothes weren't getting washed as frequently—all to save water because that's what the government were telling people to do.

He should have taken his dad up on the offer of a lift, but his stubborn streak had got the better of him. The other boys had walked in yesterday, so could he. He hated being the odd one out and made every effort not to be. He couldn't help having no arms, but he could do his best to fit in. If they saw him being dropped off, they might call him a baby.

The walk passed quickly because he was deep in thought. When he reached the village recreation ground, Toby looked up to see several of the boys laughing at him. They were slumped against the clubhouse, waiting for the course instructor to arrive.

One of the boys—a lanky lad with spiky ginger hair—nudged his friend and in a loud voice said, 'Look who it is? The spaz.'

'Oi, spaz, don't suppose you'd be up for a game of basketball later,' a short boy with spindly legs said. Toby wanted to tell him, just because he had no arms it didn't mean he couldn't play basketball, but something caught in his throat. He opened his mouth to speak but the words wouldn't form. 'Didn't think you would,' the boy said with a smirk on his face as he glanced at the others. 'Or a swim.' Why was he so tongue-tied? If only he could stand up for himself and tell them he could swim and play basketball. He was good at basketball and used his shoulders to hit the ball into the basket. Everything he wanted to say died on his tongue.

Toby wished he hadn't come today but luckily the instructor had just arrived and was parking his car. He could have spent the last few hours of Elvis's life watching him sleep in his cage, stroking him, talking to him. A thought struck. *What if Elvis gets thirsty?* He'd watched Elvis stagger to the eggcup. He was so poorly he needed help drinking. Someone to tip the cup towards his chin. Not to be able to drink. Imagine. How awful. *I'm going to spend the whole day worrying, why oh why didn't I bunk off today?*

In the changing rooms, Toby found a corner away from the other boys, took out his dressing stick and hurriedly put his football clothes on before asking the instructor to help him with his boots. Many of the boys were okay and he joined in their wisecracks. Toby took a sneaky peek round the changing room. Mostly he felt safe, but the one who'd called him a spaz and his mate, the short one, they made him feel nervy. He'd do his best to avoid them. If nothing went wrong out on the field and he played well, they wouldn't pick on him. But even that, Toby thought, was no guarantee.

'ALL RIGHT, boys, it's too damn hot,' the instructor shouted across the field, wiping his brow with the back of his hand. 'I can't take this heat any longer. We'll pack up early. Anyone due to be picked up or is everyone okay to walk home? Toby, what about you?'

All eyes turned to Toby. It was just after lunchtime and the course wasn't due to finish for another hour. He'd enjoyed the morning and didn't want the attention to be on him, to be singled out as different.

'I'm walking home.'

The boys headed for the changing rooms, a few pulling their t-shirts off as they sauntered across the field. The heat felt like a serpent coiling around Toby's limbs. Warm sweat trickled down his back and his thick hair cut in layers to resemble his hero, Kevin Keegan, clung to his head like a blanket, locking in the heat. He was desperate for a shower.

'It's hot enough to fry a breakfast on the pavement today,' the instructor said yanking open the door to the hut, the boys swarming through, kicking off their boots, tossing socks across the floor where crusts of bread, an apple core and satsuma peelings lay among the discarded clothes. The air was thick with sweat and smelled of damp towels and old trainers. There were no windows to let in fresh air.

'You played well, Toby,' the coach said coming over to Toby. 'You've got good spatial awareness.'

'Yeah, mate,' another boy added. 'Wish I could dribble like you.'

'You don't need to come on a course like this,' someone else said. 'You're a great player.'

Their comments boosted Toby's confidence. They were just what he wanted to hear because most of the time he didn't think he was that good at football.

The boys bumped and elbowed each other as they rushed for the shower, leaving a trail of clothes in their wake. There were three showers in a large communal area and Toby welcomed the streams of water needling his skin. With his eyes to the ground to avoid looking at the other naked boys as they laughed and joked, comparing their willy sizes with silly comments to each other like, 'you need a magnifying glass to see your worm,' he watched the water swirl into a little cyclone down the drain. Why were they so bothered about the size of their willies? At least they had normal arms and hands. At least they could touch their willy, hold it. That was something that Toby was never going to be able to do and lately that had started to bother him because things were happening to him, usually in bed at night. But he was learning, exploring, experimenting. With every new life experience he was finding his own way.

'You boys not ready yet?' the instructor called through. 'Come on, I'm waiting to lock up.'

Not wanting to walk into the village with the others—although he would have liked to get to know them if they'd shown an interest in him—Toby loitered for a few minutes outside the hut with one of the boys, Greg.

'One day I want to play like Kevin Keegan,' Greg said.

'In your dreams, mate.' Toby laughed.

After a short chat with Greg, he said goodbye and left the football grounds, slipping into the twitten—the path running adjacent to the recreation ground. A few paces in, he saw them. A small group of boys hanging around at the far end of the path. Cold fear ran through him. He recognised the boys from the course. The shortie, Dave, was leaning against the fence and the other two, Steve and Mike were standing opposite, next to the brambles tumbling down the wall. He stopped walking. Was there another way to get home? No. Anyway, why should he turn round, why be frightened? He didn't want to carry this fear. He'd done it for the past three years. He willed himself, *be brave, act normal, deep breaths.*

'It's a wonder you can see the ball on the pitch with all that hair in your eyes. You look like an overgrown sheepdog,' Dave said, smiling as he approached. If they were going to take the mickey out of his hair, then that was fine. He could cope with that.

'Hot work, wasn't it, lads?' Toby replied.

Steve stepped out, blocking the path so that Toby couldn't pass him. The sun was beaming behind Steve's head, obscuring his vision, but without arms, Toby couldn't block the light. Steve's head, shaped like a potato, sat on his shoulders as if he hadn't got a neck. He let out a laugh in Toby's face, but it wasn't an ordinary laugh. No sound came out of his mouth. His entire body shook. Taking a piece of bubblegum out of his pocket Steve unwrapped it and shoved it into his mouth, crushing the wrapper in his fist and flicking it over Toby's shoulder. Why did bullies always chew gum? Did they think it made them look hard? Through cold eyes like bullets, Steve stared at Toby, chewing his gum hard and fast. His mouth twisted and Toby waited for a big strawberry bubble to emerge from his mouth. They were inches apart and Toby didn't dare move. Steve was standing, his legs wide apart threateningly. For one awful moment he thought the boy was going to lean towards him and let the bubble splatter all over his own face. Steve popped the bubble, then made loud cracking noises as he sucked it back in.

Steve stepped aside with a chuckle, and Toby prepared to leg it down the path. 'Not so fast, Sunny Jim, we've got a few questions to ask you,' he said with an intimidating grimace on his face as he stood in front of him, his hands in his back pockets in a relaxed manner as if he sensed that Toby would not challenge him. 'Not s' fast.'

Toby peered up at him. He was at least a foot taller. His face and neck were sprinkled with freckles, an entire galaxy of them. Toby wondered how many there were; it gave him something to think about because it felt as if he was being held at gunpoint.

'What do you want to ask?' His voice sounded weak and pathetic, and all he wanted to do was crumble.

'We'd like to know…' Mike said, taking a sharp intake of breath, a smirk on his face as he twizzled round to glance at Steve and Dave before turning back to Toby, 'how you wipe ya arse.'

'What?' Toby's mouth fell open. He felt his face redden and hoped the boys would mistake the red face for sunburn. 'I think I'll go now,' he muttered, looking at the ground.

'Not till you've answered the question,' Dave said, sniggering.

'That's private.'

'But you're different,' Steve said, folding his arms. 'You can't blame us. We're just curious, aren't we, boys?'

'Well it's a dumb question. You need to wipe your minds. It's a private thing.' He'd said too much, there were three of them, one of him.

'Don't get all smart with us, spaz,' Dave said, moving towards Toby, making him back into the prickly brambles. 'It's a private thing,' he said, raising his voice to mimic him.

'Yeah, he's too cocky for his own good,' Steve said, spitting onto the pavement a foot away from Toby's trainers. 'Answer the bleeding question. You ain't got no arms, so how do wipe ya arse? It's a straightforward enough question.'

'I'll give you my brand new Parker pen if you tell us,' Mike said.

There was no way that Mike would hand over a brand new Parker. He was teasing him.

The three of them were standing in a semi-circle. Toby shut his eyes and wished the ground would open and swallow him. What were they going to do to him if he didn't give them a proper answer? He thought of the worst things that could happen: a hand around the neck, being pushed over, a thump in the chest.

'We're waiting, short arms,' Mike piped.

The air was spiky with hostility. He wanted it to be over. And then, from somewhere deep within, Toby felt shoots of strength take root. He was going to be brave; he was fifteen for God's sake, he couldn't cower in his cave every time he was picked on.

'How do *you* wipe your bum?' he asked, pushing Dave aside with a hard nudge of his shoulder. Dave was short, he could tackle him any day. The boys stared at him with confused expressions. 'Do you fold the toilet paper, or do you crumple it?

Do you wipe from back to front, or front to back? Do you have books to read while you're sitting on your thrones? Which hand do you use? Do you whistle while you wipe?' The questions were coming thick and fast and although Toby's heart was banging in his chest and his voice was wobbly, he felt strong. Mike, Dave and Steve weren't expecting this, they were rooted to the spot, silent. Toby stepped aside.

The spell broke. 'That's none of your business, spaz,' Mike said with a snarl.

'Come on, lads,' Steve said, 'leave the kid alone. He's good at footie, he's not s' bad.'

Toby looked Mike in the eyes, smelling the victory of the conversation. They weren't going to hit him. He was just the object of curiosity. They were teasing him. He let out a sigh of relief. 'See you all tomorrow,' he said.

And with those words he turned to continue along the path, looking ahead and not daring to turn around, terrified they were going to take him from behind and wrestle him to the ground.

4

Toby lay on his bed staring at the ceiling listening to Deep Purple. Despite the comforting warmth of the late afternoon sun streaming through his bedroom window, his mind was clouded. He'd enjoyed the football course and had learned some new moves and even won the praise and admiration of a few of the boys and the instructor. But he felt down. Was this because of the encounter with Dave, Mike and Steve or the fact that he was about to lose Elvis? He felt sad about his hamster, but he'd recover from the loss, forget in time. It wasn't like losing his mum. He'd never forget her, never recover, but had learned to accept the pain. People told him that time was a healer, but every morning when he woke the first thing that came to mind was that his mum was no more. He missed the soothing click of her knitting needles while she watched the telly and he still had all the jumpers she'd knitted for him. No one could replace her. When his mum left, a part of him had died too. He was a different person, although how, it was hard to say. Toby felt sad—the kind of sadness that seeped into your bones rather than the type that exploded in a cascade of tears. Tears were for girls, for sissies.

He reached for the photo frame on the windowsill with his

foot. It was laid on its front, glass side down. He couldn't turn it over, not today, it was just too painful sometimes to see her face. Knowing she wasn't there to support him.

He kicked the frame to the floor. Why did he even have a photo of her?

His mind ricocheted between feeling positive and despairing. Dave, Mike and Steve were just teasing him, poking fun. He was different, they were naturally curious. In just a few weeks' time he'd be applying for the local college. He'd have to get used to the sort of thing he'd encountered today. But the thought left him feeling leaden. Would he fit in at college? Toby often dreamt of living on another planet where everyone was like him and where everything was set up for people like him. It was going to be a struggle to fit in. They'd have to learn that he did things differently to them. That meant failing until he got it right. He hoped they wouldn't step in to make his life easier. How could he learn if people never gave him the chance to give something a go?

What course should he apply for? His dad wanted him to go into a trade, but their close friend Jasper said he was bright enough to take A levels and go on to university provided he worked hard. He valued Jasper's opinion more than his dad's and felt guilty for feeling this way, but Jasper was a smart and successful man. He knew what he was talking about. Or did he? He'd been successful without qualifications. He hadn't needed exam certificates to get into journalism. He had drive, ambition and flair. Toby admired him for that and wished he could be like him. His dad, on the other hand, had no ambition and wanted him to do an apprenticeship. He didn't see the point of long years in education. 'It's a waste of time, son, you need to be out earning money, paying your way.' His dad had freely admitted to having messed around at school, bunking off on numerous occasions. 'I get by,' he'd say. 'I use what's up 'ere,' pointing to his head. 'Common sense is all you need in life.'

Toby considered himself lucky. Many of the children at St

Bede's would be going on to residential care. His best friends, Christine, Julie and Sara, were going to John Groom's. They had no limbs, and their reading and writing was poor. Their future would be full-time care and support.

Toby looked around his bedroom. He had purple wallpaper and leather-effect tiles behind his bed and various posters adorned the walls: *Planet of the Apes* and *Doctor Who*. His room was the Battersea Dog's Home of books—a collection of discarded volumes that other people hadn't wanted, including ones left by the previous occupant of the cottage. He certainly had no interest in *The Reader's Digest*, or learning about tree felling, crocheting, or the *Museum of Cricket Bats,* but he'd read the *Observer* books on astronomy and birds. None of them were what he'd choose for himself, but he valued the shelf of *Encyclopaedia Britannica* his mum had bought to help with homework, and his collection of classics. He loved Thomas Hardy, George Orwell, Dostoevsky and Dickens. In places the stories were difficult to understand, but nevertheless he found them inspiring.

Growing up with a dad who didn't read much, Toby devoured everything there was to read. His worst fear was to end up thick. Even at breakfast he'd read the back of the cornflakes packet, then attempted to make the cardboard lion that Kellogg's had printed on the back.

Toby got up and went over to his record player, lifting the needle with his toe, then he went downstairs to turn the television on. It was Friday, five to five and time for *Crackerjack*. But just as it was about to start, he heard the key turn in the lock and his dad walked in.

'Come on, turn that racket off, the appointment at the vet's is at 5.10. Have you checked Elvis?'

'I had a quick look when I got in. He's still hanging in there.'

THE DEATH of a childhood pet was a rite of passage and even the loss of a small creature like a hamster with its very short life cycle would become a defining moment for Toby. Bill remembered his own adolescent years. His parents hadn't allowed a pet. Fairground goldfish were their limit and all because of his mother's experience with a pet parakeet called Flossy when she was young. On the morning of her sixth birthday, she ran to Flossy's cage to sing to her and found the bird dead on its back.

Best get this over, Bill thought, heading to the kitchen to pick up the cage. 'How was football?'

'It was too hot to play,' Toby said as they left the house.

'And it was too hot to work.' Bill laughed. 'I'm looking forward to some rain. Never thought I'd hear myself say that.'

They climbed into the truck and headed off down the lane. Toby sat with the cage between his feet as the truck bumped over the rough track towards the main road. 'Slow, Dad, slow. Elvis won't like it.'

'I can't help it, the road's bad and the suspension on this old thing is ropey.'

'Why do we have to drive this old pile of crap, Dad? Why do we never go in the Allegro?'

'Dunno. I might sell the Allegro. It was an extravagant buy. Can't afford to run two vehicles.'

'But this thing is dented and rusty and it belches out black smoke and what are those funny popping noises it's always making? Time to send it to the knacker's yard.'

Bill raised his thick eyebrows and glanced at Toby. 'Over my dead body.'

'Why are we so poor, Dad?'

Bill put his foot on the brake pedal and gave him a withering look. 'We're not poor. We get by.'

Toby gave him a look that said, *you sure about that?* It felt as if they were poor. 'You're always selling stuff. Anything we don't use, you flog it.'

Bill's shoulders slumped. 'We're never going to be millionaires, son. Not like Jasper and Sandy. They're what I'd call rich. Much richer than most folk with their big detached house, colour television and all the mod cons you could wish for. You can't compare us to them.'

'I wasn't.' He sighed. He couldn't help feeling envious of Jasper and Sandy. They didn't scrimp on food. Bulking out soup with porridge, making one can of beans last three days and relying on the farmer's goodwill for eggs and milk. When had his dad become this mean? He couldn't understand it as his dad was in full-time work. 'It's just that...' He shrugged. He couldn't change how his dad was.

Bill reversed into a space outside the vet's. Looking up at the Victorian building, he realised that he'd never visited a vet's before and didn't know what to expect. Strange. Even at his age there was a first for everything.

Bill picked up the cage. Elvis was curled up in the corner, asleep. Toby wondered what it would be like to be a vet, injecting animals all day. He couldn't imagine the owners would want to be in the room when that happened. How awful for the pet to be frantically looking around for their owner. To transition from life to death in a room of strangers sounded horrible. Toby decided that he'd hold Elvis while the vet injected him. He owed it to him. Like a gift for being his companion for the past two years. He'd look away when the needle came out. Elvis would sense his presence and would be less frightened and more at peace.

'I'll buy you another hamster for your birthday if you like.'

'My birthday's not till February. Can we get a dog instead? A dog would be more fun.' Toby's eyes sparkled and gleamed.

Bill made a few noises in his throat before speaking. 'Dogs are hard work. They need a long walk every day. And they're really expensive.' Bill thought of the costs, the vet bills, vaccinations, and food. Why were kids never content? He'd been nagged to death for months for a hamster and had finally grown used to Elvis, but now the lad was upping the game. They weren't getting a dog.

'I'd love a dog. We could get a rescue one free.'

'I'd end up having to walk it.'

'I could walk it,' Toby pleaded.

'Erm, not really, Toby. It would be a bit tricky.'

'No, it wouldn't.'

'How would you hold the lead?'

'You can get a special belt for me to wear round my waist with a hook on it to put the leash on. I've seen them.'

'You've got an answer for everything, son.'

Toby eased out of his flip-flops, leaving them in the footwell. In the summer he rarely wore anything on his feet. It was easier. He needed them to perform basic tasks. His feet were his hands. He lifted his left leg and hooked his big toe under the latch to open the door. 'But a dog would be good company. It could sleep on your bed, keep you company and stop you missing Mum.'

'Hey,' Bill scoffed, joining Toby on the pavement with the cage in his arms. 'A dog can't replace a wife. Stop pulling at my heartstrings.'

They walked up the steps towards a side door marked 'entrance' and went through to a large white room with bright spotlights beaming down and a reception desk in the corner.

'Sit down a minute,' Bill said to Toby as he headed towards the lady smiling from the reception. Toby spotted a couple of free chairs.

After checking in at reception, Bill carried the cage over to Toby. 'Sit down then, it's going to be a long wait.'

Bill plonked himself down and wiped his sweaty brow with the back of his hand. The lady sitting next to him turned to glance at him and uttered one word. 'Thalidomide?'

Bill looked at her but couldn't be bothered to reply.

The door opened and a child and its harassed mother

clutching a small dog entered and walked towards the reception. As they waited for the receptionist to end a phone call the child swung round and, spotting Toby, she dropped her mother's hand and headed over, halting in front of him. Her mouth was wide open, her head tilted to one side as she stared at him. She blinked frantically. Toby felt like an insect behind a sheet of glass. He closed his eyes briefly and shifted uncomfortably in his seat. Taking a deep breath, he imagined he was living on his own private island with turquoise blue sea and golden sand. Back to reality. He opened his eyes to find her still staring, so he gave her a broad smile. It was the best way to break the spell. She quickly looked away with a coy expression on her face Toby had seen many times before on other children.

'Oi, stop staring. Come 'ere,' the mother said, grabbing the child's hand and hurriedly pulling her away.

The vet popped his head round a wall at the far end of the room and called, 'Elvis.'

In his consulting room the vet took Elvis out of the cage with great care. He had a concerned look on his face and, observing him at his job, Toby knew that he treated every creature, no matter how big or small, with the same love and importance. He was a professional man. He examined Elvis and made it clear there was nothing he could do. Toby liked the way the vet didn't rush them. He led them into a back room where he talked them through the procedure. Toby was inspired by this man's passion and wondered fleetingly as he was talking whether he himself could be a vet. He only knew about hamsters, but he loved animals. Wasn't that enough? He wanted to ask the man about the requirements for the job, but it was embarrassing with his dad in the room. He knew his dad would laugh at the suggestion and tell him it wasn't the sort of job he'd be able to do.

'Can I hold him while you inject him?' Toby asked the vet.

When the vet hesitated and glanced at Toby's lack of arms with a sceptical look on his face, a tiny part of Toby lost respect for him. How did the vet imagine he'd spent the last two years caring for Elvis?

'How do you normally hold him?' he asked.

'With my feet.'

'Okay.' The vet looked thoughtful for a moment. 'Can you hop onto my consulting table, and I'll put him between your feet.' He pushed a chair next to the table so that Toby could climb up. Toby sat on the table with his knees up and made a cradle with both feet for the vet to place Elvis. With no energy left in him, Elvis made no attempt to escape. Toby quickly looked away when the euthanasia solution was administered.

It was all over quickly. 'He's gone,' the vet said.

Afterwards Toby thought the experience was surreal but also peaceful and in some ways a relief after watching him suffer for days. As soon as they got back to the cottage, Bill went to find a spade in the shed and dug a hole in the garden to bury the small cardboard box.

5
———

The following morning Toby set off towards the village. It was the last day of his football course.

Reaching the main road, he walked towards a footpath that wove between thick bracken leading to the village. Hearing a car pull up behind him he twisted his head, squinting into the already bright sun to see Jasper waving from behind the wheel of his red Jaguar XJS. The car pulled onto the verge, crushing the foliage beneath its tyres, and Jasper flicked the passenger window down, leaning over to speak to Toby.

'Hey, nipper. Want a lift to the football hut? I'm going that way.'

'No thanks, I'll get there too early, and I don't really want to hang around with the other boys.'

'What's up, big fella?' Beneath his casual tone Toby knew that Jasper was concerned for him. Since moving to Haslemere three years ago, Jasper had become a good friend and Toby, Bill and Jasper spent a lot of time together. They were like the Three Musketeers. There had been weekend camping trips, days out to see football matches, long hikes through the countryside, Brands Hatch. His dad and Jasper were so different, but they got on well, because of and despite of their differences. They often laughed at each other's humour and habits. Jasper was posh and his dad, Toby thought, was a bit rough and ready. 'Is someone bothering you?' Jasper had become increasingly protective towards him, and Toby quite liked that. He was an uncle figure, someone to whom he felt he could turn for advice if he needed to.

'Nothing I can't handle.' Toby tried to sound upbeat, brave even. He'd handled the boys yesterday—he could do it again. But a sick feeling sat at the base of his stomach. Why did he have to go through all this? Why was life so hard? If only people would accept him for who he was.

'What time does it end?'

'Midday, because it's so hot.'

'I'm just nipping into Guildford this morning. What if I picked you up? We could find a nice pub for lunch. We can sit in the garden. Any excuse to avoid going home to the typewriter.'

Toby couldn't remember if he'd ever spent time with Jasper without his dad being there. Would it be awkward? He was so used to their little threesome. It would give him the chance to talk freely without his dad making unhelpful comments or talking too loudly like he usually did.

'That sounds fab.' Toby's mood lightened. Jasper had the type of lifestyle Toby aspired to when he was older. Free time to swan off to a café or pub or play sport. Working from home with the occasional day in London. Much better than his dad's hard life, grafting all hours, coming home sweaty and dirty, moaning that he didn't earn enough, which meant scrimping on essentials. Like soap; gathering up small bits of old soap and moulding them into one piece. Ghastly.

He was looking forward to it already, especially the ride in Jasper's Jag. Dave, Mike and Steve would be dead jealous when they saw the Jag. They would think Jasper was his dad. That didn't bother him. Let them think it. 'See you at twelve,' he said.

After saying goodbye, Toby watched the car speed off down

the road. He felt mean for thinking badly of his dad. But sometimes he was embarrassed to call him Dad. He lived in jeans with worn knees and when he bent forward his hairy bottom and crack were on full display. And Toby hated driving around in a beaten-up old truck with rust patches and rubbish in the footwell. There was always something not working: a brake light or front light or the time when the exhaust needed replacing but couldn't be fixed for several weeks until his dad got paid. It was like taking a ride in Fred Flintstone's car.

But worst of all, Toby loathed his dad's bad habits, his loud, piercing cough. The way he cut his toenails in the lounge while Toby was trying to watch *Morecambe and Wise* and using the end of a spoon to clean out his ears. And why did he spill food down his t-shirt? Usually egg. Often blackberry juice. Addicted as he was to blackberries, pips got stuck between his teeth—the cause of two abscesses.

'Look who it isn't, it's the spaz,' Dave said, glancing at Mike and Steve before smirking at Toby. They were leaning against the peeling paint of the old football hut as Toby arrived.

'Hey, give him a break,' Greg said, picking his football kit up from the grass when he saw the instructor arrive, his car crunching over the gravel.

'Butt out of it, div,' Dave said with a hard edge to his voice.

Toby was glad he had an ally. At his old school in Blackpool nobody had defended him. He liked Greg. Maybe he'd ask for his phone number so they could arrange to meet up sometime.

'Do you even know what a div is?' Tom asked. 'Dumb arsehole.'

'I don't care. Expect you're gonna tell me, anyway.'

'It was one of the worst jobs in prison, which is where you'll end up, one day.'

'I suppose your old man's served time in the big house, that's how you know that piece of useless information.' Mike laughed. 'How come you're in all the bottom sets?' He stepped over to

Greg and smirked at him. Greg didn't flinch. His dark eyes bored into Mike's. He wasn't going to weaken. *Probably used to them*, Toby thought.

'Right then, you waifs,' the instructor said, joining them at the hut entrance, 'let's get you in and changed. It's a short day today, our last day. I'm sure some of you will be upset not to see me again, but that's life,' he jested. 'We're finishing at midday, pronto.'

AT MIDDAY on the dot the eleven boys spilled out of the hut into the bright sunshine. Jasper was already waiting, leaning against the Jag, his arms folded, looking as if he was posing for a TV commercial. The long bonnet gleamed in the light. He'd parked adjacent to the hut and Toby wondered if this was deliberate, so that the boys would see the car as soon as they left the hut. He wasn't a braggy boy but smiled inwardly. If they were jealous of his ride in a super car, good—let them be.

Toby headed over to Jasper who smiled and stepped towards him, ruffling his hair. From behind him, Toby heard Mike's voice. 'Must be his dad, looks just like him.'

'If that's his dad in a fancy motor, who was the short fat guy in the old truck I saw him with in town the other day?'

Hearing this, a stab of sadness washed over Toby, and he felt a rush of love towards his dad.

Jasper walked round to the passenger door, opening it for Toby. 'Hang on a tick,' Toby said. 'I need to get a friend's phone number.' He called over to Greg who was a few metres away, sauntering towards the oak tree to wait for his mum in the shade. Toby ran to him. 'Can I have your number, maybe we could meet up sometime?'

With a sheepish look on his face, Greg glanced towards Dave, Mike and Steve who were watching. 'I don't get much free time, sorry. And we'll be back at school next week.'

Toby turned away feeling deflated. Jasper must have seen the disappointment etched on his face because he swung an arm around Toby's sagging shoulders when he reached him. 'Some you win, some you lose. I learned that a long time ago, nipper.'

Toby leaned down and got into the car, breathing in the welcoming smell of leather and wood. It had an old library aroma. He'd always found the car cramped and claustrophobic, rather like walking into an old cottage thinking he might hit his head on the low beams. But today it was a welcome refuge. The car was solid, well-built. It was also powerful and imposing. The car engine coughed to life and roared as they swung out onto the road, heading along the winding lanes. Toby glanced at Jasper's smooth hands. He'd never done a day's manual work in his life but unlike his dad's gnarled hands and calloused podgy fingers, these hands were in control. He'd watched Jasper's long fingers dance across the keys of his typewriter many times, forming the rhythm of a song as each fresh white sheet of paper became a work of art. Jasper made life seem so effortless and masterful. Like now, clutching the huge steering wheel, like Sir Francis Drake at the helm of the Golden Hinde.

Jasper turned on the car radio and pushed a cassette into the tape deck; a song by his favourite band, Abba, floated out. Their music was a bit tame and clean for Toby. He preferred heavy metal and rock, but he could see their appeal and why Jasper liked them so much, especially 'Waterloo', the winner of the Eurovision Song Contest two years back. The tunes were catchy, hummable and uplifting and their fabulous costumes were amazing —all sequins, bright colours and spangled jumpsuits. If only he could get his dad into rock music. Toby really wanted to go to a concert. That would be incredible, a dream come true, soaking up the atmosphere, seeing so many people gathered in one place, to sing and dance all night. The dynamics of the musicians on stage—the whole sound experience. It would be out of this world.

Feeling a buzz of excitement, on impulse Toby asked, 'Could you take me to a concert? I really want to see some live music. Dad won't take me, it's not his thing.'

Jasper turned the volume down and glanced at Toby with a frown on his face. Toby shifted in his seat and cringed with embarrassment. It was a cheeky question. No wonder Jasper was taking his time to answer.

'Hell, yes,' Jasper yelled, turning the music up and stepping on the accelerator. 'Let's do it! Let's go to a concert.'

Toby smiled across at him. Something inside him had been ignited and being with Jasper right at that moment was the most fun thing in Toby's world. He loved that flash of impulsiveness, wished his dad could be like that, but Bill was the opposite, always cautious.

'Who have you got in mind? Frank Sinatra, Bob Dylan?'

His excitement waned. Was he being serious or taking the mickey?

Jasper threw him a playful smile and Toby knew he was teasing. 'Queen? They're playing in Hyde Park on the 18th of September. It's free.'

'Really?'

'I believe so. They want to pay their fans back for their loyalty over the years.'

'That would be so groovy,' Toby said with a gasp.

'We're gonna have the funkiest evening ever. Ask your dad to come too.'

Toby hesitated. 'Do I have to? Can't it just be us two for a change? Anyway, it's not Dad's thing.'

'That wouldn't be fair, would it? You've gotta ask him, even if he says no. We always do stuff together. We're the Three Musketeers.'

Toby's head sagged as disappointment hit.

'It's tough being a teenager. I remember how I used to feel about my parents. It's all part of growing up. You're trying to find your own identity. I can see you want to make something of your life.'

'It sounds horrible, but I don't want to end up like Dad. Going into manual labour.'

'I vehemently resisted following my dad through the factory gates. I didn't want to settle for a job on a production line. I can sense chasms opening up between you and your old man, Toby, but it's not fair to exclude him.'

Toby made a grunting sound and didn't speak.

'Let me see if I can get tickets first,' Jasper said, glossing over their disagreement as he slowed the car turning down a steep hill. The pub—the Jug and Pitcher—had a thatched roof speckled with moss and lichen. It was nestled at the bottom of the hill between several matching limestone cottages, all with thatched roofs. 'This is one of my favourite boozers. It's got a great atmosphere.' He found a space in the car park to the rear of the pub, and they made their way round to the entrance, dipping their heads as they went through the door into the dark interior.

6

Toby peered up at the oak beams and marvelled at the rows of hanging tankards. There was a smell of woodsmoke despite it being August. This was such a treat. Ever since his dad had taken to making beer from a Boots the Chemist home brew kit—storing it under the stairs in kegs—Bill rarely went to the pub. Home brew was disgusting and a few mouthfuls of the foul stuff one evening had given Toby a terrible headache. How his dad could drink it, he'd never know. He couldn't see the appeal other than to save money. Surely his dad wanted to get out to meet new friends, and even meet a lady, but he didn't seem that bothered and always complained that he was too knackered after work. Maybe it was just as well. Toby didn't know how he'd feel if his dad met a woman. Nobody could replace his mother. Anyway, it wasn't likely to happen. He always looked such a wreck: face covered in stubble, hair wild and unkempt, and grubby trousers. No, that was not something Toby needed to worry about.

At the bar, Jasper ordered a pint of beer for himself and a bottle of pop for Toby.

'The lad will have to wait outside, I'm afraid,' the barman

said.

'Yes of course.' Jasper grabbed a couple of menus from a stand, and they headed into the back garden to sit at one of the wooden tables with a view over the North Downs. Toby studied the menu. He couldn't decide.

'Whatcha having then? You're as thin as a rake, you need feeding up. You've shot up in the past few months.'

'I'm taller than Dad now. I call him shorty.' Toby laughed. Standing next to his dad they looked a funny pair, like Laurel and Hardy, their bodies were so different.

'I'll have a ploughman's,' Jasper said.

'That sounds nice. Dad only cooks boring stuff, like egg and chips.'

'You could cook. He works long hours. He'd appreciate somebody doing the cooking occasionally.'

'Dad would never let me cook. Anyway, I'll just have a sandwich, thanks. I'm not very hungry.'

'You should be hungry, after your football. At your age I didn't stop eating.' Jasper got up and grabbing the menus to take back to the bar said, 'I'll order you a big bowl of chips on the side.'

'Go on then.' Toby smiled.

'Would you mind feeding me?' Toby asked Jasper when the food arrived twenty minutes later. The garden was crowded, and he didn't like strangers staring at him when he ate using his feet.

'Sure,' Jasper said, stabbing a chip with Toby's fork. 'When I was your age, I remember my teacher saying to us, *you're all approaching the big three distractions: boobs, birds, bikes*. And he was right. You need to focus now, with your O levels coming up. How do you feel about leaving St Bede's?'

Toby pondered his answer while he ate his food. 'I'm worried about going to college,' he blurted. 'I don't even know what I want to do. I wish my life was different. I want to be accepted, I don't want to be everybody's object of curiosity, I'm sick of being me. Sick of people patronising me.' He'd said too much, Jasper would think he was a right moaning Minnie, but hearing himself speak made him aware of how he was feeling.

'But, Toby,' Jasper said leaning in, chewing his food. 'This is who you are. People will love *you*. You have a choice, to keep going or give up. We all put ourselves down, you're not unusual. Nobody's happy with who they are.'

'Really?' Toby asked, squinting because the sun was bright.

'Yeah,' Jasper said. 'You've just got to find your purpose in life. We all have a purpose. There's going to be ups and down, but you'll be okay. You trust me when I say that?' He raised a fist and tapped it lightly on Toby's shoulder.

Jasper's simple words were encouraging. He wanted to ask more. 'Look at me. How am I going to get anywhere in life?'

'You've lived in your body for fifteen years. You've coped, what are you worried about?'

'Everything's about to change.'

'You're overthinking. You've just got to take one step at a time.'

'That's a bit ironic, given that steps are all I can take.' Toby laughed.

'Hey, stop running yourself down.' Jasper fed Toby a mouthful then took a huge bite of his loaf. They were quiet while they ate. Wiping his chin with a napkin he said, with a thoughtful expression, 'You don't know what you can achieve until you try. Anyway, why all these doubts? I've seen how adept you are at using your feet. You can do most things.'

Toby hesitated before speaking. He wanted to share his thoughts with someone. Things were getting to him. 'Dad doesn't want me to do A levels. He doesn't see the point. But I love reading and I write fast.' Toby wrote using a pen gripped between the toes of his right foot, but he could also write holding a pen between his lips. 'And I can use a typewriter. I want a desk job, Jasper. I don't have the skills to go into a trade. Dad's just not thinking. He wants me to follow some of my classmates to John Groom in London. But I don't want to be locked away in an institution.'

'John Groom? What's that?'

'It's a charity that houses handicapped people. It's in North London. They have a factory workshop next to the home. Their houses were originally only for women. In return for lodgings and care, the women make silk flowers and do other crafts which are sold in the shop they have on site.'

'But what about men?'

'They've got one for men in Edgware. I don't want to live somewhere like that, having to share a room with someone else—someone who might be a lot older than me, who knows? An old lady who'd lived at John Groom's since she was sixteen came to give us a talk to encourage us to apply. She said the home was bright, airy and gay and everything adapted for our particular needs and that we'd feel secure and happier. And we'd be given work. And famous people come to visit, like Cliff Richard. Who cares about seeing him? I don't want to be put away, Jasper, and forgotten about. I want to live at home. Not in a place for spastics, paralysed people, and the blind, sharing meals like we're still at school. It would be horrible. But Dad heard the talk and wants me to go. It's as if he just wants me off his hands to make his own life easier. That's how it feels.

'My own dad had fixed ideas about my future, but your dad means well.'

'I want to make something of my life. But how will I ever do that? Please don't let him make me go to John Groom.'

Jasper had such a gift with words, Toby thought, he'd point him in the right direction.

Jasper's elbow was on the table, and he rubbed his chin with his fingers for a couple of moments before speaking. Looking directly at Toby with a serious expression he said, 'You need to decide who you are. What you are.' He pointed a finger at Toby to emphasise his point. 'Change what the label says so that people see the human not the handicap, you're a victor not a victim. It's not about having strength on the outside, it's how strong you are inside.' He balled his fist and banged his chest. 'I was a poor kid and not expected to do well. I sat in my attic bedroom studying hard under bad lighting night after night. I wanted a new label. I wasn't going to be pigeonholed: poor kid equals failed kid. I was going to push the boundaries. That fire inside me came when I was about your age.'

'I wish I had fire inside me,' Toby said despondently.

Jasper frowned and it was a few moments before he spoke. 'Do you know what I think?' Jasper tapped the side of his beer glass with his fingernails. 'I think you need extra help to get you through your O levels. From what I can gather, St Bede's isn't particularly academic. Good O level grades, particularly in maths, English and science are so important. I could help you. We could go over past exam papers together.'

Toby's eyes lit up. 'Really? That would be great. There are some things I'm finding difficult and I'm not very good at organising myself and revising for exams.'

Jasper swigged his beer. 'Whatever I can do to help, I'd love to.'

Toby's eyes widened as he processed his thoughts. 'But exam certificates won't make a scrap of difference. Disability is a wall and other people can't see over it. Out on the street grown-ups look at me with pity. I can't imagine it will be any different in the workplace.'

'Don't forget most of the kids at St Bede's are in wheelchairs. They might need somewhere like John Groom, but I wouldn't say you do.'

'What if I get good grades and employers turn me away because I'm handicapped? Whatever I do in life, I'm going to have a hard time proving to people that I can do things.'

'In the time I've known you, you've overcome many challenges'. Like learning to swim for starters. Doing well at school is the first passport to a successful future. You can do it.'

'Dad doesn't think so. Because he didn't take exams and thinks he's done alright for himself he doesn't see the point in me taking them.' Toby's shoulders sagged and his head drooped. 'When I ask for his help with homework, he says he's thick or is too tired.'

Jasper chewed his lips. 'Ask me instead. I'm more than happy to help.'

'It's okay, I'll ask the teacher.' Toby's voice was flat. He didn't want Jasper going to all that effort, but he felt as if he was sticking a pin in Jasper's bubble of enthusiasm.

'Come on, lad. I want to see you do well. What are you up to this afternoon?'

'Not much. Dad's working till six.'

'How about we go back to my house?'

Toby stared at Jasper as if seeing him for the first time. Why was he putting himself out like this, didn't he have better things to do with his time? Sandy, his wife, was heavily pregnant. Surely, she needed his help around the house. Jasper's eyes were sparked, his veins shot through as if with gunpowder, clearly enjoying this. Toby quivered, an experimental guinea pig waiting for the torture to begin. He didn't want to be used as bait, his pictures across the papers, the local celeb, singled out for special treatment. He just wanted to blend in with the crowd. He'd be picked on and the other kids at St Bede's would think he was being offered special treatment. After all, they were mainly boarding kids and didn't have the luxury of going home to a family each evening. That wouldn't be fair.

Was he being cynical? If Jasper could help him, get him better grades, he was all for that.

Toby went to say something, but somebody was heading towards them. Turning his head, Jasper put his hand in front of his eyes to block the sun and to see who was calling his name.

'Jasper. I thought that was you.'

'Ronny.'

Noticing Jasper's face tense and a flatness in his voice, Toby knew this wasn't someone Jasper particularly liked. He certainly wasn't a mate.

'Don't see much of you, as you're working on a different floor.'

'No, and I don't go in the staff canteen so much, now they have new caterers. Food's a bit rubbish.'

A grin played on Ronny's face as he glanced from Jasper to Toby. 'My oh my, your son. My God, you're the spitting image of ya father, but I bet everybody tells you that.' He laughed then took a swig of his beer. 'How old are you, young man?'

Toby's mouth fell open. He was about to answer him, but Ronny had spun round and was waving to an old man at a table on the other side of the garden.

'Sorry, got to go. Can't leave my old dad on his own for long, he gets confused. Let's meet for a drink sometime.' He fumbled in his pocket and taking out his wallet pulled out a card with his phone number and address on. 'Here, give us a ring sometime if you fancy a jar or two.'

Toby watched Jasper's face, the curious expression, the hesitation, the confusion. *You're the spitting image of ya father.*

Ronny wandered back to his table.

'Why didn't you correct him when he thought we were father and son?'

'You heard him,' Jasper said with a hint of aggression in his tone that Toby couldn't fathom. 'He was like a runaway train, hardly gave me the chance. But if he thinks we look alike—which maybe we do, maybe we don't, people see what they want to see. Consider it a compliment.' Jasper winked at him. Then he was downcast. 'No way I'm meeting that geezer for a pint.'

Toby was desperate to stay on the topic of their likeness. 'Got any photos of yourself at my age?'

'No, my parents didn't own a camera.'

'Shame. Would have been interesting to see what you were like as a kid.' Toby could tell that Jasper was only half-listening. He was too busy eying Ronny warily, so changing the subject, asked, 'So how do you know that bloke?'

'Ronny Steadman. I don't like the man. We work together but I try and avoid him. We often clash and he's a strange guy, got a massive chip on his shoulder. Thinks the world owes him a favour. He has a woe-is-me attitude. I heard he'd moved into the area. Not sure where.' Jasper, still holding the card Ronny had given him, read the address. 'Larchwood Close, Haslemere. Oh God, he doesn't live far from me.' Jasper folded the card and slotted it between the grooves in the table. 'Don't look like that, nipper, I don't like him. And he's annoyed because I was asked to go to Willesden last week to the Grunwick Processing Laboratories.'

Toby looked blank. 'Why? What's going on there?'

'The workers were promised air conditioning, but it didn't arrive. Imagine it, in this heat. The workers snapped. Trouble broke out. Not at all surprising. The managers rule with an iron rod, keeping the staff cooped up for long hours and just not caring. I was up there yesterday when the workers walked out. We'll see what happens next.'

'You're lucky to have such an interesting job,' Toby said in admiration.

'No two days are the same in journalism. But the people I work with don't change. Ever since I pursued the thalidomide story, Ronny's had a grudge towards me. God knows why he was being so friendly just then, asking me to come out for a drink. He must have an ulterior motive. Anyway, do you fancy coming back to ours for a while?'

'Okay.'

'I'll ring your dad when we get back, tell him where you are.'

7

Toby gasped. He'd never stepped inside Jasper's study. It was not at all what he was expecting. It was a large square room, as big as Sandy and Jasper's lounge, and had a leather-clad desk, a small velvet settee and coffee table. This was somewhere he'd happily spend hours, cut off from the rest of the world but learning about it in this welcoming hideout, lying stretched out and immobile like a cat across the carpet, or flicking through the pile of dog-eared newspapers on the coffee table. Bookcases hugged three of the walls from floor to ceiling, heaving under the weight of old volumes. A large expanse of glass in a sliding patio door opened into the garden. What an incredible room. His eyes scanned the vast collection, a swathe of political biographies: Churchill, Harold Wilson, Anthony Eden and more, a section on American history and literature, books by Salinger and Ernest Hemingway, John Steinbeck and a section for English literature, books by Charles Dickens, the Brontës and more. He had a sudden urge to pick books at random and read snippets. It was all here in the power of the word, filling the mind, offering the key to success. And in an instant like a light pinging on in his brain, Toby knew what he would do—

take A levels and aim for university. Then he noticed what looked like a stack of photo albums on the top of one of the shelves.

'Are those photos up there?' He looked up at the top shelf, surprised.

'Yes, of our wedding, honeymoon, special occasions. Nothing of me when I was young though.'

'That's a shame. After my mum died, I caught my dad burning all our photos. I managed to salvage just one of Mum. I keep it safe.'

'That's sad, Toby. It's hard losing someone. Maybe he did it in a moment of madness. I'm sorry I never got to meet her. I bet she was a lovely lady.'

'Yes, she was. I really miss her.' Toby kicked off his flip-flops to feel the deep red carpet, not wanting to be drawn into talking about his mum, because it made him feel sad. 'This room's amazing. If I had a room like this, I'd never leave it.'

'There's only one thing it lacks.' Jasper had a serious look on his face.

'What's that?'

'A bell cord to ring for fresh coffee and biscuits.'

Toby laughed. 'You need to train the dog to do that. Or get a secretary.'

Sandy appeared at the doorway. 'Hi, Toby, did you enjoy lunch?'

Jasper and Toby looked at each other and laughed.

'What's funny?' Sandy asked.

'I was just saying I need an assistant to bring coffee. Then you arrived.' Jasper touched her arm then turned to Toby. 'I just need to make a quick phone call.'

Jasper disappeared, leaving him with Sandy. Toby, now sitting on the carpet, digging his toes into the thick pile of carpet glanced up at her long sleek tanned legs and glossy blonde hair sweeping down her back. Without a shadow of doubt, she was

47

the most stunning woman he'd ever clapped his eyes on. Movie-star stunning and knew it.

Why couldn't Jasper have waited till she went back into the kitchen? Now he had to be alone with her. He never knew what to say to her, that was the problem. And for some reason he couldn't relax and found himself either stuttering or tongue-tied when she made conversation. What she must think of him, it was embarrassing. Why was he like this? Sometimes he hated being a spotty teenager. But never mind having to talk to her, just looking at her made him squirm and that left him breathless. She was so beautiful, even with a neat bulge in her belly that looked like a giant football. But he couldn't avoid it, she was talking to him, asking questions, he had to meet her eyes and as he did so, he felt his cheeks burn. Images popped unannounced into his head—Jasper and Sandy having sex. He winced, ashamed that he'd let his mind wander.

As Sandy chatted to Toby about their dog, his mind drifted. In recent weeks he'd increasingly wondered what it would be like to have a girlfriend—just to know that a girl liked him and that he liked her too. But would a girl want to bring a boy who looked like him home to meet their parents or friends? It was unlikely. Unless he went out with someone who was also handicapped, but there was nobody at school he fancied.

'Jasper was saying he doesn't have any photos of when he was young,' Toby said to break his wandering thoughts.

'Really?' She frowned and glanced up at the shelf where the albums were kept. 'He's got plenty.'

Surprised to hear this after what Jasper had told him, he was careful with his words, not wanting to contradict Jasper but wondering why he'd fibbed. 'I thought perhaps his parents were too poor to own a camera.'

'They were, but he had a rich uncle who took plenty of photos. But who wants to look at old pictures, they're boring, don't you think?'

'Yes.' Toby decided it was easier to agree than risk her pulling them off the shelf just as Jasper walked back in. But it was odd. Maybe Jasper didn't like the look of himself as a kid.

Jasper was back. Sandy left the room promising to bring tea and biscuits and thankfully didn't mention the photos.

~

As Sandy stood watching the kettle boil, she had one of her 'moments', when she found herself stricken with guilt. Toby's presence sometimes brought on these attacks. She couldn't help it. He was a living reminder of the child she'd lost. Like Toby, her child would be coming up to sixteen. She imagined a party in the garden or a disco in the village hall. Laughter, loud music. What would he look like, what sorts of things would he be into?

She'd always had such mixed feelings about Toby. Irritation and resentment because Jasper spent so much time with him. She felt left out. Jasper always seemed to put Bill and Toby first, arguing that they needed his support. Was that the real reason she was having another baby? A family of her own? So that Jasper would spend more time with her? At times she felt annoyance towards Toby simply because he could be a brat. But she also felt sadness and compassion because of his handicap.

What she needed in her life never seemed straightforward. At the heart of everything was simply the need to be loved. Growing up she hadn't received love, and everything she'd worked towards as an adult had been about validation, confirming she was worthy of love.

Pouring the boiling water into each mug she thought how uncanny it all was. She wished she'd met Toby's mother, Rona. To have had a friend, an ally, someone who shared a common ground. Except for one massive difference. Rona's child had lived—was now a tall strapping lad. Would she have been proud of how he'd turned out?

Sandy wondered if it had been the same for Rona. How had she lived with the guilt? Did she punish herself each day for having taken those pills? How many had she taken?

∼

Sandy came back with tea and biscuits while Toby was telling Jasper what he was studying in English literature. Toby watched her lean over the desk as she put the tray down. He felt his heart rate rise and with colour returning to his cheeks, he wished he could control the spread of pink. He felt under a spell—it was hard not to stare. If he'd seen his reflection in a mirror, his face would have been mottled ham.

'What do you think, Sandy, about my helping Toby with his schoolwork?'

Sandy frowned. 'Are you struggling, Toby?'

'A bit.'

'I remember school days. I couldn't wait to leave. I wasn't interested in all that academic stuff.' She turned to Jasper. 'Don't forget you work long hours, Jasper. You're not always around. Don't get Toby's hopes up.' Then she looked at Toby. 'Jasper spreads himself thinly.' She winked but Toby saw a serious message behind her eyes. Then she seemed to mellow. 'It's okay, pet, you can always ring us if you want some help.'

'I'll make time. Toby wants to do well, and I want him to do well.'

Toby felt uncomfortable and didn't know where to put himself. It was awkward, they were talking about him as if he wasn't in the room. Jasper was being overambitious, and Sandy at first seemed dismissive, One minute she was cold, then she was kind. He couldn't work her out.

'I think I better get home,' Toby said, feeling despondent.

'What does your dad think about Jasper helping you?' Sandy asked.

Another adult's opinion. Toby groaned. 'He doesn't know. Jasper and I were just discussing my exams over lunch, that's all,' Toby replied in a flat tone.

'Well really, Jasper, you're not his dad. Bill might not like it.'

Jasper flinched. 'I'm just trying to help, that's all.'

Sandy smiled. 'I'll be in the kitchen if you need me.' She swept from the room leaving a cloud of perfume in her wake.

Doubt crept in. Even if Jasper could help him, his dad wasn't going to like the interference because it would look bad on him—and show up his own weaknesses. His dad was funny like that. Sensitive to outside interference. He liked to do things his way.

Jasper flopped into his chair and picked up the pen on his desk. Putting it between two fingers and flicking it around, he seemed to be in deep thought. 'Look at what you can do,' he muttered to himself, in a barely audible tone, as if addressing the table not Toby.

It was several moments before he spoke and when he did, Toby saw a spark in his eyes as if he'd come up with a brainwave. 'Let's make a list of all your skills, lad. I think you're lacking in confidence. It's an age thing. But I want to boost your confidence if I can.' He opened a drawer and, taking out some paper, placed it on the coffee table. He sat down on the carpet next to Toby. 'You see it's not what you can't do, it's what you can do that matters. It's about being positive, and I know there are lots of things you're perfectly capable of doing. But I need to hear it from you.' Toby didn't know why they'd gone from discussing help with his O levels to writing a list, but he'd go along with it. He had nothing better to do if he went home. Jasper was a crackpot, but lovable and that made him smile.

'Think hard, Toby. Let's make a column for all your hobbies first, because I know you've got a lot of them.'

'My hobbies aren't going to help me with exams or get me a job.' Toby's eyes narrowed in confusion.

Jasper looked brightly at Toby. 'Wanna bet? Hobbies are very important because they teach you a whole set of skills.'

Toby's posture slumped. Unsure, but prepared to hear Jasper out, he said, 'Well you know what my hobbies are. Just write them down.'

'No. You tell me. This is your list of achievements and interests.'

Toby sighed and stared at the carpet for a moment before answering. 'I like reading but that's not going to get me a Saturday job, or swimming. And I like football. And music. And I used to enjoy helping Dad collect money from his clients when we lived in Blackpool. But that's not a hobby.'

'We'll come back to that in a minute. Music. What can you play?' Jasper's tone was upbeat and encouraging. He liked Jasper's idea of making a list although wasn't yet sure where this was heading.

'I love music, you know I do, but I don't want to earn money from it. I play the guitar.'

'I remember you played at last year's school concert. Amazing. I don't know how you manage to play using your feet.' Jasper's excitement seemed to burst out of him, and his eyes were sparky.

'It's easy. And I can play the piano.'

'Wow, I'm really impressed. You should be very proud of yourself.'

'Why?'

'Oh, come on, Toby,' Jasper said in exasperation then in his upbeat tone added, 'Which do you like best? Piano, guitar or drums?'

'The guitar, but I'm not very good,' he said.

'Stop putting yourself down. Can you sing?' Jasper asked. God, he wasn't giving up. What was it with adults? They were hard work. Toby felt like slinking off and forgetting they'd ever had this conversation.

'No! My voice is really screechy.' Toby let out a sound, mimicking himself.

'I bet it's not. But singing's not for everyone and lots of people hate the sound of their own voice. I dread Christmas carols at the church service. I only go for the sherry in the crypt afterwards.'

'My voice always sounds tight and strained.' Toby moved his legs into a butterfly position.

'You can learn to love the sound of your own voice with professional help, but we'll leave the singing for the moment.' Jasper scribbled on the paper, and they were quiet for a while. 'Aren't you forgetting something?'

'No, I don't think so.' Toby yawned.

'Oh, come on, Toby. What other things are you good at? In fact, very good at? I don't think I know of anybody with as many hobbies as you.'

'I don't know,' Toby shrugged, aware that he was emitting powerful negative vibes. 'What else am I good at?'

'Painting, you great wally.'

'Oh yeah.'

'Don't you oh yeah me.' Jasper chuckled. 'I've seen that drawing you did of the hamster. Such an incredible talent to be able to hold a brush in your mouth and paint. It's an ability I just can't comprehend. You're so gifted and I don't think you realise it. You're an inspiration, Toby, never forget that.'

A flush crept up Jasper's neck and with water glittering in his eyes he looked away and sniffed. Jasper was a softie and clearly felt deeply for Toby, he could see that. Toby was used to this reaction but never in Bill. His dad wasn't the soppy type, didn't easily show emotion, but there were times when he would have liked to see tears in *his* eyes because that would be proof of his pride.

'Most people see us thalidomides as monsters, like the Hunchback of Notre Dame.'

Jasper sniffed and ignored the comment. 'Tell me about when you used to help your dad.'

'I miss helping him on his rounds.' Staring thoughtfully into the carpet, Toby hadn't noticed the door ajar, nudging open, their Tibetan spaniel wandering in. He went straight to Toby, sniffing his toes. Toby gave him a stroke with one foot. 'I used to like walking round the estates, looking at the different houses. If it was night-time and people hadn't closed their curtains, you could see in. Dad and I would make guesses about the people's characters and personalities based on what wallpaper and pictures they had on their walls. I liked chatting to his customers. And sometimes I'd help Dad deliver flyers round when he wanted to drum up more business.'

'Ah, so how did you manage to put leaflets through the doors?'

'Dad folded them, and I picked each up with my mouth, careful not to make them wet, nudged them through the letterbox with my nose. If the letterbox was a difficult one with brushes, it was hard. Sometimes I'd put it between my toes and push it through. It wasn't too bad, and Dad carried the bag. It was okay as a pair. Much easier.'

Jasper looked like a doctor, listening carefully, seemed about to make his diagnosis. 'I've got it. Well in fact I've got two ideas. One of them needs some thought and enquiries. Come round on Monday if you can. It's a bank holiday and, Toby, bring your dad too.'

'Do I have to?' Toby groaned, pouting his lips.

'You can't exclude your dad.' Jasper winked at him.

Toby wasn't looking forward to getting home. Despite it being a testing afternoon, he'd enjoyed himself with Jasper. Jasper understood him a lot better than his own dad. They were on a similar wavelength particularly when it came to the arts. Jasper understood the importance of following your creative passions—something his dad hadn't got a clue about.

8

The temperature had dropped and there was a light breeze as Toby hurried back from Jasper's. Black thunder clouds rolled above, sucking light from the lane as Toby arrived home. Before reaching the back door, he felt the first spots of rain on his t-shirt. Looking up at the sky, he wondered, was this the end of the long hot summer? A heavy deluge had been forecast that morning, lucky he was home before the heavens opened. He plonked himself down at the kitchen table as the first crack of lightning lit the room, then an explosion of thunder, followed by pounding rain.

Bill was preparing dinner while complaining about yet another flood from the twin-tub and that he couldn't afford a replacement.

Toby wasn't listening to Bill's grumbles. He went to the window to watch the rain. Something was niggling him. The photographs.

'Rain.' Bill tutted. 'Days after they appointed Denis Howell, Minister for Drought. Pointless. What did you do at Sandy and Jasper's? You were ages.' Bill put drinks and cutlery on the table, a straw in Toby's glass of water.

'This and that.' He was deliberately vague.

'How are they?' Bill sat down and they tucked into sausage, mash and peas.

'Okay. We're invited round there on Monday as it's bank holiday.'

Bill stared at Toby. 'You know how precious bank holiday is to me. I've been working flat out.'

Toby knew this speech off by heart. *To put a roof over your head and food on the table.*

'To put a roof over your head and food on the table. When I was your age—'

Toby hadn't asked for his dad to support him. He had no choice in the matter. 'Kids these days expect to have it all their own way. At your age I wasn't a burden.'

'I'm a burden?'

'Of course not. Sorry. Wrong choice of words. You're never a burden, far from it. You know what I mean.' Bill looked embarrassed at his clumsy choice of words. 'I just need a day out, doing something fun for a change. The letterbox fair is on Monday.'

Toby groaned. In the past couple of years Bill had developed an annoying craze—collecting miniature red letter boxes. It had to be the dullest thing ever. Bill had recently joined the Letter Box Appreciation Society—a group of crusty old men with bad haircuts and wild beards. They sat at trestle tables displaying their collections, guidebooks and leaflets about the next exhibition they were going to, clutching flasks and Tupperware boxes containing cheese and pickle sandwiches for their lunch. 'I'm not going,' Toby said defiantly. 'I'd rather go to Jasper's, they're doing a barbecue and I like their barbecues, especially the toasted marshmallows.'

Toby saw Bill twist as if he was upset. 'In a few days you'll be back at school. It's the last chance I'll get to spend time with you.'

'Can't we do something else then? Anything. I really don't want to walk round a hall or a field looking at a load of stupid red ornaments.'

'You liked it last year. And there was an ice-cream van.'

'I found it funny—watching grown men play with letter-boxes, like toys. As if they're still young boys. I'm not going again.' He wanted to add that Jasper didn't have embarrassing hobbies, but he thought he'd better not. It might upset his dad.

'There's a lot to learn about letter boxes. And you like learning.'

'So you keep saying. I'm fed up of hearing about the very rare Penfold.'

'I'm sorry if I bore you.'

Bill was so out of touch with normal life. 'I like learning about important stuff. Things that matter. Letterboxes are trivia. So are AA badges.' Toby stabbed his fork into one of the sausages. He loathed his dad's stupid hobbies, taken up since his mum had died: collecting various stuff and displaying it in on the wall. No wonder his dad was always broke. That's what he spent all his money on—pointless junk. His mum would never have allowed it if she'd still been alive. Recently it felt as if his dad was trying to rebel against her memory, doing all the things she would have hated.

'My hobbies might seem trivial to you. But it's about stopping to appreciate the small stuff. All the things we pass each day but ignore or don't even notice. If more of us did that, then maybe we would relax, enjoy life and not get down.' He chuckled. 'That's the most sophisticated thing I think I've ever said in my entire life.'

Toby was surprised at Bill's words and glancing at him, he noticed a shadow pass across his face—one of sadness, rawness. And in a flash, he saw his pain. Getting by each day, having to carry himself. These weird new hobbies of his—they were about coping. His dad had always said that hugging was for sissies and a sign of weakness, but in that moment, Toby wanted arms to throw around him to make him feel better and lift his spirits. His dad looked so lost.

And under the poor lighting Bill seemed older, weary, giving Toby a glimpse of his grief and what his dad might look like in a decade's time.

'What I worry about, son, is Jasper turning you into someone you're not.'

'How do you mean?' Toby sat back in his chair, puzzled.

'Giving you ideas above your station.'

'He just wants me to do well. And he's offered to help with homework.'

'Has he now?' Bill bristled and pulled himself upright, jerking his head back, showing his insecurity. 'And does he think I'm incapable of helping you myself?'

'Sorry, Dad, but you know you can't do half my homework. You're always too tired to help. And you get bored easily. You don't have as much patience as Jasper.'

'Is that so?'

'I'm not being horrible,' Toby quickly said when he saw Bill's wounded face. 'I'm just being honest.'

Bill rubbed the bristle on his chin and looked dismissively at Toby. 'I'm sure you'll pass your O Levels, with or without his help.' His voice was flat, cold.

'But I want to do A levels after. Maybe one in English literature. I need good grades, not just passes.' Toby's voice had risen a few octaves, showing his enthusiasm.

Bill rubbed his forehead and sighed. 'It worries me. You dismiss the things I enjoy when half the stuff you're learning at school will be of no use in the real world. You need solid practical skills, not the romantic claptrap of a Brontë novel. And all that bloody Shakespeare. Who speaks like that these days? A load of mumbo-jumbo words nobody understands.'

'Well actually, Dad, did you know that Shakespeare invented about 1,700 words and phrases that we use today?'

Bill sniffed. 'I suppose Jasper told you that.'

'No.' Toby felt put out. 'I was reading about Shakespeare in a book I found in my room.' Keen to change the subject, Toby added, 'Something really weird happened today. We bumped into a friend of Jasper's, and he was convinced I was Jasper's son.'

'Why?' Bill stared at him.

Toby shrugged. 'I don't know. Maybe he thought we looked alike and assumed we were father and son. Do we? Look alike?'

'Never really thought about it, son.' Bill sniffed and rubbed his nose as if he were uncomfortable.

'I don't really look like you though. Am I more like Mum?'

Bill squirmed in his chair, twisting his body towards the worktop. 'Where's the ketchup?' There was tension in his voice and his evasiveness made Toby wonder if he was deliberately avoiding the question.

'You don't need ketchup as well as gravy.' Toby frowned. His dad was behaving oddly.

'I like both.'

Toby persisted. 'Am I more like Mum?'

'Maybe, although we've both got dark hair and you've got fair hair. Your Great Aunt Maud had fair hair. You look just like her. Same eyes too.'

Toby pulled a face. 'Have I met her?'

'No, long dead.'

Toby was frustrated with Bill's short answers. He rarely discussed anything and often spoke in monosyllables. Toby could hear his English teacher barking, *don't speak in monosyllables.*

'Have you got photos of when you were my age? I really want to see them.'

'I burned everything in that fire, after your mum died.'

'Not everything. I'm sure I saw a box of old photos when we

moved down here. Where would they be?' Toby glanced round the room as if expecting the box to jump out.

'I burned the lot,' Bill snapped. 'What use are old photos anyway?' Bill leaned towards his plate and shovelled peas onto his fork. After swallowing them he stuffed sausage into his mouth, leaving a small drop of gravy on his chin. He had a chin that stuck out like a cartoon character, or one drawn by a lazy artist, and it acted as a landing stage for bits of food.

'You've got gravy on your chin.'

'Yeah, all right.' Bill sounded irritated and reached for the tea-towel.

'You always spill food, Dad.'

'We can't all be perfect.'

'I don't have arms and I never spill food.' If his mum had been here, he wouldn't have eaten like that, but since her death, Toby noticed how uncouth his dad had become. He was a different man. He didn't seem to care any more about manners. Toby was glad he hadn't inherited his dad's chin. 'Who do you think I take after most, you or Mum?'

'The milkman!' Bill laughed.

'Stop teasing, I'm being serious. Maybe I looked like you when you were younger, or Mum when she was younger? I could ask Grandma if she's got any photos of Mum.'

That was another thing that adults were good at—being evasive when they couldn't be bothered to answer questions or turning things into a silly joke. In his dad's case he put it down to laziness.

'Come on, eat your dinner. The mash isn't lumpy tonight.'

'Your mash is always lumpy,' Toby squished a lump. 'Dad,' Toby said cagily, 'Jasper thought I should cook dinner now and again.'

'Did he? Interfering in our domestic life too, is he?' Bill bristled and Toby could see that he'd hit a raw nerve. 'He shouldn't

plant ideas in your head without running them past me first.'
Toby was surprised at how sensitive his dad seemed.

'He was just trying to be helpful.'

'Your mother was all for trying out new things with you, but I'm more cautious.'

'But you've made me gadgets so that I can do things. That was the whole idea, to encourage my independence.' Toby realised how little he'd helped around the house since his mum had died. His dad never asked for help. 'We cook at school. And Mum used to let me.' He didn't see what the problem was. He could climb onto worktops, turn the gas on and fry bacon. He could do lots of things with his feet. And he was fast, moving around the worktop on his bottom from the oven to the sink. He had even learned to turn the tap with his foot. 'Why can't I?'

'I don't want you burning the house down or having an accident, all right?' Bill looked irritated. 'It's all very well for Jasper to make these suggestions but he's not your dad and it's not his kitchen to worry about.'

'But one day I might need to cook,' Toby said in a pleading voice.

'Stop arguing, I've had a long day. It's easier if I do it. Anyway, you won't need to be an expert at cooking. You'll either have a wife or you'll be living in residential care. All I want to do is clear the dishes, put my feet up. Shame *The Two Ronnies* isn't on. That's usually the highlight of my Saturday night.'

Bill rose from his chair. Watching his dad put the kettle on and take a teabag from the caddy, Toby wondered why Bill was building a pile of festering teabags into a pyramid on the windowsill if he wasn't going to ever reuse them. His mother would never have put up with this. It was horrible. But every time Toby complained, Bill said, 'When you're grown up you can do as you please, but this is my house and my way of doing things.'

'I'm going to my room to listen to music,' Toby said.

'Keep the racket down, will you?'

'I think I might hunt for the photos before I go up.'

'I told you, we don't have any,' Bill snapped, heading into the tiny front room. Toby lingered in the doorway as Bill switched the telly on, giving it a smack on the side to make the picture settle.

He'd wait till his dad was out, then see if he could find any photos. 'Call me when *Starsky and Hutch* comes on at nine,' he said before turning to the stairs.

9

At his desk after Toby left, Jasper buried his face in his hands. The hours he'd spent with Toby had wiped him out. He was determined, desperate even, to help the lad onto that first rung of adult life. He would do whatever he could to guide him, pull strings, call in favours. Life was always going to be hard for Toby.

Despite feeling tired, Jasper was fired up. Although it was the weekend, he knew it would be okay to call his friend, a local town councillor. He picked up the telephone on his desk and dialled his number.

'Henry, how are you, mate?'

After chatting for a few minutes, Henry asked, 'So to what do I owe the pleasure of your call?'

'Town Week is coming up next month and I remember last year there were entertainers playing along the shopping street. A young lad, he's nearly sixteen, might be interested in playing the guitar.'

'I'm sure that wouldn't be a problem if he's any good.'

'I've seen him play in his school concert. He was fantastic. He goes to St Bede's.'

'He's handicapped?' Jasper picked up alarm in Henry's voice.

'Yes, you'll be amazed. The lad can play the guitar with his feet. He's got no arms.'

'Oh.'

There was a pause and Jasper thought the line had gone dead. 'Henry, you still there?'

'Yes.' Another pause. 'I'm not sure it's such a good idea, Jasper. I want to give the lad the opportunity to play, but…'

'But what?'

'I'm not sure how the public would take it, what people would think and what about his feet? Wouldn't they get sore? We need to think of the welfare of our participants.'

'Henry, his feet are his hands.'

'Right. But we could be accused of exploiting him, like one of those freak shows in Victorian times.'

It sounded like an excuse. A daft one. 'What if I bring him over sometime and you can meet him, hear him play?'

'I suppose,' Henry said cautiously, 'it wouldn't do any harm. But I can't make any promises. Town Week is very soon. You best bring him over tomorrow.'

Jasper came off the phone, disappointed with Henry's attitude. He had the distinct feeling Henry was going to turn Toby away and what would that do to the lad's confidence? He wanted so much to make a difference to Toby's life, it almost pained him, but he was also conscious he mustn't step on Bill's feet. He hated that lack of control, having to run every idea past Bill first. Goddamn it, Bill wasn't Toby's dad. Not in a biological sense. Jasper was. If Bill hadn't wanted Jasper to be involved in the boy's life, he shouldn't have confessed.

Jasper rang Bill to clear it with him, but busy cooking dinner, Bill had passed the phone over to Toby. Toby loved the idea of playing the guitar at Town Week and agreed to discuss it with

Bill and if there were any problems, Toby promised to ring Jasper back.

Resting his head on the table, Jasper closed his eyes. He was to blame. For everything. For the tough life that lay ahead for Toby. He wondered how Sandy would react if she knew the truth—that Toby was theirs. Telling her scared him to death.

A niggling voice pricked his conscience.

She's your wife, she's Toby's mother, she needs to know, you can't keep it a secret.

He could have told her three years ago—as soon as he'd found out. God knows he'd agonised for long enough, but it was a huge dilemma. Bill had begged him to keep it a secret, worried he'd be in trouble with the police and social services if it came out. But Sandy, go to the police? Would she actually? He couldn't say for sure, even if she swore not to. He thought he knew her, but people could be unpredictable, acting irrationally, without thought, especially when emotions were running high. It was simply too big a risk to take. Bill might flee, go into hiding and then Jasper would never see Toby again.

He'd always had the feeling that Sandy had been relieved to be told her handicapped child was dead. He couldn't remember what had given him that impression—the vibes she'd given? Maybe it was time to probe, clarify how she'd felt, surreptitiously ask questions. More than anything, he was curious.

He heard the door open, felt Sandy's warm hand on his shoulder and her soft voice. 'Darling, what's wrong?'

He straightened his back and turned to look at her. He put his hand on her swollen belly and smiled.

'Come into the garden and I'll fix you a drink. Time to relax, now Toby's gone.'

Jasper bristled. 'Relax?' he asked, getting up and following her through to the kitchen, where she pulled across the sliding door stepping onto the Yorkshire paving, where there were two loungers, side by side. 'His company *is* relaxing.'

The beautiful summer's day was tipping into a Gothic evening as grey clouds gathered above. There was a smell of sulphur in the air, a light breeze picking up. A storm brewing? He was glad Sandy had coaxed him away from his study. The evening would have disappeared behind his typewriter; he always had work to do.

She gave a half-laugh. 'Whoever said teenagers were relaxing?' She disappeared inside and came back with two glasses of non-alcoholic fruit punch, and they settled on their loungers to sip their drinks while the weather held.

'Teenagers are the most misunderstood people on the planet.' Jasper sighed, still pondering Toby's future with that heavy feeling of helplessness. 'Don't you remember how you felt as a teenager? Defying your parents but learning how to conform all at the same time? The teen years are the beginning of wisdom, of discovery.'

'Maybe.' Sandy looked thoughtful. 'But pregnancy stole the last year of my teens.' He sensed regret in her voice. 'When I could have been out having fun, with friends and with work.'

'Don't you ever wish things had been different?'

'I wish we hadn't split up, but I know you had to go to Manchester.'

'I'm sorry. It was a great opportunity.'

'And to be fair, my career was important too, otherwise I would have gone with you.

'It's okay. I understood. You had to stay in London.' He sipped his drink.

'It was the wrong time for us to reconnect. But a part of me wished I'd found you, told you I was pregnant. I wouldn't have felt so alone.' She swept her fingers through her hair.

'You didn't want to put me under pressure. I admired you for that.'

'It was the wrong time for a family. We were young. I accepted the baby would have to be adopted. Mum and Dad weren't very understanding though and after our baby died, they just wanted me to forget the loss.'

'What if the baby had lived and we'd brought him up together? Surely you think about our first baby sometimes?'

There it was—that familiar blankness. He could see it in her eyes. What it meant, he wished he knew. It wasn't possible to erase trauma by pretending it hadn't happened, despite her valiant efforts over the years. In that moment all he wanted was for her to offer him a glimpse of her pain. But she didn't speak, and as the minutes ticked by, it was left to him to fill the void.

'I find it exciting watching Toby's life change and helping him to make decisions that will shape the rest of his life.'

'That sounds very grand and noble of you, Jasper. Poor kid, it'll be a rocky path,' she said, with a look of pity. And then turning to him, in a teacherly tone, she added, 'But, Jasper, you have to remember, he's not your son.' Was she warning him not to get too involved in Toby's life, because they had a child of their own on the way? It certainly felt like it. 'Part of me is glad we were spared what Bill's going through. I think that's because I've always put myself first. Does that make me cruel, heartless, glad that our child died? Think how different our lives would have been. Being married, you learn to think of someone else's needs. This baby will change our lives. Just think, a human that's totally dependent on us. It's scary.'

'We would have coped with a handicapped child. You can't prepare for parenting. Life occasionally throws curve balls—you just get on with it. People are remarkably resilient when faced with difficulties.'

'Even if the baby had been healthy, I was far too young, on my own and I wanted a career. Is that such a bad thing? It feels as if you're subtly trying to have a dig at me, Jasper, for the choices I made. Mum was right to encourage me to have the baby adopted.'

'I'm not doing that at all, I wouldn't dare judge. But don't you ever wonder—what if Toby had been ours? How would you feel?' Jasper crossed his legs and clenched his fist behind his back. He'd gone a step too far; his questions were supposed to be subtle.

'I don't know, Jasper!' She looked flabbergasted. 'He's not, so it's not relevant.' She huffed, looked irritated and took a sip of her drink. 'Are you asking because you're worried we're going to have another handicapped child?' She sat up and swung her legs, hauling the cargo of her pregnancy, bare feet connecting with the paving slabs as she faced him. He noticed her skin tone, now a deathly pallor, and hoped he hadn't raised alarm bells in her mind.

'God no, of course not. Bad luck doesn't come in twos. Just pure conjecture, that's all.'

She stood up and waddled to the patio door. 'I need some ginger biscuits. Another craving's coming on.'

∽

HE WAS WINDING her up and she was glad to escape into the kitchen. She stood at the cupboard, momentarily forgetting what she'd come in for, hands gripping the side of the worktop.

She couldn't believe it. He thought her cold, heartless. She opened a cupboard door, groping for the biscuits, reeling in shock.

Of course she looked at Toby and thought about the child they'd lost. How could she not? She didn't need Jasper to ask her such an obvious question.

It was cruel of Jasper to rub her nose in it. To think she lacked human emotion.

Jasper didn't understand the circumstances surrounding the birth. How her parents had made her feel. A baby out of wedlock—what would the neighbours say?

It was all right for him. He'd done the easy bit. Leading her astray in that Brighton hotel, making her believe it would be okay not to use contraception. She didn't hold it against him, the fact they'd split up. After all, he wasn't to know she'd been pregnant. And really, he would have stood by her, if he'd found out. He was a loyal man.

Returning from the kitchen she plonked herself back on the lounger just as the first raindrops came down.

'I'd have felt ashamed. Giving birth to a handicapped child. Because that's who I was back then. I was shallow. And back then handicap was harder to accept. We were somehow made to feel ashamed if that makes sense. I'd have had a hard time coming to terms with it. What giving birth to a child with profound difficulties meant for me. I don't know how I would have reacted if he'd lived. It was beyond the realms of my life experience.' She looked up at the sky. 'We better head in, weather's turning.'

∾

HE STARED AT HER, words failing him. Her vanity astounded him. Was she so incapable of accepting imperfection? Once a model, always a model? Ever since he'd known her, Sandy had strived for that perfect, unblemished look—immaculate teeth, flawless make-up, gazing in front of the mirror for ages each morning, checking her reflection in shop windows, hours at the hairdresser. There was no doubt she was stunning: long slender arms and legs, so pure and unsullied, it was no wonder heads turned. *But ashamed—of her own flesh and blood?* How could she be so callous?

'I'm sorry,' she said, heading into the kitchen. He followed behind and they went to sit at the table. Sorry? Sorry didn't even cut it. 'I'm not explaining myself. My mother would have made me feel ashamed, she would have blamed me, even though she'd been delighted when the doctor offered me thalidomide. For her it sorted one problem—her daughter puking up every five minutes, time off work which meant I couldn't pay my share of the housekeeping. Neither of us knew at the time the dangers of thalidomide.'

Mrs Lambert. He should have known his mother-in-law was behind Sandy's negativity. The woman was poison. Always had been. Thankfully, Sandy thought so too, which was why they didn't see the Lamberts often.

'You've never really said much about your mother's reaction to the baby dying.'

'She was relieved, I could see it on her face, not that it concerned her, because the plan had been to have the baby adopted. If he'd lived and I'd changed my mind and kept him, all hell would have broken loose.'

'You would have been the family outcast. The black sheep with her deformed child.'

'Exactly.'

'She would have looked at me as a massive failure and couldn't have coped with the gawping in the street, the stigma, three hundred pairs of eyes watching us.

'Your mother is a very private woman.'

'She is. Doesn't like to be on show so there's no doubt that a thalidomide grandchild would have changed her narrow world. So yes, Jasper, I'm glad I don't have a Toby, or a Robbie or Jimmy. I'd be struggling, he'd be struggling, and she'd knock us down further and treat him like the family curse. I've never mentioned our friendship with Bill and Toby. I think she'd be horrified.'

Jasper felt his neck muscles tighten. He stared at her. 'Why does her approval matter so much? You're under a spell.'

'A good way of looking at it. I think I've always felt under my mother's spell. I am who I am because of who she's made me. Everything I do, I subconsciously or consciously think about whether she'd approve.'

'What are you afraid of?'

'Nothing.' She hesitated. 'I don't think I'm afraid.'

'Maybe you're in denial.'

'All I crave is her smile. A real smile that reaches her eyes. Is that too much to ask for? Just warmth. But that's asking for too much. When I was young, I used to compare her to other mothers, and it pained me to see what the other children had, and I didn't have.'

'I think we all do that.'

'Something was missing.' Sandy had been gazing off into the distance, her eyes trancelike. She turned to Jasper, with wet eyes.

They were quiet and then Sandy added, 'I wonder what she'll be like this time around. She's not shown much interest in the pregnancy so far.'

'Ignore her.' It was feeble advice, but he didn't know what else to offer. Mrs Lambert was a miserable and twisted woman—why, he had no idea, and didn't think Sandy knew either. But he was aware of one thing—if he told Sandy the truth, he'd be playing with fire.

Sandy didn't need to know. It was easier that way. Bill wanted him to keep quiet and it would be devastating for Toby. Adults close to him who'd lied. Jasper couldn't imagine that amount of pain. How would the lad ever trust a soul again? And how would they explain it all, the deception, the chain of events? And what that would do to his state of mind.

And now Mrs Lambert. A new factor in the equation. That sour mother-in-law, the thorn in their marriage. He didn't want Sandy taking on the burden of her mother's deeply held prejudices. The passing years hadn't made Sandy braver. He'd seen her cower, put up with her hurtful remarks.

Suddenly and inexplicably, he knew he had to do something. It troubled him that his work colleague thought he and Toby looked alike. How long before others put two and two together?

After dinner, the rain started lashing at the windowpanes.

Jasper slipped into his study. He opened his drawer and took out his stationery set and treasured Montblanc fountain pen, and decided that if he couldn't tell her, he'd write a letter instead.

Dear Sandy,

You know how much I've always loved you and I hope you never have cause to open this letter.

In case my death precedes yours, there is something you need to know. Toby is our child. The midwife who delivered our baby was Rona, Bill's wife. When the doctor saw Toby's deformed arms he didn't think the little mite would live and thought there were internal things wrong with him too. Rona was asked to put Toby in the cold room, to let nature take its course. Rona couldn't do it and pleaded with the doctor to let her take the baby home. She didn't believe he would die. She blackmailed the doctor, threatened to expose the marital affair he was having with the secretary. The doctor caved in and helped cover up the deceit. Bill wanted Rona to take the baby back, but desperate for a baby and infertile, he accepted Toby as their own. My love, you were planning to have our baby adopted. He was never going to be your child, our child.

I HOPE you can forgive me for keeping it a secret. There are so many reasons why I couldn't tell you. Please ask Bill.

I HAVE LEFT some money in my will to Toby.

YOUR LOVING HUSBAND, Jasper

HE TUCKED the letter into the envelope, sealed it and wrote on the front. *To Sandy. To be opened in the event of my death.* If he died, at least she'd know the truth. He'd speak to his solicitor next week and get his will changed. He wanted Toby to be provided for in the event of his death. There was no guarantee that Toby would become a beneficiary of The Thalidomide Trust. Bill still hadn't heard if he was eligible.

10

Jasper stepped out of his house into the outdoor glare. It was the afternoon, and white sunlight spread over the driveway and out across the parched lawn. Jasper hadn't spoken to Bill. He'd left it to Toby to tell him about Town Week.

He arrived at Bill and Toby's cottage. About to knock on the door, he heard them shouting at each other. Trying to gauge what they were arguing about, he leaned toward the door listening. From what Toby had told him, things weren't great between them. Jasper remembered what it was like to be a teenager. The rebellious moods. And something hormonal going on. Talking to his parents in simple sentences because they came across as thick and uneducated, fading them out of his consciousness, pretending they didn't exist because they had nothing of any value to talk about.

Jasper glanced at his watch and knocked. Bill, with Toby standing behind him, opened the door and blinked at him as if he was an unexpected room service person. Toby looked embarrassed when he saw Jasper, who picked up on the strained atmosphere.

'Has Toby told you where we're off to?' Jasper asked.

'Only just.'

It felt wrong of him to just turn up like this. 'I'm sorry, mate, it's my fault, don't blame the lad. I should have spoken to you first. I did try but you passed the phone over to Toby because you were cooking dinner.'

'Yes, you should have asked me,' Bill said. Then, turning to Toby, said, 'Go upstairs a minute while I talk to Jasper.'

'Dad, please. I think it's a great idea. I didn't want to tell you because you always say no.'

'Get upstairs,' he barked, pointing his finger towards the stairwell.

Toby gave up his protest and slunk off down the hall. Guilt sat heavy in Jasper's head as he listened to Toby's feet thudding up the stairs. Jasper winced and managed to smile at Bill. Jasper had always been impetuous. It was often hard not to be. It was his greatest weakness. The scrapes he'd got into over the years and all because he hadn't taken time to think things through. He could remember being a ten-year-old kid, being egged on by his mates to throw a brick through the vicar's window. Without a moment's thought, he'd picked the brick up and thrown it. Jasper shuddered. He could have killed someone. He reminded himself of the words of the Greek historian Thucydides. 'Few things are brought to a successful issue by impetuous desire, but most by calm and prudent forethought.' Such true words, but hard to follow, especially when all he wanted was the best for Toby—his son.

'Why didn't you run this past me first? I'm his father. You had no right to make plans,' Bill said.

Jasper glanced up towards Toby's bedroom window. Bill referring to himself as Toby's father felt deliberate. It stoked a kernel of rage deep in Jasper's chest. He wanted to correct Bill, remind him of who Toby's real dad was, but with Toby within earshot all he could do was glare at him with gritted teeth. After all, Bill was trying his best, despite the difficult circumstances.

'I'm sorry. I should have spoken to you first. I wasn't deliberately trying to undermine you.'

'That's exactly what you were doing.'

'The lad's talented, Bill. I don't think you see it.'

Bill, with arms folded, face expressionless, stared at Jasper. 'People are going to laugh at him.'

'This could open up opportunities for him.'

'You've put me in a really awkward position. If I tell him no, I'm going to look the bad guy. Cheers for that, Jasper. Next time, run things past me first, all right?'

'Look I'm sorry, mate, I can't apologise enough.'

Bill shook his head, a resigned look on his face as he turned and called for Toby to come down.

~

'You should have cleared it with your dad,' Jasper said crossly to Toby, as he slowed the Jag into the curve of the lane, the car bouncing over ruts and loose gravel. Its interior was clean, and Toby breathed in the pleasant chemical scent of pine air freshener. 'You put me in a difficult position. It was embarrassing.'

'I'm going to be sixteen in February. I can make my own decisions. He treats me like a baby.'

'He? Your dad. Have some respect, Toby.'

Ah, it was that respect speech again that adults frequently gave. 'I can't help it. He annoys me.'

'He's just old school, your father. It's a generational thing.'

'No, it's an arsehole thing.'

'Hey, don't call your father an arsehole.'

'Sorry.' Toby didn't like behaving like a teenage prat but sometimes it was hard to control what came out of his mouth.

'He loves you.'

'He's got a funny way of showing it.'

'Whatever you think, try and be nice to him, it's hard work being a parent.'

'How would you know? You've never been a parent.' He'd done it again. His words sounded rude and cocky.

Jasper bristled, his face hardening as he stared ahead through cold unwavering eyes. Toby felt uncomfortable. He knew that Jasper and Sandy had lost a baby. Having now upset Jasper, Toby didn't know what to say.

'I'm sure I've a lot to learn, with a baby on the way,' Jasper said coolly.

As they approached Henry's house a girl who looked a bit older than Toby was standing in the sunlight on the front drive wiping her oily hands on the back of patched jeans and admiring a gleaming bright orange moped. She looked as if she'd recently been out for a spin because she was still wearing her helmet.

'A Fizzy,' Jasper said smiling as he parked the car in front of the moped.

'What?'

'It's a Yamaha FSI-E. Lucky girl.'

'What did you just call it?'

'A Fizzy. That's its nickname. Great machine. When Ted Heath changed the law limiting sixteen-year-olds to bikes with a 50cc engine he didn't expect manufacturers to introduce a new breed of motorcycles like this one. The government's looking to change the law again though, because these beasts can nudge up to 50 mph. What do you think? Like it?'

'It's the colour of orange Spangles. My favourite sweets.'

They got out of the car and Jasper introduced himself and Toby to Henry's daughter, Lucy. She absently wiped a smudge of oil across her brow and holding a chamois leather in her other hand, polished the black vinyl seat.

'What a fantastic little machine you've got there,' Jasper gushed.

'Like it?' Lucy asked. 'I've been working on it all morning.

Checking the oil, polishing it. It goes like a dream. Mum and Dad bought it for my seventeenth.'

Jasper ran his fingers along the globe of the front lamp. 'Very nice.' His hand rested there for a moment while his eyes travelled over the bodywork for a second look, nodding before turning to the front doorstep where Henry was standing.

'Hey, Jasper, do you like the new bike? Cost me £199, but it means we don't have to drive her into college. She passed her test with flying colours.'

Toby thought Henry was a bragger. Did he need to mention the cost? He watched Lucy unclip her helmet and tuck it under her arm, then shake her long honey-coloured hair hanging sweaty and dull where the helmet had pressed against her head. She raked her fingers through it. 'The helmet plays havoc with my hair. There's so much static.' She shook her head from side to side, her hair falling into Farrah Fawcett flicks, then reached into her pocket for a hairband before twirling it into a bunch.

Toby felt breathless, as if the atmosphere between them had been sucked of air. Briefly comparing his pale skin to her chestnut tan, he averted his gaze and stared at the bike, a convenient distraction. Lucy was gorgeous. She reminded him of the actress Raquel Welch in the film *One Million Years B.C.* Wild, carefree, she oozed something. Freedom, courage, he wasn't sure. As if she knew her mind, her place in the world. He imagined Lucy on the bike with her nose to the wind. An intense feeling of admiration for her made Toby's heart beat fast and left his mouth dry. There was something about her though that scared him. Was it her confidence? He wasn't sure.

'Dad told me you play the guitar with your feet.'

'Yeah, I'm 'armless as you can see.' Toby laughed and waggled his fingers at her. She smiled but he could see uncertainty on her face, wondering if she should laugh at his self-deprecating joke.

'Henry,' Jasper said, 'meet Toby.' Toby turned to Henry, a

tall, burly man whose belly strained under a tight-fitting shirt. But when Toby looked at Henry's eyes, he felt unnerved and wanted to look away. They were black as a raven and didn't align. 'I'll just get the guitar out of the car.' Jasper turned away and walked back to the car, leaving Toby to make polite conversation with Henry.

'Won't you find it difficult to play at Town Week, Toby?' Henry asked in an Irish accent. Toby wasn't sure if it was from the north or south of Ireland and didn't want to embarrass himself by asking. Henry smiled through thin lips that looked like a scribble on his chubby face. But there was something about his expression that told Toby this was all a waste of time. Henry wasn't going to take him seriously, he was just going through the motions, agreeing to hear him play because he wanted to keep in with Jasper. Jasper had told Toby on more than one occasion, everybody wanted to stay on the good side of journalists. Jasper's favourite quote, *the pen is mightier than the sword.* 'We are the ones who expose the truth. Like we did with the Watergate cover-up and the Thalidomide scandal.'

Toby frowned. 'Difficult, in what way?'

Henry laughed and Toby saw an expression on Henry's face. A look that said, 'be a good boy and go back into the corner where you belong'.

'How long have you been playing the guitar?'

It was as if Henry thought Toby was just at the messing around stage and saw only his limitations. Toby was sensitive and aware of people's reactions to his disability. He was tired of being branded thalidomide, handicapped and judged. To his mind handicap wasn't about how he felt because of the way he looked, but more about how others felt about him because of the way he looked. In his own mind he was normal. They thought he was weak and incapable and sometimes spoke to him as if he was a shilling short of a pound.

'I've never had lessons. I just started goofing around on a

guitar at school, a few years ago.'

Henry lifted a single eyebrow.

'My dad didn't believe I could play. I had a hard time convincing him to buy me a guitar.'

Henry scratched his jaw. 'Interesting lad,' he said to Jasper who had joined them at the front door carrying the guitar case.

Henry beckoned them in, but after clocking the disbelief on Henry's face, Toby's enthusiasm was draining away.

Lucy followed on behind and that buoyed him. Although he wasn't keen on her dad, there was something about his daughter that Toby warmed to, something dazzling. He wondered how she saw him. Did she see his face, his smile, or could she only see his lack of arms?

They went into a lounge with a small window overlooking the next-door neighbour's house. Sunlight glinted on a dusty TV.

'Do sit down,' Henry said.

The walls, carpet and settee were dark green and made Toby think that he was in a forest. It was oppressive and cluttered. He wondered what Henry did for a job. Something to do with the town council, Jasper had said. There were oil paintings adorning the walls in heavy gilt frames and even a piano in the corner. Nothing about the room put him at ease, and neither did Henry's stiff manner.

'I don't know how much Jasper told you about the event,' Henry said. 'It's over two days, Saturday and Sunday. The third weekend of September. That's not long to practise. You sure you're up to it?'

Of course he was up for it, otherwise why was he here? Henry seemed intent on dampening Toby's spirit. 'I went to Town Week last year but don't remember there being music other than from the fairground rides. There were lots of trestle tables selling cakes and knitted toys, that kind of thing, a coconut shy.'

'This year we're trying something slightly different and

hoping to raise money for the local hospice. We're setting up a stage for young musicians who live in the town. A few are at performing art colleges. It's an opportunity for them to show off their skills to their friends and family as well as the general public. But they have been practising for months.' Henry winced and pursed his lips–, clearly trying to put Toby off. But why invite him along for audition? Toby loved the idea of playing on stage, but the other musicians were semi-professional and he'd be made to look a fool without sufficient practice.

Jasper straightened his back and held his hands in his lap. Toby could see the fight in Jasper's eyes. This was important to him—more than it was for Toby who reckoned Jasper was just using the occasion to write a piece about the thalidomides as teenagers. After all, Toby hadn't forgotten the circumstances in which he and Bill had first met Jasper. They'd been living in Blackpool at the time and Jasper was travelling the country interviewing thalidomides. Their unique stories were published in the newspaper, highlighting their plight, and putting financial pressure on the government to compensate the affected families. 'You're already proficient, Toby,' he said, looking from Toby to Henry. 'You've just played in the school concert.'

Henry raised his eyebrows, feigning interest. 'What did you play?'

Jasper answered before Toby had a chance. Why did people always do this? He had a voice of his own. 'He plays 'Country Roads' by John Denver really well and 'Love of My Life' by Queen. But best of all, and he'll melt your heart when you hear him, he plays it so beautifully—'Killing Me Softly'.

To Toby's surprise, Lucy clapped her hands enthusiastically and beamed at him. 'That's my favourite song. I absolutely love it. Let's hear you then.'

Jasper, who'd been holding the guitar, positioned it on a mat on the carpet next to where Toby was sitting. It was a standard acoustic guitar. Placing the toes of his left foot over the sound hole, Toby began to pluck at the strings. And with the toes of his right foot, he strummed along the neck of the guitar. After testing each string, from E, to A, D and down to E, he launched into playing the song, humming along as he went. No matter what his small audience here in this dark lounge thought, playing felt therapeutic, made Toby feel calmer, and suddenly everything felt right. He loved this song and although he couldn't sing along, he felt a great sense of personal pride. He could feel pent-up aggression, sadness and anxiety leave his mind and body as he focused solely on the notes. Towards the end of the song, he knew he could do this. He wanted to perform at Town Week. The thought of it made him feel part of something bigger than his own small world, it would help him connect with other like-minded people.

Lucy clapped. 'Extraordinary. Vivid, passionate and utterly compelling.'

Toby, all too aware that someone would always tell him what he wanted to hear, wasn't particularly moved by her excitement. Her clapping should have drawn him in, given him a rush and made him want to play again, but all he thought was, would she react like that to anyone else playing, or was it because he played with his feet? He was more concerned with Henry's mediocre reaction.

'And if I asked you to play the piano, could you?' Henry said, nodding towards the piano in the corner of the room.

'Dad, don't be mean,' Lucy squealed. 'Can't you just show some praise for what he can do? I thought he played beautifully.'

'I can play the piano, but I'm not that good.'

'And you can't sing?' Henry asked flatly.

'It doesn't matter, Dad. Stop being so negative. I can sing. We could perform a duet.'

Taken aback by this suggestion, Toby felt overwhelmed and was speechless for a couple of moments.

'You'd like that idea, wouldn't you?' Lucy urged.

Flustered, Toby couldn't get his words out and stuttered

something before saying a decisive, 'Yes, I'd really like that, if you're up for it.'

'We've already discussed this, Lucy. I don't want you involved in Town Week this year. You need to concentrate on your studies.' Glancing at Jasper, Henry added, 'She's going into the final year of college.' His tone turned steely as he addressed Lucy. 'You've got your future to think of.'

Toby could see the coming storm. At least he didn't get pressure from his dad where schoolwork was concerned. If anything, he got the opposite. He wondered how much thought Lucy gave to her future. Whether she had it all mapped out.

'This isn't going to take up much time. Anyway, singing helps me relax and it would make Toby's act so much better, more powerful.'

Toby, aware of Lucy next to him, her floral scent mingling with engine oil from the moped, felt strangely energised by the power he felt in her presence. She had an aura about her, and he felt a frisson of excitement. He wanted this duet, but Henry was deliberately scuppering the idea. He tried to imagine them practising together. Hell, she wanted to hang out with him. Why? He couldn't fathom it and she was older than him by at least a year. Surely there were other guitarists she could sing with.

'You're taking A levels next summer?' Jasper asked Lucy. 'What are you going to do after your exams?'

'University. That's what we're hoping.' Henry cut in, taking back the reins of the conversation. 'But she won't get there without hard work.'

Toby noticed the tense body language between father and daughter before Lucy looked at Toby and gave a weary sigh. 'If Dad changes his mind, we could pull off a great act. Leave your phone number with me, Toby.' She walked over to a bureau for paper and a pen, glancing back at her dad with a mischievous look spreading across her face. 'Think of all that money for charity we could raise. Double acts are always better.'

11

The day after meeting the loveliest girl he'd ever seen, Toby lay in bed recalling Lucy's face, exploring its contours in his mind, her perfect shaped nose, neither too big nor too small, her cherry-tinged lips and hazel eyes. How that face had made him feel—warm and tingly inside. Her face told him many things about her character. But suddenly, he remembered his mother's advice on women shortly before she'd died: 'look beyond the make-up and glamour. Scratch the surface, get to know her, before your mind is made up. But be on your guard.' After saying that, she'd reminded him that he wouldn't be able to have children. He wondered now, as he sometimes did, how she could possibly have known that. At the time he'd dismissed her end-of-life ramblings and utterances; she hadn't been well. Back then, adulthood had seemed so far away—it wasn't something at that point in time he needed to worry about. He'd been too devastated, consumed with losing his mother to give it much thought. All he knew was that several others at St Bede's had been told the same thing by their parents, leaving him with the idea that maybe thalidomide had affected his fertility.

Lucy's face was fading fast. Getting dressed, he had a crazy idea to draw her—a few lines, a gesture, the way she tugged at the back of her denim jeans or tucked her hair behind her ear. Until now he'd concentrated on drawing insects and trees in the school grounds and around the cottage, but he wanted to capture her spirit. Taking a pencil between his toes, he summoned up her features in turn: the curve of her waist, her dainty nose and chin, the soft layers of her hair, before making the first strokes across the paper. After sketching her face, he stopped. A great surge of jealousy towards her boyfriend took hold, without even knowing who he was or if he even existed. She must have one. And why would she be interested in a boy like Toby? What was he thinking?

He flung the pencil across the room and scrunched the paper between both feet. The emotions coursing through him were new and unexpected. None of what he was feeling could be spoken out loud—who to? Best not spend too much time dwelling on her. She wasn't going to ring. Her father would see to that. He no longer wanted to play the guitar alone. He'd only agree to perform at Town Week if they were a duet.

A COUPLE OF DAYS LATER, to Toby's delight, Lucy phoned.

'Do you want to come round, to practise for Town Week?'

Confused, he didn't know what to say. 'Are we doing it then?'

'Yeah, of course we are.' She laughed in that high-pitched voice of hers.

'Oh, it's just I thought…'

'Dad says you're very gifted.'

'He didn't look as if he wanted either of us in the performance.'

'He can be a right jerk. I swear he doesn't know how to smile or pay compliments. It's so embarrassing.'

'When are you thinking of?' Toby, having played out various

dialogues in his head and how he'd wanted to come across, was aware of how flat he sounded.

But she was upbeat. 'What are you doing today?' She was keen, on him, or on singing with him?

His brain froze, today felt too soon. He needed time to overcome his nerves. He hesitated before blurting, 'Not much.'

'Come round at two?'

'Okay.' Then he remembered and his heart sank. 'Oh no, Dad's working. He can't give me a lift.'

'Hang on a tick, Mum won't mind picking you up.' He heard a crackle and voices in the background.

Toby wished he could ride pillion on her moped—how amazing that would be. A wave of sadness, rather like grief, washed over him. He was fed up with missing out on all the fun other teenagers were having. Riding a moped was just something else he wouldn't be able to do. He visualised her coming to pick him up on the bike, heading towards his cottage, a cloud of dust in her wake. She'd pull a spare helmet from the storage box, they'd climb on. In his dreams, he'd circle her waist. Just like in the movies. He tried to imagine how it would be. Scary. No barrier around him, like in a car. But oh, that sense of freedom, the smells, the rush of air—a whole new world opening up. He wondered if she appreciated just how lucky she was and whether that initial excitement wore off. Not having to ask her parents for lifts everywhere. Taking off whenever she fancied.

Minutes later she was back on the line. They'd be over at two to collect him.

Toby was waiting on the doorstep at two, his guitar in its case beside him. He'd left a note on the kitchen table for Bill who was working till six-thirty.

A navy Ford Capri turned into the lane, Lucy in the passenger seat next to her mum who was driving. As the car pulled up in front of the cottage, a new thought slammed into him. He stood no chance with Lucy. She'd have to make sacrifices for him. Cadging lifts every time they went out together, because he couldn't ride a bike of his own. Her sad face, the moped left on the driveway. How terrible—the thought of her losing her independence when she'd just gained it. He didn't want to be a burden, not to her, not to any girl.

Setting off in the car, Lucy's mum asked Toby who was sitting behind them, 'Looking forward to going back to school?' Her hair was similar in colour and texture to Lucy's. It was piled high on her head, as if a bird had built a nest there.

He was barely given a chance to reply when Lucy slammed a cassette into the built-in player on the dashboard. It sounded like Fleetwood Mac.

'Lucy.' Mrs Rogers, batted Lucy's hand from the dashboard and pressed the button to eject the tape. 'Don't be rude. I was talking.'

'Why d'you have to ask about school?'

'It's called conversation.' Her mum glanced in the mirror, rolling her eyes at Toby.

'Course he's not looking forward to school.' Lucy turned to glare at her mum. 'No one looks forward to school.' Toby stifled a smile at her cheeky comment and stared down at his feet.

Ignoring her daughter, her mum ploughed on. 'Did you go away this summer, Toby?'

'Yes. We went to Dorset.'

They arrived at the house, got out the car, and headed towards a side door which led straight into the kitchen.

'Lemonade and crisps, Toby?'

'Yes please.'

'I'll bring a tray through to the playroom.'

'Mum,' Lucy said, blushing, as she stretched the word out, looking as if she was squirming inside. 'It hasn't been a playroom for years.'

'It's what we call it though.' She raised her eyebrows to Toby.

'It's a *den*, not a playroom.'

'Whatever.'

Mrs Rogers huffed. Toby caught a look of resignation on her face as he turned to follow Lucy along the hallway and into the den.

Now alone with Lucy, Toby couldn't think of what to talk about. He wanted to ask her all about college. 'D'you prefer college to school?'

'Yeah, it's ace.' She flung herself onto one of the matching brown settees that occupied the centre of the room. With tatty cushions and threadbare arms, they'd clearly seen better days. Feeling awkward because she hadn't invited him to sit, he remained standing as he glanced round the room. White bookcases along the wall. He reckoned they came from the furniture store, MFI. Along the opposite wall there was a large unit which housed a record collection and a whole array of *Jackie* magazines and make-up. 'Don't eat the bread rolls in the canteen though. They're horrible and dry.'

'It's okay. I'm used to a lot worse.'

Mrs Rogers came in, holding a tray with two glasses of lemonade and a plate of biscuits. 'You must have eaten all the crisps, Lucy. All we've got are these Rich Tea biscuits, until I do another shop.'

'I haven't. I always get the blame for everything. You'll find a pile of wrappers under Sarah's bed.'

'Do *you* fight with your brothers and sisters, Toby?'

'He doesn't have any.' She threw her mum a look which said 'why can't you be more tactful?'

Mrs Rogers put the tray onto a coffee table and picking up one of the glasses was about to hand it to Toby. Her hand froze in mid-air. He knew at once what she was thinking. Why people couldn't ask him simple questions about his needs, he'd never know. Jumping up from the settee, Lucy rushed to his rescue. 'Hang on a tick, I'll get you a straw.'

Her mum left the room. Lucy, now returned from the kitchen and having popped the straw in his drink, made Toby feel feeble. Although she hadn't said much, there was something about her that gave him the impression that she was popular at college. Way out of his league. Why had he allowed himself to consider she might be attracted to him? More likely she'd offered to sing out of pity—had a tender spot in her heart for cripples and broken things.

'How shall we begin?' Toby asked, lacking in ideas.

'Assume we're playing 'Killing Me Softly'? Have you practised?'

'Yes.' The lie caused pinpricks of sweat to emerge on his forehead. He felt like a naughty schoolboy who'd forgotten to hand his homework in on time. The truth was, he hadn't touched his guitar since they'd met because he hadn't believed that she'd ring.

She took the lead. 'I think we should tackle each section of the song separately. Get the chorus right. Then go on to the verses. Start with some down strums, Toby,' she said, putting the guitar on the floor in front of where he was sitting.

'We could record ourselves. That way we'll learn where we're going wrong. Do you have a tape recorder?'

'Great idea,' she said going over to a cupboard and pulling out a tape recorder before searching for a blank tape. 'Try some different strumming patterns first. Keep it simple though, muted strums, then we can establish a pattern. The pattern's got to line up with the lyrics.' She pressed the recorder on and walked over to him, standing beside him tapping her feet as he strummed. 'One, two, three four. Loosen up, feel the beat.'

Lucy nodded her head as he plucked at the strings, a thoughtful look on her face as she tried to establish the pattern and timings, interjecting with the odd hum here and there, testing her vocals. 'We can do this. We just need to simplify things, separate the challenges, know our individual parts really well and repeat, until it becomes second nature.'

They practised for three hours. It was harder than Toby had imagined but he enjoyed the sense of achievement at the headway they were making.

'Cut.' Lucy stopped singing and walked over to the door. 'Coffee?'

'Please.' He took his aching feet off the strings and gave them a shake. It had been an intensive session. He thought it was polite to join her for coffee, but his stomach was growling and what he really wanted was to get off home for dinner.

She returned a few minutes later with mugs and put them on a low table. Going to stand at the window, she pulled a packet of Rothmans from her pocket. 'Sorry, Toby, bad habit I know, but I'm gasping for a ciggie.' She turned slightly. He knew she was gauging his reaction, to see if he was one of those people who took offence at the smelly habit. He felt a surge of revulsion and tried not to look disgusted and shocked. He eyed her judgingly, but in that moment as she tilted her head, her hair catching the low evening light, the ends curled into perfect commas, she looked glamorous and mature. The way she pursed her lips, blowing out a plume of smoke. Sophisticated—mesmerising even. A flutter of butterflies moved across his stomach.

'Why are you staring, Toby?' It was hard not to. Heat rose to his face and his gaze fell to the floor.

'Sorry, I wasn't aware I was.'

Now it was her turn to stare at him. 'Can I ask...?' She was frowning but her face showed concern.

He looked up at her. 'Why I've got no arms? My mum took thalidomide,' he said matter-of-factly.

'I did wonder.'

'But didn't like to ask?' He smiled, trying to put her at ease because he knew she felt uncomfortable having asked about his disability. People always were.

'Bet your mum feels bad.'

'Why would she?'

Flicking the ash out of the window, she shrugged. 'For taking the tablet.'

'Don't know. She's dead.'

'I'm sorry.' She frowned. 'Did I know that?'

'Don't think so.' He looked away, fixing his gaze on the guitar lying on the floor, aware that she was looking at him now as if seeing him for the first time. They were from different worlds. How could she ever understand him? She was heading towards amazing things but felt suffocated by them. He was from a cossetted world, his opportunities blighted.

'Fancy a drag?' she asked.

'No,' he replied without a moment's thought.

She smiled, her eyes teasing, daring him to be defiant. She flicked more ash out of the window not seeming to care if it ended up in the pot plants on the window ledge.

'Do your parents mind you smoking?'

She gave an arrogant laugh. 'Course not, everybody smokes.'

After their practice, Toby was sitting on one of the settees. He leant forward and took a sip of his coffee. 'I should be getting home.'

'Yep, Mum won't mind running you back. We can practise again at the weekend if you can get here. My parents are away so we can make as much noise as we like.'

'Okay, I'll get Dad to drop me off.'

12

Arriving back from Lucy's and sitting down to tea, Toby found his head buzzing with excitement as he chatted to Bill about the afternoon he'd had, and how much he was looking forward to Town Week. Spending time in Lucy's company, working together, anticipating the thrill of being on stage. Everything about their time together had felt special, even the awkward moments between Lucy and her mum. He glowed with a wonderful feeling of achievement—leaving him warm and hopeful.

Bill looked directly at Toby, before slopping custard into their pudding bowls. 'You really like her, don't you?'

'She's very pretty.' Toby smiled.

'You're all starry-eyed.' Bill chuckled and winked as he put one of the bowls in front of Toby. 'Is she as pretty as Sandy?'

'Yes,' he said thoughtfully. 'But in a different way. Lucy's hair was messy, and she was wearing a white shirt that was way too big for her, but even if she'd been wearing a bin bag, she'd still have looked gorgeous.'

'I can't wait to meet her.'

'You'll see her at Town Week.'

'Maybe I can meet her before that.'

'No, you'll be embarrassing and say something weird like you always do. I'd like to ask her out, I don't want her to be put off by my annoying dad.'

'Charming.'

'It's true.'

'You've got it bad, son, but don't get your hopes up. The lass might have a boyfriend.'

'We're just friends, that's all,' Toby quickly said.

'No harm in that.'

A sudden thought flashed through Toby's head. 'I remembered something the other day. Don't know why, it just popped into my head. Years ago, Mum told me that I wouldn't be able to have children. Is that right?'

Toby noticed Bill flinch. 'What's made you remember?'

'Is it true?'

As Bill stiffened and rubbed his forehead, a serious and concerned expression on his face, Toby wished he'd not asked. 'You're much too young to be worrying about marriage and children. You're only fifteen, you've just met this girl.'

Toby stared at Bill through glassy eyes. 'It's got nothing to do with meeting Lucy.'

'There are no guarantees with anything in life.'

'I know that. I'm not a baby. But what Mum said was big. How did she know I wouldn't be able to have children?'

'Did she actually say that?' Bill scratched his head as if he was either struggling to remember or wondering how he would reply. 'The mind can play tricks. Memories get muddled over time.'

'We were in a park when she first said it and then she said it over the phone, not long before she died.'

'She wasn't herself at the end.'

'She sounded normal to me.'

'People say all sorts of things just before they die. Why didn't you mention it to me at the time?'

'I was upset. She was dying. And after she'd gone, you were drinking all the time. It felt as if I was in your way. You didn't want me around.'

Bill slumped in his chair, his arms falling to his sides. 'My head was all over the place. I'm sorry.'

'It's okay.' Toby fixed his gaze on the cooker and tried to tamp down the emotions swirling in his stomach. A pool of silence formed between them. Toby half expected his dad to reach out, touch and reassure him with loving words. But that wasn't his dad's way and never had been.

Glancing at Bill, Toby saw his eyes had dissolved into misery and that faraway look he'd seen so many times was back. And then, as quick as a storm cloud it was gone. 'Don't let it worry you. Eat your food.'

Realising his dad was upset, he carried on. 'Why would she say that?'

Bill looked flustered and uncomfortable. 'I don't know. She was in nursing. She knew about the human body.' He shifted his weight in the chair.

Toby was more confused than ever. He had to get answers. 'Not everyone is the same. All the thalidomides are damaged in different ways.'

'What do they tell you at school?'

'Some of my friends have been told the same thing, that they'll never be parents.'

Bill winced and when he spoke, his voice sounded scratchy. 'That's sad, but for some of them, how could they be parents, how would it even be possible? You just have to look at them to know that.'

Toby felt a flicker of anger. 'With help and support there's no reason why they can't be.'

Bill raised his arms in mock defeat, his words coming out

like a shotgun. 'Maybe their parents asked a doctor. Maybe they've had examinations, X-rays, scans. Or maybe their parents told them that because they didn't want to build up their hope.'

This last comment was something Toby hadn't considered.

∼

BILL GOT UP–, his pudding unfinished. He scraped his chair back and went to look out of the window. With his arms folded and his back to Toby, his mind reeled back to the past.

Rona had been a strong woman, but she'd also been a worrier, and nothing worried her more than Toby's future.

All that fretting had prevented her from falling pregnant—Bill was convinced of that. He'd heard that stress affected fertility. Or maybe that was an old wives' tale. If only she hadn't worked such long hours, if she'd relaxed more, let nature do its thing. But she'd also been strong-willed, thinking she knew best, which was why he was standing here now, facing not the biggest juncture of all—bloody hell, if that ever came out—but a huge one all the same. Whether to tell Toby the truth—that his mother had lied to him. A white lie, she'd called it. Toby had been around seven at the time and watching a baby wriggle on a rug in the park had said, 'I want a sister or a brother.' When Bill had told him that wasn't going to happen, Toby had replied, 'When I grow up, I'm going to have a baby boy and a baby girl. Then they can keep each other company.'

Bill had been so shocked by Rona's response, he'd stayed quiet. At the time he'd been reassured by the thought that Toby was young and would forget. That evening in bed, Bill had asked Rona why she'd said it.

'It's about being cruel to be kind. We don't want to build his hopes up, stand by and watch his heart be broken when women reject him. Better to prepare him for the harsh realities of life.'

'But he might meet someone who will love him and stay with him despite his handicap,' Bill had said.

Bill hadn't known about Rona's end-of-life speech over the phone. Typical Rona—even on her death bed she was leaving him to pick up the pieces.

∼

TOBY SAW the truth in his dad's eyes.

'Was Mum lying to protect me?'

Bill faced him. 'Protect you? From what?'

Toby needed time to process his own words. Bill turned and stared out of the window.

When Toby spoke again, Bill was back at the table and seated. 'Life. Women. Rejection.'

'Life, women, rejection?'

'Stop repeating everything I say. Was Mum worried that women wouldn't be interested in me? Did she make it up to soften the blow in case I ended up alone?'

'I don't know, son.' He sounded pathetic.

'You do,' Toby insisted. He got up and towered over Bill. 'Without tests there's no way she'd have known.'

Bill's shoulders slumped and he lowered his head.

'I want to see my medical records.'

'Calm down. Fetch me a beer from the fridge.'

'Not until you tell me the truth.' Toby's voice splintered. 'It's my life and I've a right to know.'

Toby sat down and they faced each other in limbo. He watched as Bill hesitated. When his words came, they were barely more than a whisper. 'She made it up.'

The words cut through Toby, like a saw through steel. He'd always had the greatest respect for his mother, she was the one person he'd never stopped loving—until now.

'To protect me?'

'I'm sorry. She had your best interests at heart.'

'That may be, but you went along with it.'

'Don't think badly of her, son. Please. She loved you very much, just didn't want to see you get hurt.'

'This morning when Lucy rang, I considered asking her for a ride on her moped. I know it would have been reckless, I'd have fallen off. Got hurt. But at least I would have been responsible for myself. For my life.'

'I'm glad you didn't.'

'From now on, Dad, the lies stop.'

'Okay.'

'I'm sixteen soon. I don't need protecting.' Toby got up and rushed upstairs to his bedroom, flinging himself onto his bed. He just wanted to be alone.

13

It was early morning and Jasper dashed downstairs for the phone. He was surprised to hear the urgent voice of Sam, his editor.

'I need you up at the Notting Hill Carnival.'

Jasper was familiar with the Notting Hill part of West London, a poor area where many West Indians lived. It had first hit the headlines in 1958 when four nights of rioting between blacks and whites had tested the ability of the police. In the past ten years an annual carnival had been held and was starting to attract huge crowds.

'Why?' He didn't normally cover community events. His stories were more headline-grabbing.

'This year there's a smell of trouble brewing. It should have been held in Battersea Park or White City Stadium like the police wanted it to be. It was utter chaos last year, and they couldn't control it on the streets, so they've been flooding the place with bobbies this time.'

'The police often take a heavy-handed approach to any large group of black people. We've known that for a while.'

'It won't take much for trouble to erupt. Some of these

communities hate 'stop and search.' Any excuse the police can think of, they haul them in. Plenty deserve it, especially if they're carrying drugs or weapons. And just to warn you, the place is teeming with thugs and pickpockets. Watch your wallet, Jasper.'

Jasper groaned inwardly. How could he get out of it? 'What about Steadman covering it?' Jasper suggested, as Sandy stood beside him, sweeping her fingers through her hair. He gave her an apologetic look. She shook her head and clicked her tongue against the roof of her mouth.

Sam hesitated. 'Not this one.'

'If it turns into a big story, he'll be cross. Steadman's never forgiven you for letting me cover the thalidomide scandal. Has always claimed that I nicked his idea.'

'He needs to bloody well get over it. That was four years ago now.'

'He hasn't forgotten it. It feels as if he's waiting to stab me in the back.'

'Don't worry about him. He's not important. If it wasn't for the union, I'd sack him.'

'I suppose he has his uses.'

'If you can get up to Notting Hill, I'd appreciate it.'

'Okay, will do. I don't have any body armour though,' he joked.

Sandy was staring at Jasper when he replaced the receiver.

'I'm sorry, honey.' He put his hands on her shoulders.

'I can't believe you said you'd go. We've hardly spent any time together this weekend and today's a bank holiday. You've spent so much time with Toby lately, now this.'

He wrapped his arms around her, pulling her into a kiss. Their relationship was steady contentment after years together, but he still felt lightening bulbs and butterflies when he kissed and touched her. She magnetised him and especially now, heavily pregnant, she glowed with radiance. His tongue searched her mouth hungrily and his hand tugged her blouse. Damn it, he'd be late up to London, but she was hard to resist.

ON THE TRAIN, Jasper fiddled with his camera. He shouldn't have brought it with him, but it was still fairly new, and he was still trying it out. He emerged from Ladbroke Grove tube station. He passed a stall selling newspapers. *'Dancing In The Rain'* read the headline in the *Daily Mirror* showing a policeman laughing with a black woman in the rain at the carnival the previous day.

He headed towards Ladbroke Gardens and onto the Portobello Road. The place was alive with the sound of Bob Marley's hymns of freedom and the beat of steel drums. The sweet smell of ganja mingled with Caribbean cooking, and a whiff of burgers and chips filled the air. Fast food sellers were serving sizzling hot spicy food: Jerk chicken, goat curry, creamy fish stew, as well as tantalising sliced coconut, mango and pineapple. The smells were mouth-watering. His nose picked up ginger, rum, lime, chilli, papaya. He deftly avoided a scattering of oranges, inched past a wooden wheelbarrow, and wove an awkward path through a gaggle of loud-mouthed traders and their customers.

A sea of people, bright colours, flowing robes, streamers in hair, turbans, happy faces. Glancing around, he smiled. People having fun, enjoying themselves. He wanted to join in, chat to folk, get their picture, their story. Everybody had a story. The street was scattered with litter, the debris of partygoers. He wandered along the pavement, weaving through the throng, his feet kicking litter scattered across the street, watching black and white people mixing happily. He couldn't see any trouble. A false alarm, a wasted day? And then he came to an abrupt halt at the side of a building. Graffiti. Words of hate that bled into the hearts and minds of those who lived here, an insidious reminder that tension bubbled under the surface.

Let's look after our own first.

And further along, more spray-can weaponry. *Keep Britain White.*

Jasper shuddered.

Then he saw it. A huge police cordon, from one side of the road to the other. People were shouting at the police. He heard someone say, 'This is a police carnival.'

He rushed over to see what was happening, asking, 'Excuse me, officer, I'm Press,' flashing his union card. 'Please can I get through?'

The officer stepped aside but looked at him through cold, hard eyes. 'Why do you want to join all those…?'

Jasper's brain stuttered for a moment in stunned surprise at the disgusting word the officer had used to describe black people. Every part of him went on pause as he stared at the copper. 'I don't like your tone, officer. They're human beings and deserve to be treated as such.'

But before the officer had time to answer, a black youth came running from between the police and jumped on top of another black guy. Jasper reached for his camera hanging from his neck and took the cap off the lens, raising the viewfinder to his eye in a fluster. He loved his Hasselblad. He didn't normally take his camera because he wasn't a photojournalist. But photography was his passion, a hobby and if he could get some great shots while working then all the better. His camera was satisfyingly heavy in the hand and made wonderful mechanical whirring and clicking noises. Time was of the essence. Events were moving fast, too fast to capture it all, hear what was going on.

A fight had started. Jasper ran over, wanting to be part of the action, soaking up the detail as it unfolded, careful not to end up in the thick of it, in the dance of violence, trampled on, wounded. There were women, children—and police moving into the crowd with truncheons extended in front of them, grabbing, shoving people at random as they surged forward. Jasper smelled the fear, the anger, the shock on the faces in the crowd.

A black woman next to him was screaming at a policeman, 'why are you hurting people, just stop, you're fucking filth.'

Jasper heard glass, a shop window shattering, bottles hurled, screaming, people scattering. And in the distance he saw a fire—a car ablaze. His senses were on high alert, this was descending into a war zone. Every colour grew suddenly brighter, every noise louder, the heat of bodies packed against him, his heart beating fiercely, spiking adrenaline. From the corner of his eye, he saw a beer bottle hurtle towards the wall next to him and turning, panicked, watched it shatter and fall, the liquid fanning out, splashing the hem of his trousers. The crowd pushed forward, the boys in blue were running towards the car, down the street, grabbing metal bin lids for protection as bottles flew at them.

Got to get out of here and fast, Jasper thought. But it was too late, the crowd were pressing forward. He saw a flash of someone he vaguely recognised in the sea of sweaty revellers, just a few feet away. He lost his balance, he hadn't seen the pushchair, or had someone rammed it at him? He crashed sideways into the crowd, the sound of tarmac connecting with his face, the sting of glass on flesh, the thud of the metal casing on his camera hitting the ground. The pain in his head was indescribable, like hot knives. A wave of blackness tried to drag him under, his brain wanting to shut his body down. A shred of survival instinct fought against it. Somehow he found strength, kicking, flailing, screaming an inaudible scream, fought to escape the crush of feet, terrified he would be trampled to death. *Give in,* said a voice inside him. *Let go. No.* He refused to let go. He refused to die. His last thought before blacking out was, *shit, my time's up, I'll never see my unborn child.*

∽

AFTER JASPER HAD LEFT for London, Sandy carried the Agatha Christie novel she was reading to the bottom of the garden and positioned her sun-lounger to face the mid-morning sun, already bright and warming the air. The dog followed her, sitting on the grass, lifting his head to regard Sandy before curling up to sleep, snoring gently.

Half-way through the fourth chapter, the words began to swim in front of her eyes. She felt groggy, yawned and closed her eyes, the book falling onto the grass. Sometime later she woke, shivering despite the heat on her skin, a flash from the dream she'd just had—so real. Before it floated away, she clutched on to it. There was a rawness and misery in the emotions it conjured. In the dream, as had happened in real life, she'd been lying in bed hours after having giving birth to her first baby. Why hadn't they brought him to her? The agony of that wait mixed with the torment of her doubts, regrets about the planned adoption. The doctor coming to tell her the news: her baby had no arms and had died. But in the dream reality blurred with fiction. Her mother stood over her, taunting, sneering, jeering, waggling her finger. *Think you're so perfect do you, Miss Glamour Model? All you can produce is a deformed baby.* Then the emotions: shame and embarrassment.

Sandy got up and headed to the kitchen, hoping a cup of tea would shake the dream from her thoughts. But it had been so stark, it was hard to erase the images and she dwelled for some time on the birth of that first baby. There was no doubt in her mind she was scared of giving birth a second time. It was the unknown of what could happen. Any technology offering to stop the pain, ease the suffering, fight against nature—she'd jolly well take it. Because she hated pain, didn't want prolonged agony, but what about the side effects of pain relief, the harm they could do to the baby? And after thalidomide, she didn't want to take any chances.

She had neither the soul nor the romanticism to look at childbirth as a miracle, a great defining moment in her life's achievement, something to be venerated. She hoped the impact on her body would be minimal. That was something she dwelled on. No scars or hideous stretch marks and gravity working to pull everything downwards. What a depressing thought.

Women were supposed to forget the pain and remember it as the happiest, most profound day of their lives. It was hard to imagine that. She got the impression that her mother had certainly never forgotten the pain and distress, telling her, 'The day I watched the doctor stitch my private bits was one of the worst days of my life.' She might as well have said Sandy's birth was one of the worst moments of her life.

Sandy spent the rest of the day idling around the house, grooming the dog and rifling through her wardrobe with a desperate longing to be able to wear her dresses again.

When early evening came, glancing at the kitchen clock, Sandy was surprised Jasper hadn't rung, but imagined him holed up in a Notting Hill pub chatting to revellers and making mental notes before heading into the office to write the story for publication in tomorrow's paper.

The phone rang. It had to be him. She hurried into his study to take it there. Disappointed to hear her mother's voice, Sandy hoped she wasn't going to endure her moaning for the next half hour about something trivial and tedious. She needed to keep the line free.

'Mother, I can't talk long, Jasper might phone.'

'Isn't he home? It's bank holiday, he shouldn't go out and leave you all by yourself, you need to be firm with these men. Don't stand for it.'

Sandy sighed. She was in one of her sour moods. 'He's had to work.'

'On a bank holiday? Are you sure it's just work?' She gave a spectacular tut. 'Where is he then?'

'Of course I am. He's only up at Notting Hill, covering the carnival.'

'Notting Hill? Didn't you watch the six o' clock news?

There's been riots, lots of people injured, taken to hospital. Bloody hooligans, the lot of them, but honestly what do you expect?'

Feeling suddenly light-headed Sandy slumped into the leather chair. 'Oh God.' Her brain froze over. 'I better get off the phone.' He would be back at his desk in Fleet Street working to beat the 9.50pm deadline when the newspaper went to press. 'I'll call you another time.'

Sandy had to find out if Jasper was okay. Rushing into the lounge, she turned on the television, pressing each channel. On Thames, *Man About the House* was just starting. On BBC One it was the film *Chitty Chitty Bang Bang* and John Denver was singing on Two. She didn't want to wait till the nine o' clock news came on. She needed to do something now, even if it meant ringing all the hospitals to check their admissions. Back in his study she plonked herself on Jasper's chair, clasping her hands together as if in prayer, and brought them up to her lips. She tried to remain calm, even though she found herself in the grip of panic. She eased the desk drawer open with a trembling hand and rummaged inside for Jasper's phone book. Rifling through the pages she found the office number and picked up the phone.

'I'm sure he'll be fine, but if you don't hear from him by nine, ring me, will you?' Sam told her.

Coming off the phone, she felt foolish. Her hormones had been all over the place lately and her mother shouldn't have worried her. She slipped the book back into the drawer and, about to close it, she noticed an envelope nestled between a stapler and a booklet of stamps. She took the envelope out to take a closer look, her heart skipping a beat when she read the handwritten words on the front. *To Sandy Cooper, my wife. Only to be opened in the event of my death.* She regarded it curiously for several moments, turning it over and in capital letters this time, Jasper had written the same words, *only to be opened by my wife in the event of my death.*

When had he written it? What could he possibly need to tell her after his death that wasn't already in their will? Holding it for several moments, she considered opening it, but thought better of it. It was clear that she should not open it. Respecting his privacy, she thrust the envelope back into the drawer.

14

Jasper woke up in hospital. The pain in his head had subsided—maybe they'd pumped him full of painkillers. He tested his arms and legs, fingers and toes. Everything seemed to work but his whole body was bruised and he couldn't move his left arm. He felt sick and shaky. He pushed himself into a sitting position, careful not to disturb the tube that ran from a drip into his arm. He gingerly he touched the back of his head, which was covered in a bandage.

A nurse spotted him and came over.

'Mr Cooper, you need to take it easy. The doctor wants to examine you. I'll let him know you're awake.'

She was about to go when he said, 'Wait. My wife, does she know I'm here?'

'Yes. She called this morning. She's coming this afternoon during visiting hours.'

Jasper glanced round the ward at the other patients. Opposite him were several men of a similar age. They were bouncing light-hearted insults at each other, like a kid's rubber ball, a verbal dance that seemed weird to an outsider like himself. Just at that moment a police officer came onto the ward and smiling at them said, 'Don't think you lot are going to be resting for long, and they all replied, 'Morning, sarge, you come to check up on us?' And then it dawned on him, they were police officers and like him, they'd been injured at the carnival.

While the sergeant spoke to the other patients, the doctor arrived on the ward. He gave Jasper the once-over and told him he was fine—apart from having a broken left arm that needed plastering. They were going to keep him in for a couple of days for observation. They were mostly concerned about his head injury.

'It's not as bad as it must have felt,' the doctor said. 'You banged your head when you fell, or your head was hit in the commotion. Your skull isn't fractured. We've already carried out an X-ray and scan and there doesn't appear to be any internal damage. You have a tough head, Mr Cooper. We've given you twenty stitches. But we want to monitor you for concussion. There's a risk of subdural haematoma developing, but I think you're going to be all right.'

'You think I was hit? All I remember is smacking my head onto glass.'

'Yes, hence the need for stitches but it does appear you were hit with something hard. Maybe that's why you fell?'

'I don't remember, it all happened so fast.'

'Take it easy, get some rest and I'll see how you're doing tomorrow.'

Jasper closed his eyes, but it was hard to find sleep amid his thoughts. He replayed what had happened, but there were gaps in his memory, and he couldn't recall coming to hospital and having stitches and an X-ray.

Someone said his name. He opened his eyes to see a man standing over him. He introduced himself as Sergeant Peter Hainsworth.

'Are you feeling up to answering some questions?' He pulled up a plastic chair.

'Of course. But can you answer one of mine first? Did anyone see what happened? Did I stumble or did someone hit me?'

The constable formed a fist with his hand and put it to his lips, clearing his throat. 'There were so many people at the carnival. We're just trying to piece together the chain of events for everything that happened yesterday. If I can just take some notes from you, everything you remember, please.'

Jasper's mind was hazy, but he told him all he could and after the sergeant left, he rested his eyes, longing for Sandy to appear at his bedside.

Drifting off to sleep, he jerked awake on hearing a scraping sound as the curtain around his bedside was pulled back. Sandy managed a smile through her sad eyes. 'My poor love. When I heard there'd been a riot, people injured, fighting, and you were so late home—I thought you were dead.' Tears filled her eyes. She grabbed his hand, leaning down to kiss his forehead. 'I've brought the newspaper.'

Jasper tried to make light of it, but his headache was coming back with a vengeance now. His vision was soft around the edges, a steady pain pulsing out from his forehead, but it didn't stop him looking at the headline—'*All Out War on London Streets,*' and turned to the editorial report that he would have written. 'I wonder who wrote this.' His eyes flicked over the first few pages, which were full of photos and news of the riots. 'Oh Jesus, Ronny bloody Steadman. How the hell did that weasel write this when he wasn't even there?'

Jasper read the first lines of the report and folded the paper, horrified. 'Unbelievable. So quick to blame the West Indian community. The Met were far too heavy-handed, flooding the street with officers. The stance I would have taken, if I'd written this, would have been quite different. And wait... these photos look very much like mine.'

'Calm down, love, don't get yourself all worked up. You're lucky to be alive. From these pictures it looked like a battleground. They said on the news this morning it was the worst violence seen on the streets of London since the Second World War.'

'Where's my camera?' Jasper glanced round the bed as if the camera was about to jump out at him.

'I think it must be lost, Jasper, you didn't come in with anything, apart from your union card.'

'And my wallet?'

'Your wallet is gone.'

'Must have been nicked. Thieving bunch of...' Then he glanced at the nurse and didn't continue. 'These photos look very much like the ones I took.' He stared off into the distance, pondering a new thought. 'It's odd. I know this sounds really far-fetched, but what if Ronny was there and stole my camera?'

'Jasper,' Sandy said in a stern tone, 'just drop this thing between you and Ronny Steadman. If you go into work accusing him, they'll think you're mad and you might even lose your job. Leave it. The camera's gone.'

Sandy was perched on the edge of the bed. 'Careful, love, if the ward sister sees you sitting there, she won't be happy. They're very strict.'

Visiting time was very short, the hour went quickly and then a bell indicated that it was time for Sandy to leave.

JASPER WAS DISCHARGED a few days later. The doctor warned him to look out for symptoms like drowsiness, poor tolerance to light, disorientation and confusion, and to ring the hospital if he was at all worried. He was given an appointment to return in ten days' time, to have his stitches removed and they would check his arm, which had been cast with plaster of Paris. Thank God it had been his left arm and not his right. He'd be able to type with one hand, that was easy enough.

Hopefully he'd be driving again in eight weeks. It seemed a long time away and would be bloody inconvenient. It was just one of those things. He was alive. That was all that mattered.

A few days later a familiar unshaven face appeared on the doorstep. Bill.

'Look at you, the war-wounded soldier, risking life and limb in the line of duty.'

'Bill, thanks for coming.'

'Surprise.' Toby came into view, joining Bill at the doorstep.

'We heard the news, we were very worried,' Bill said.

'We didn't think you'd appreciate flowers,' Toby said, 'but I've got a good joke to cheer you up.'

Jasper stood aside and let them in, nodding for them to go through to the kitchen. 'Oh yeah,' Jasper smiled. 'What's that, sunshine?'

'What's the worst place to hide when you play hide-and-seek in a hospital?'

'Ow, I'm not sure.'

'The ICU.'

'Very good, very good. I've got a friend who works in dermatology. He started his career from scratch.'

Bill tutted, Toby looked blank and as they went through to the kitchen Sandy was standing by the kettle about to offer them tea.

'Fancy a cuppa?' she said, reaching for mugs and teabags.

Gathered round the kitchen table, they sipped their tea and Jasper told Toby and Bill the story of what had happened to him at the carnival.

'At least we have the concert to look forward to. That'll cheer you up,' Toby said.

Bill frowned. 'What concert?'

Dipping his head, Toby looked sheepish. 'Sorry, Dad, I forgot to tell you. Jasper's booked tickets to see Queen in Hyde Park on the 18th September.'

Bill shook his head and sighed. 'How much is that costing?'

'It's free. It's being organised by the entrepreneur, Richard Branson. Toby said he'd never been to a concert before.'

Fiddling with the collar of his t-shirt, Bill was clearly put out and Jasper was embarrassed. Toby should have told Bill.

'Nice of you to plan this behind my back. Is it just the two of you?' He'd adopted a sullen look.

'I've ordered two tickets, yes.'

'Why not three?' Sandy asked. 'Why would you exclude Bill?'

'Sorry, mate, but the lad said you wouldn't want to go.'

'Maybe not—but nice to be asked.'

'Dad, it's not your thing.' Toby raised his eyebrows at Jasper and tutted.

'Looks like you'll be taking him, I won't be driving, not in this state.'

'You could drive us up there, Dad, and wait in the car, as long as we don't go in your old truck.'

'You're ashamed to go to a public event with your dad? And ashamed to go in the truck?'

'How's Town Week practice with Lucy going?' Jasper asked, trying to defuse the tension.

'Great.'

'I've had a brainwave,' Jasper said. 'Why not ask Lucy to the concert? You'd enjoy it far more with someone of your own age group.'

Toby frowned, a thoughtful look on his face. 'But she might say no, then I'd look a right div.'

'Don't ask, you don't get.' Jasper winked.

'I'll think about it.'

'Don't think too long, these hot chicks don't stick around for long, kiddo.'

Sandy looked curious. 'What's she like, Toby?'

'She's okay, I suppose.'

Bill elbowed Toby. 'Come on, she's more than okay.' He winked at Sandy. 'He's smitten.'

Toby's face went a shade of beetroot.

15

'Good to see you, mate, come in.'

Sam was standing by his office window beaming. With a wave of his arm, he beckoned Jasper into the room. It felt like a hero's welcome, as if he'd been gone for months. Two weeks, that was all. And he still wasn't right. He'd spent several days in bed with the curtains drawn. His head was foggy and occasionally it throbbed. Sandy had tried to stop him returning so soon. She could be persuasive, but he didn't want to stay in his pit any longer.

He needed to be back. In the driving seat. Two things were preying on his mind.

His camera. And Ronny's editorial. It was a shite piece of writing. Plain and simple. And blatantly racist. A gross distortion of the truth. And Sam had approved it! Unbelievable. The editor's standards were slipping. Jasper felt almost ashamed to work for the paper.

'So glad you're back.' Sam's arms flew into the air. What a sentimental old bugger he was.

Sam's excitement made Jasper cringe as he joined him at the window, a copy of the newspaper for Tuesday 31st August, tucked under his arm. His editor was friendlier than normal, gushing even, which meant one thing: after a welcoming chat about something pointless and irrelevant he'd launch in and ask him to cover a new story. He was so predictable.

'Don't you just love this view? I bet you've missed it.'

'It's okay.' There were more pressing matters to discuss.

'Look.' Sam pointed to the buildings in Fleet Street and beyond. 'St Paul's Cathedral and its cluster of church towers. And opposite us, Edwin Lutyens' finest of buildings. I love walking past that imposing building each morning. Its grandeur, it makes *me* feel important.' He banged his chest, turned from the window, and looked at Jasper. 'We're a factory. That's what we are. We're like bees going about our work, racing to get the paper to press, working hard to beat that all-important deadline. God, I've missed you.'

Christ. He wasn't here to discuss the bloody view. It was time for serious conversation. Now. Before the phone interrupted them.

Jasper stepped forward and slammed the newspaper onto Sam's desk, scattering letters, memos, empty crisp packets. Messy git. How could he work in such chaos?

'This.' He jabbed his finger at Ronny's editorial. 'Is a pile of racist crap.'

Sam stood back looking alarmed.

'Gutter journalism. *Battle at The Carnival.* Sensational words. Who chose them, that wanker Steadman? *Last week it was Soweto, this week it's Notting Hill.* We'll have blood on our hands at this rate. You're playing right into the hands of politicians like Enoch Powell, people whose only goal is to divide the nation.'

'What would you have written?'

'The bloody truth for a start. The police were bastards, heavy-handed and provocative. Steadman paints the revellers as violent animals, out of control. The tension's bubbled away in these West Indian communities for years. They've had decades of discrimination, prejudice, hardship—then the police arrived and there was a massive backlash.'

'I thought he wrote a good piece,' Sam muttered weakly. 'Without his presence, we would have been stuck, given what happened to you.'

'He shouldn't have been there,' Jasper hissed. 'You asked me to go. You didn't want him there.'

'It's a free country, Jasper, he can go where he likes.'

'And who took these pictures? Was our cameraman there?'

'No, they're Steadman's pictures. He's into photography. Think he's got a Nikon. It was a day out. Told me he'd wanted to capture the Caribbean vibrancy—the beautiful costumes, the musicians, the faces. He's got his own darkroom at home, but he dropped the reel to us, so I included his best shots.'

'I need to see every single one of those negatives.'

Sam moved away from the window, a puzzled expression on his face. 'Why?'

Jasper stared at him, incredulous. 'Because they're my fucking pictures.'

'Oh, for God's sake, Jasper,' he snapped. 'You're not the only person in the world to own a bloody camera.'

'I'll prove it. There were pictures of Sandy on that reel. And Toby. My camera was stolen,' he shouted. 'I felt it being wrenched from my neck.'

'Do you know how you sound? Barking mad.'

Jasper felt about as small and insignificant as a schoolboy.

'Are you seriously accusing Steadman of stealing your camera? What were you even doing with a camera on you? You were there to write, not take pictures. You can't do both.'

'I didn't expect it to turn violent. Thought it would be a breeze of a day, but it was anything but.'

'I did warn you about pickpockets.'

'You didn't warn me about thieving colleagues.'

'Oh please. Just claim on your bloody insurance and buy a new one.'

Jasper's voice was cold, and he was struggling to contain his anger. 'You know that Steadman's a nasty piece of shit and you believe his word over mine, your friend of what, twenty years?'

'Jesus, you're overreacting. Just stop it.'

'He's got it in for me because you chose me over him to report on the thalidomide scandal.'

'That was years ago.'

'He's harboured a grudge ever since.'

'You won't be able to prove the camera, so you may as well drop it. We handed all the negatives, apart from the ones we used, back to Steadman. It's what he wanted.'

'Now why does that not surprise me?' Jasper tilted his head back and gave a mocking laugh. 'How bloody convenient.'

'Did you say the film contained pictures of Sandy and Toby? Isn't Toby your friend's kid? The thalidomide boy?' Sam had a habit of deflecting when he was losing the argument or didn't want trouble.

'Yes. So those pictures—pictures of a minor, are now in Steadman's hands.'

'Challenge him if you want, but I'd think very carefully before you do. You can't just go around accusing people. Oh, by the way, Steadman said he saw you with Toby in a pub garden back in the summer. He commented on the likeness between you. Even speculated that he might be your son.'

'The bloke's weird. He's got no right to speculate about my private life and spread his thoughts round the office.'

'Like him or loathe him, he's your work colleague. I always appreciate your professionalism. Now.' He snapped his fingers to signify the conversation had ended. 'I'd like you to write a piece about Chairman Mao.' The long-time leader of Communist China had died very recently. It would be an easy piece to write, but Jasper couldn't get stuck in until he'd confronted bloody Steadman.

JASPER WAS SHAKING with rage as he left Sam's room. Ronny *had* stolen his camera. And knocked him to the ground? He couldn't be sure, but he was convinced that's what had happened. He wished he could piece the events together, but his memory was fuzzy. Not to be able to remember—how infuriating that was. And his bloody head, it was throbbing again. He needed more painkillers. Maybe Sandy was right, it was too early to return to work.

With trembling hands, he pushed through the swing doors, heart pounding in his chest. He steamed down the stairs at full pelt until he reached the first floor where Ronny worked. The floor vibrated because it was above the noisy machine rooms and the smell of spirits and ink drifted up. It all mirrored what was going on in his head. He felt sick to the core and couldn't control the emotions coursing through him. He hovered in the stairwell rubbing his sweaty palms, wondering what the hell he was going to say to Steadman.

The door onto the corridor swung open and he found himself staring into the eyes of his nemesis.

Ronny Steadman.

Steadman swaggered over to him with a cocky expression on his face. In that moment, Jasper just wanted one thing. To punch his lights out.

'This isn't your neck of the woods, Cooper.'

'We need to talk.'

'I'm just on my way to the gents,' Steadman called from over his shoulder as he passed.

Jasper followed him into the gloom—the furthest part of the corridor where the men's toilets were situated. He hovered outside, his nerves jangling as he waited. A few moments later he heard a toilet flush and, clenching his fists with mounting anger, kicked the door with his foot and went through to the communal area where basins lined the wall. Steadman was washing his hands, his back to him. Jasper glanced towards the urinals. Good. They were alone. Steadman stared at Jasper's reflection, a cold, arrogant look in his eyes.

'What do you want?'

'I think you know.' Jasper's blood was simmering, but his voice was hard and in control. Ronny flicked the water from his hands before grabbing a paper towel to dry them.

He shrugged. 'No, mate, sorry, you've lost me.'

'I'm not your mate.'

'What the fuck do you want, Cooper?' He threw the towel in the bin and turned to stare at him.

'My camera.'

'What of it?'

'You stole it. The carnival pictures were mine.'

Stepping closer, Ronny sneered. His manner was defiant. As their eyes locked, he spat his words. 'Tosser. Prove it.'

'Show me the negatives.'

'Or you'll do what?' Steadman pulled his shoulders back and gave an amused laugh.

The periphery of Jasper's vision was fast blurring. That mocking tone, it echoed in his head. Ronny's smugness—it needed wiping from his face. Vile creature. He despised him. A wall of anger rose inside him, making him crack. Grabbing his collar, he twisted it, slamming him hard against the laminate partition panel of the toilet cubicle, causing the adjoining door to ricochet on its hinges.

'Fuck off, Cooper.' Steadman tried to wriggle free. Pinned against the panel, the bastard wasn't going anywhere and if he struggled, Jasper would knee him in the balls.

He tightened his grip as Steadman coughed. Right in that

moment, Jasper didn't care if he choked to death. This feud had to end.

'Toby's your son. And your wife doesn't know.'

His words were a blow and he felt the impact—he melted, shoulders sagging, hand falling to his side.

He stared into power-hungry eyes that glittered and sparkled with triumph. A chill swept through him.

How could Steadman possibly know? None of this made any sense.

'What does your missus think about your cosy relationship with the boy and Bill? All those clandestine meetings to hand over money.'

The lie had to be contained. The mess he'd created. How he wished things had been different. He was a liar and he'd lived with that stain for so long. Too long. The thought of it all coming out into the open—he felt sick to the core. Bile rose in his throat. He leaned over the basin and swallowed hard, wanted to throw up. Behind him, Ronny laughed.

He couldn't lose them. Sandy. Toby. His unborn baby. They were all he had. They meant the world, made each day worthwhile. His heart ached for them. Without them, what was the point to his life? The thought of trust—gone. He was better than this. He splashed water over his face. He'd always prided himself on his integrity, his strength of character, but now he wasn't so sure. No matter how he explained and justified his secret, it would be hopeless. Because it tarnished everything else, every good he'd ever done, none of it mattered and would be forgotten. Because this one thing, this dirty and scandalous lie was just too big.

How the fuck had it come to this? He wiped his face with a paper towel and stared at Ronny's reflection in the mirror.

'Meet me at five in The Old Bell Tavern,' Ronny said.

'What do you want?'

'All in the fullness of time, my friend.' He smirked and

tapped the side of his nose. 'I'll see you at five. Be there.' Ronny turned to go, leaving Jasper frozen to the spot staring at his own reflection in the mirror.

Pulling himself together, he left the gents. Joining the main corridor, he heard laughter. A crowd of workers were standing around a new apprentice who'd been slung in a hand cart wearing only his underpants, smothered in glue, paper shavings, ink and tea slops and was being driven around the various departments for all to see and jeer at. This was an age-old ritual in the firm and across the printing industry. Fearing he'd be stopped and asked how he was, Jasper dipped his head and hurried into the waiting lift to take him to the solitude of his own office where he could process his thoughts before starting his piece about Chairman Mao.

He couldn't keep putting it off. He had to tell Sandy the truth.

16

The Old Bell Tavern was the Fleet Street boozer of choice among the printers and journalists working nearby. Hardly private, there was often a three-foot-deep crowd of drinkers gathered around the wooden bar—the circular hub in the middle of the premises.

Somewhere off the beaten track would have been more discreet, Jasper thought as he yanked open the door, his eyes adjusting to the dark interior as he scanned his surroundings. Surprisingly, it wasn't busy. Steadman was already there and had chosen one of the best seats, a table near the stained-glass window where a kaleidoscope of colour danced on the floor and bounced off the pint of beer he was cradling.

Jasper stood at the bar waiting to be served. All day he'd been in a tortured state, trying to work out how the hell Steadman could possibly know that Toby was his son. More than anything he wanted to mull it over with someone else, a confidant, someone he could trust. He had to discuss this with Bill, tell him their secret was no longer safe.

Jasper went over the events of fifteen years ago trying to work out how the secret had fallen into Steadman's hands. Could it have been the doctor who'd delivered Toby? Revenge over what had happened after Bill's wife, Rona, had stubbornly refused to follow his orders?

No, how could it be the doctor? He was dead.

He had to silence Steadman. How, when his enemy had all the winning cards?

Shit, if all this were to come out, the police could accuse Bill of being an accomplice to kidnapping a child. The very last thing Jasper wanted was to see Bill convicted and sent to prison. What that would do to Toby. Destroy him. Imagine discovering the facts of your life were fiction: who your parents are and how you came into the world. Everything, one giant ugly lie. It stank. Both men had agreed to keep the lie going. Jasper felt ashamed, deeply ashamed. If only he could turn back the clock. If only. He wouldn't be here now having to face Steadman.

Now was not the time to dwell on regrets. Everything hinged on this meeting with Steadman. His relationship with his son. Toby's future. Protecting him, whatever it took. Bill was the only father he'd known. And even though their relationship was difficult, Bill and Toby needed each other. This massive act of betrayal threatened to send it plummeting over a cliff.

Jasper ordered a double whisky—he needed it. Then he wandered over to the table, pulling out a velvet padded stool.

Steadman cut to the chase. 'Your secret is safe with me, but only if you do what I say.'

Jasper took a swig of his whisky, feeling it burn its way down his throat and warm his insides. He glanced at Steadman's pint which was three-quarters empty and raised a placatory hand. 'Sorry, I forgot to ask. Want a top up?'

'No.' Steadman's voice was icy.

'Come on, Ronny, let's talk about this man to man. Whatever makes you think that Toby's my son?'

Steadman folded his arms, leaned back and laughed. He

tapped the side of his nose and winked at Jasper. 'I have reliable sources. That's all you need to know.'

'Sources? What sources?' Was he bluffing? Playing games?

'I've had someone follow you.'

'Jesus Christ.' Jasper went cold. 'Why? What am I supposed to have done?'

The man was a complete lunatic. Had a screw loose. Might even be dangerous.

Steadman swigged his beer and said nothing.

'You'd better tell me what's going on, or I go straight to the police,' Jasper said angrily.

Steadman smiled. 'We both know you're not going to do that.'

He had the upper hand. What the hell was this *really* about? It was serious stuff. And wasn't just about Toby.

'If you go to the police, I'll tell her. That wife of yours. And your son.'

'Are you trying to blackmail me over some sort of fantasy? You think I've been banging your wife or something?' Jasper kept his cool. 'Why would you have me followed? What have I done that's pissed you off?'

When Steadman said nothing, Jasper drained the rest of his whisky and went to get up.

'Not so fast, Cooper. Stay right where you are.'

All he wanted was this slimy git off his back.

'Your life's over. All your castles are about to come tumbling down when the shit hits the fan. Which it will. And I'll enjoy watching it happen.' He leaned back in his chair, adopting a relaxed posture. 'Unless of course…'

Jasper wanted to grab the bastard's face and twist the sarcasm out of it like juice from a lemon, but violence wasn't in his nature. He was normally a calm man, but this piece of filth was testing him to the limit.

'Unless what?' Jasper's stomach churned with fear.

'Money would keep me quiet. You earn more than me. I bet you got a big bonus after the double-page spread about the thalidomide scandal. As senior reporter, you can afford it.' He tapped the side of his beer glass with fingernails that needed cutting.

Jasper's heart pounded in his chest. Blackmailers were never satisfied, kept their victims locked in fear. He'd be back for more until he'd bled him dry and destroyed his entire life. Everything he'd worked so hard for—he was over. Finished. Ruined.

Steadman's voice fell to a whisper, but there was a menacing edge to it. 'Get me a £1,000.'

A thousand quid. What the hell! Kowtow to arsehole Steadman, yield to extortion.

'I haven't got that kind of money.'

'Sell your car, re-mortgage the house. I don't care how you get it.' He sniggered.

'Get lost, Steadman.'

'The clock's ticking. You've got a week to come up with the cash.'

'Fuck off. You don't know what you're talking about. You can't even make up a story of who these sources are. That's how pathetic you are.'

Steadman looked straight at Jasper through cold, serious eyes and ushered him to sit. 'You want to know? Then I'll tell you.'

Jasper sat. His heart was banging in his chest. What the hell was Steadman going to say?

'Actually, not now, all in the fullness of time.'

Jasper was fuming. He couldn't leave him hanging like this.

'You'll have to be more careful if you want your private life to remain private. There are things I know, going right back to Toby's birth.' He chuckled as if he'd made a joke.

. . .

A COLD CHILL swept through him. He didn't need to hear any more. Steadman knew. Jasper stood up, his legs wobbly, stars dancing in front of his eyes. He felt physically sick, as if he was about to throw up. 'Get lost.' He turned and staggered out of the pub.

Outside, he loosened his tie and took several gasps of breath, feeling his lungs expand. His forehead and neck were sweating, and it was a huge relief to be away from Steadman and out in the fresh air. He couldn't believe what he'd just heard. He hadn't seen that coming. But what to do? How was he going to deal with it? Inside he was screaming, *don't give in to blackmail—tell Sandy*.

Telling Sandy the truth was going to be the hardest thing ever. The thought scared him to the bone and yet he'd always known at some point he'd have to. He had no idea how she would react. She'd go to pieces. She'd find Jasper's deceit abhorrent. She'd be beside herself with rage. It was a complete unknown. If he could just put it off for a tiny bit longer. Give himself time to work out with Bill what he planned to say. Because despite months of mulling this over, he was totally unprepared—hadn't a clue.

Walking towards Temple tube station, although his pace was brisk he felt dazed. If he handed the money over, it would be an admission of sorts.

On the other hand, he had a choice. He could ignore him. But was that wise? It was a massive risk given Steadman's threats.

During the journey from Waterloo to Haslemere he closed his eyes and tried to imagine what it would be like for poor Sandy finding out the truth after fifteen years of believing her baby had died. To discover that he was very much alive and well and living nearby. It was hard to imagine the shock she'd feel. It was going to be devastating.

If he told her the truth, he'd have to tell her every sordid detail. And even though Sandy had planned for her baby to be adopted, Jasper didn't imagine her feeling anything other than disgust. The barbaric and wilful neglect of the doctor ordering her baby to be put in a cold room to die. A professional she'd trusted. When he'd told her the baby had died, she had no reason to disbelieve him. But not just one professional, two. The midwife. Who'd been kind and caring during the delivery, but quick to seize the opportunity to snatch her baby. All of it—it beggared belief.

Jasper rested his eyes for the remainder of the journey, but he felt deeply troubled.

Back home, having paid the taxi driver, he stood on the driveway gazing up at the house. He was proud of what he'd achieved and knew that his parents were proud of him too. A detached house in a quiet, desirable close. Something that no one in his family had achieved. And to think of how his life had begun. Growing up in a two-up-two-down, his parents barely having two halfpennies to rub together. A tin bath in the scullery and a lav in the garden. Pushing an old pram three miles through the snow in the bitter winter of '47 to nick coal from the yard. He'd come a long way. He'd saved hard for the deposit, and applying for a mortgage hadn't been easy.

But it was theirs. Every brick, every pane of glass.

And he wasn't about to lose it all. And certainly not to that bastard Steadman.

Opening the front door, he stepped inside to the delicious aroma of his favourite dish, coq au vin. Domestic bliss hit. Then, when Sandy's smiling face appeared in the hall to greet him and kiss him, his resolve melted. He couldn't do it. Couldn't risk hurting her.

To see the admiration and love in her eyes as their lips touched. All thoughts of telling her and the confrontation that would surely follow were dissolved in a kiss.

Damn it, he hated himself for even considering giving money to that thieving arsehole. The man was a criminal. The lowest of the low. But this was huge. He couldn't risk upsetting her before the baby was born. If paying hush money to get Steadman off his back gave him more time, it might be worth it. And by the time Steadman demanded more, he'd have told her. But never again would he give in to threats, not from Steadman, not from anyone.

'You're just in time. The baby's kicking. Here, feel…' She grabbed his hand and put it to her swollen belly. 'Can you feel him moving?' Her eyes sparkled with excitement.

Why would he want to risk losing all this? He couldn't. He just couldn't.

'Wow,' he said, trying to forget the dreadful day he'd had. 'Is that a fist? I think the little blighter just punched me.'

They both laughed.

He felt tears prick his eyes and he stroked her hair. 'You're wonderful, darling, and I love you so much. Just think, in a few weeks' time, we're going to have a baby.'

17

Jasper longed for his brain to find sleep and his mind to switch off. Now, at two in the morning and feeling groggy, he stood bare-chested at the bedroom window looking out. The sky was still and blistered with stars. The moon, a marble. He wouldn't be going to work today. He didn't feel up to it.

Jasper had always thought he had his life under control, that he was the architect of his future. But in the cold clarity of hindsight, some of his decisions would have been different.

He should never have got so involved in Bill and Toby's life. He'd overstepped a personal and professional boundary and that always came with consequences. In befriending them, he'd gone way beyond the scope of his role as reporter and ended up opening a box of trouble.

Would he have been better off not knowing that he had a son? Blissful ignorance was a better state to be in than flailing in this mess.

Maybe he shouldn't have covered the thalidomide story at all. Motivated by his own loss of a thalidomide baby, he'd been too personally involved. It never paid to cover a story that would result in the unearthing of deep emotion. Passion had driven him, the fight for justice had burned. Considering everything now, he wondered if he should have passed the story over to Steadman who'd been clamouring to take it on.

And then he remembered one of the reasons why he hadn't wanted Steadman involved in the thalidomide story. Steadman had wanted to take the story off in a different direction, but Jasper had insisted they stick to the main theme of the investigation—which was a series of interviews with thalidomide-affected families to show how they were getting on with their lives. How they were coping or not coping as was the case, and with the aim of putting pressure on the government and Distillers, the pharmaceutical company that had supplied the drug, to help those families.

Did Steadman's campaign of vitriol have anything to do with his bitterness about not being involved in the thalidomide investigative story?

Jasper slipped back into bed and stared at the swirling patterns of the Artexed ceiling and then at his wife sleeping peacefully beside him, her body the shape of a question mark. It was a nuisance that his arm was still in plaster. Otherwise, he'd have been tempted to slip out of the house and go for a head-clearing drive.

His car. Shit. He'd have to sell it to pay Steadman. They'd ploughed all their savings into buying the house. He loved his motor, it was part of who he was, who he wanted to be. It felt so good to drive. No other car could compete with a Jag. The smooth braking, the fast acceleration. It made him feel in control of his own destiny. It was fun, loud, empowering. But that bastard had him backed into a corner.

It was the finest car he'd ever driven. Jasper often retreated to his lair, the garage, to spend time with his pride and joy. Men and their cars. That was something Sandy would never understand. 'If you had testicles,' he'd once told her, 'you'd understand.'

He couldn't afford to be sentimental about the vehicle. If he wasn't going to tell Sandy, it had to go.

WITH THE SUN brightening the room he rose, needing coffee to ignite the morning. He told Sandy that his arm was hurting, and he'd decided to take the day off. Waiting until they were dressed and seated at the kitchen table, he made his big announcement. Sandy was bound to be pleased. She'd always complained about the lack of leg room in the Jag.

'I've decided to sell the car.'

She put her mug down and stared at him. 'You're having me on?'

'We need a family car. The Jag isn't practical. The back seat won't be big enough for the carrycot.'

'Darling.' She reached for his hand. 'But you love it. Won't you be heartbroken?'

Yes, he would be. More than she could imagine. But he didn't want her to know that. All he could do was smile and try not to show how devastated he felt.

'You don't have to sell it. I know how much it means to you. You worked hard to be able to buy that car.' Her eyes lit up. 'Perhaps we could buy a cheap second car. That way you get to keep it.'

He was horrified. He hadn't expected that. 'We don't need two cars,' he said forcefully. 'What an extravagance. We'll drive over to Guildford. You can look round the shops while I'm at the garage. Take as long as you like, and we'll meet up for lunch.'

'You know me and shopping. I never miss the opportunity of a browse round The Army & Navy.'

Giving in to Steadman's blackmail was supposed to be the easy route out of the mess, the chicken's way out. It was proving more difficult than he'd anticipated.

He scraped his chair back. 'When you're ready, we'll head out.'

'Today? I didn't realise you meant today.'

'May as well. You don't have anything planned, do you?'

'Nothing planned. I'd love to go shopping, but why today? I just know you're going to regret this, darling. It's never a good idea to rush into decisions.'

'Actually, I've been thinking about it for a while,' Jasper lied.

'What?'

'When you got pregnant, I knew it would have to go.'

'Would have been nice if you'd discussed it with me, rather than spring it on me like this?'

'You could look round the garage with me if you like, but you'd find it boring. You know how tedious those sales guys can be.'

'Gosh yes. I'll leave that to you.'

PARTING with his Jag later that day, Jasper felt as if his right arm had been chopped off. The grief he felt was like physical pain. It had been the mark of his success. He was reminded of the time in the school playground as a child, faced with bullies who'd snatched his toy car and refused to give it back. He might as well have been five years old now. The feelings were similar.

He met Sandy in a café on the high street. She was sipping tea at a window table and several bags of shopping sat at her feet.

'Your face, Jasper. You look horrified. They're just clothes for the baby. I didn't splash out on myself. No point in buying any new dresses until I've got my figure back, although I did see one or two lovely outfits.'

'I've bought a car. We'll head back to the garage after lunch.'

. . .

'Surprise,' Jasper said when they were standing in front of the new car an hour later.

'Oh, darling,' Sandy said excitedly. 'What a lovely car and such a gorgeous colour. I used to have a dress this exact same blue. It's so cheerful.'

It was a sky-blue 5-door Morris Marina estate. Very boring and unadventurous.

'It was a great swap.' *Hardly*, Jasper thought, but he had to downplay the massive price difference. He hoped she wouldn't ask what he was going to do with the extra money they now had.

'Four doors and a big boot. And loads of room for the carrycot. I love it. Jasper you are wonderful.'

He recoiled in embarrassment. It was a pile of crap. If only she knew the truth.

She seemed so happy, giggling as she threw herself at him with a big kiss on the lips. 'You did this for us! You're the best husband.'

He now had the money to pay Steadman, which he'd slap on his desk in the morning. Get it over and done with and then that would be the end of it. He'd then decide on a right time to tell Sandy. His stomach was in knots. Was there ever a right time to find out your husband was a liar? Did he even need to tell her once he'd paid Steadman off?

Telling her was the right thing to do. It was what his head was screaming for him to do. But his gut was urging him not to rush into it. The pressure was off. He was back in control and could decide the best time. It certainly wouldn't be before the birth. The shock could induce her labour.

18

There was a pleasant stillness to the cooler air that signified summer was ending.

The melting sun was a flame across the sky, like a battle cry to the gathering night and the storm raging in Jasper's head as he entered the woods where he'd arranged to meet Bill. It was good to be out of the house, away from Sandy and the crushing guilt he felt every time he looked at her. Amid the trees stretching to the sky, this was a peaceful sanctuary, his troubles weaving with nature's sounds and smells.

The woods were a halfway point between their homes, and it hadn't taken him long to walk here. From a vantage point on the fringes of the wood, he waited for Bill's truck to arrive, his anxiety mounting by the second. How was Bill going to react to his news? Remembering Bill's warning that if the secret of Toby's birth and parentage ever came out, they'd have to flee, Jasper wondered how likely that was. It took effort and planning to up sticks, and wasn't practical. Would Bill really quit his job, a job he enjoyed, and take Toby, do a disappearing act?

The thought of never seeing his son again was unbearable. Unthinkable. They'd become good friends. Toby was about to become a brother, yet he had no idea. How was that fair, how was it morally right to deny him his blood family? With miles between them it would be impossible to hold on to the close relationship he'd formed with Toby.

Toby had to stay here. He was taking his exams next summer. It would be cruel and unsettling to uproot him. He'd been through enough change when they'd moved down from Blackpool three years ago.

Jasper rubbed his head, silently swearing to himself. Maybe it wouldn't come to that. He was overthinking. He'd talk to Bill and together they'd work out what to do.

Poor bloke. It must have been so hard raising a handicapped child alone while grieving the loss of his wife. Yet faced with a world that wasn't accessible for his child's needs, he'd overcome each problem. He'd made adaptions to the cottage and gadgets to make Toby's life easier. From calling an electrician in to fit new light switches that Toby could reach, to installing a simpler lock on the front door. People generally lacked understanding, and all that form-filling he must have done over the years and the endless hospital appointments. Bill was a good dad. He'd done his best to make sure Toby had a happy childhood. Could he himself have done any better?

Jasper watched Bill parking. He wandered over and after they'd exchanged greetings Bill led the way into the wood, as if navigating a pathway through the mess they both found themselves in. The only sound came from their feet crunching over twigs and fallen leaves. A short way in, they came to a felled tree.

These clandestine meetings made Jasper feel increasingly uncomfortable. The secret had become like a cancer, eating away at him and he didn't like how it made him; scheming and conniving. Getting it out into the open would be a relief of sorts.

'You said it was urgent. What's on your mind?' Brushing

moss from the bark, Jasper perched on the edge and as Bill joined him, the wood creaked with the extra weight.

All Jasper's pent-up worries were waiting to burst. Everything he couldn't tell a soul, now tumbled from his mouth. The confrontation with Steadman to the humiliation of being forced to sell his Jag. As he told his story, he realised the gravity of the situation and how wretched he felt. He turned to Bill who was slumped forward, shaking his head.

∼

JASPER LOOKED BLOODY AWFUL. This wasn't the confident man Bill had befriended three years ago. This one appeared to have had a personality transplant. He was meant to be a sodding journalist, used to asking clever questions, turning situations around and yet he'd cowered from this Steadman guy, meekly coughing up a ridiculous sum of money.

'I can't believe you took the fella's idle threat so seriously. Selling your car. That was drastic. Sounds to me like this guy's got you over a barrel. By paying him you've acknowledged he was right. You should have ignored him.'

Fear was streaked across Jasper's face. 'I just wanted him off my back.'

'What the hell were you thinking?' Bill asked. 'You've played straight into this geezer's hands. And I thought you were the bright one.'

'He was threatening to tell Sandy. What was I supposed to do?'

'He's got a hunch. So what? He knows something's going on, but that's it. He's not interested in your life. He just wants to manipulate you and you've given him leverage to do just that. Jesus, what have you done to piss this guy off?'

'He's never liked me.'

'Stay out of his way then.'

'You make it sound so simple. Doesn't it worry you that he's got someone following us? It bloody well should do.'

'It's hot air, that's all, to scare you. Only *we* know what happened and it's going to stay that way.'

'I must have slipped up.'

Bill grabbed Jasper's arm. 'What do you mean?'

'I don't know. I've been racking my brains. I can't think.'

'We've got to be careful. We don't want to arouse suspicion.'

Jasper rubbed the side of his head and stood up. 'It doesn't matter what he knows, how he knows. The fact is he *does* know. That makes him a threat.' Jasper made a despairing gesture with his hands. 'Look, Bill, we can't keep it from Sandy and Toby forever. It's time they both knew. For Christ sake, they've got a right to know. Even without Steadman causing trouble, at some point they'll guess. Toby looks more like me by the day. It's insane that Sandy doesn't know what happened to her baby. And Toby deserves to know who his real parents are. We're both living a lie.'

When they'd first met, Jasper had come across as caring, compassionate, and genuinely concerned for the plight of the thalidomide families. But sometimes Bill saw a different side to him. A man who wanted to take over Toby's life given half a chance. He was already trying. His wild and ridiculous suggestions about Toby's future for example. Town Week. The Queen concert. University. He had an inkling that Jasper and Toby laughed about him behind his back. Sometimes Toby acted all snarly, was critical of Bill's ways. He could see that his son was losing respect for him. Slowly slipping away. Into the clutches of his real father.

Jasper continued. 'I can't go on like this. My marriage is held together by a lie. And our relationship with Toby—all lies. I don't know how you live with it.'

'Because I have to. What choice do I have?'

Was this the beginning of the end for him? Sandy mustn't find out.

As though reading his mind, Jasper said, 'Sandy won't go to the police. I'll make sure of it.'

Bill scoffed. 'How, by tying her up?'

'Don't be ridiculous.'

Bill looked up at the trees, feeling utter despair. 'I could face years in prison for conspiracy to abduct a child.'

'There were mitigating circumstances. If it hadn't had been for Rona, my son would have died in that cold room.'

'Rona had no right to take him. That's how the court would look at it.'

'Lucky for you, the two key witnesses are dead.'

'My wife's dead. I wouldn't call that lucky,' Bill scoffed.

'I'm sorry, I didn't mean that.' Jasper's voice fell to a hissed whisper as he looked around to check that nobody was nearby. 'Bill, we have to tell them. It's the right thing to do. And you know it.'

Bill got up and walked deeper into the woods, kicking moss and leaves in his pathway. Jasper followed. It was easier to think while putting one foot in front of the other.

'You want to see me banged up?' He couldn't look at Jasper. He felt so frustrated.

'She won't go to the police.'

Bill stopped and spun round. 'She will. Any mother would. She'll demand a full investigation.'

'And would you blame her?'

'No.' Bill felt tugged in two directions. The thought of Toby knowing the truth. Of him, Bill, being branded a liar. That pivotal moment that would change his world forever. It would be traumatic, might even derail him. Knowing his whole life had been a lie. His dad wasn't his real dad, his mum wasn't his real mum.

Above all Bill was desperate for Toby's memories of Rona to

be protected. For him to continue to think of her as a loving mother and a good woman. Bill wanted the happy times to be locked away in Toby's young head undisturbed. Otherwise, all those beautiful memories would be meaningless. They'd be replaced with bitter thoughts. After all these years, it would be cruel. He'd be scarred for life.

And how would Toby feel about his real parents, Sandy, and Jasper? Bill couldn't deal with the fallout. Any of it. He couldn't handle complicated and tangled emotions. That had been Rona's department.

His biggest worry was losing Toby. That worry kept him locked in a permanent state of fear. Lying had never felt right. What sort of parent lies to their child? When Toby had asked about family and who he most looked like, Bill had felt like a fraud. He reckoned he must have told so many lies over the years. The thought of losing the one person in his life who truly mattered—the boy he'd always considered to be his son. Forget blood ties. He'd raised him and that counted for so much more. But if the truth came out, and the shit hit the fan, would Toby turn on him? He dreaded that very real possibility.

'I can't spend the rest of my days walking around with this secret. I'll burst from the pressure of it. I feel shackled by it,' Jasper said.

Bill grabbed Jasper's shoulder and their eyes locked. 'Please, I'm begging you, don't tell her. It will break me. It will break Toby.'

'I'm not making any more promises. I'll do what's right for Sandy and our future.'

The air crackled with hostility and Jasper looked angrier than Bill had ever seen him. His face had turned hard and there were deep frown lines across his forehead.

'You're the one who put me in this impossible position.' Jasper's words were like pistol shots, and then without warning he turned and stormed off.

Bill stared after him. His instinct was to run after him, beg him not to tell Sandy, but a niggling conscience pricked at him. Everything Jasper had said, he was right. Sandy and Toby did have a right to know. He looked up at the branches of the trees. Dear God, how was he going to get out of this nightmare? He stood rooted to the spot feeling totally lost and alone. He needed a stiff drink. To feel the ruinous effects on his brain. Why did Rona have to die, leaving him to deal with this mess?

19

It was Saturday and Toby and Lucy had been practising all day for Town Week. Toby's feet were aching, and he needed a drink.

Lucy went into the kitchen and returned with two glasses of orange squash.

After he'd finished his drink, he said, 'I wanted to ask you something.' His heart was hammering in his chest. Why was this so hard?

'Go on.'

'I wondered if you'd like to see Queen with me, in Hyde Park on the 18th?' He suddenly felt overcome by nerves and felt himself bottling out. 'It's not much notice. Sorry, you've probably got other plans, a boyfriend, oh look, I didn't mean it like that, I'm just asking as a friend, not as a date, Jasper can't come with me...' All that stammering and waffling. What would she think? He willed himself to try again. Pulling his shoulders back, he took a deep breath and snapped the sentence out. 'Would you like to come with me?'

She beamed at him. 'I'd love to.'

'You like Queen?'

'What sort of a question is that? They're only the greatest band ever.'

He felt a surge of joy and took a gulp of air. 'Great. We can get the last train back.'

Casually she took a cigarette from her back pocket, perching on a stool by the open window. 'Something to look forward to.' Lighting the cigarette, she took it to her lips in that sexy way of hers. Toby watched the smoke coiling lazily in front of her as she exhaled.

'Who's in the line-up?' she asked.

'Supercharge, Steve Hillage and Kiki Dee. There's a rumour that Elton John will join her on stage for 'Don't Go Breaking My Heart.'

'Love that song. No wonder it was number one for six weeks.' A smile flitted across her face. 'At Town Week, we're going to be like them, Kiki Dee and Elton John.' She winked at him.

'Hardly.' He felt the colour rise to his cheeks.

'The crowd will love us.' She yawned, stretching her arms above her head in the shape of a cathedral spire. For a moment he thought she would drop the cigarette but as with everything he'd seen her do, she was in control. She was wearing a white embroidered cheesecloth blouse and faded denim shorts; simple clothes but to Toby they looked hot. She rested the cigarette on a saucer on the windowsill, getting up from the stool and rising onto the balls of her feet, taking him by surprise when she twirled like an elegant ballerina, kicking her leg out behind her. Toby pushed the guitar away, flexing his feet and watching her. Something radiated from her.

'They'll love *you*,' she added, smiling and pointing at him. She danced towards him with dainty steps. He couldn't work her out. Did she like him—in that way? She leaned down, floral scent wafting towards him and ruffled his hair. He jerked away.

He felt like a puppy being petted, rather than someone she'd consider dating.

'I play the guitar, but I'm literally nothing special,' he said.

'You are, but you don't see it.'

About to answer her, Toby's eyes darted to the window. A ladder had appeared and a man with a cloth and a bucket was climbing rung by rung.

'The window cleaner. That reminds me, Mum wanted me to pay him.'

Sloshing soapy water over each square pane of glass, the man rubbed the smears until they gleamed, spending more time than he needed to. He kept glancing in, as if interested in what they were doing.

Twenty minutes later the doorbell rang. Toby and Lucy were in the hallway—Toby slipping into his flip-flops ready for his dad to pick him up.

Lucy flung the door open, stepping back into the hallway because the window cleaner was standing so close, his toes were touching the threshold. He wasn't smiling, which Toby found rude considering he was offering a service and about to be paid.

'Hang on a tick and I'll get your money.'

Left in the hallway while Lucy dashed upstairs to get the money, Toby glanced at the man. He recognised him from somewhere. There was a vague sense of danger about him, but he couldn't think why. Was it his greasy hair, his thin face covered in pock marks, or his long, crooked nose? Whatever it was, Toby felt edgy. He considered making small talk about the weather but didn't want to. Luckily, a moment later, Lucy was back and handing over the money. Toby felt relief when she closed the door.

'There's something creepy about him,' she said.

'Yes, I thought that too. I'm sure I've seen him before.'

Bill arrived, the tyres of his truck crunching over the gravel, sweeping to a halt next to the window cleaner's van. Toby said goodbye to Lucy, and climbing into the passenger seat, he glanced over at the van and saw the man was filling in paperwork. A cold chill swept through him. An odd thought briefly flitted through his mind. Should they wait until the man had left before going? Something made him feel unnerved. Was Lucy safe? But as Bill turned the truck round and headed out onto the road, Toby glanced round and saw the man was also leaving.

'How did you get on today?' his dad asked cheerily.

So annoying. Why did adults have to do this? Constant questions he couldn't be bothered to answer. It was like the Spanish Inquisition. Toby smiled to himself. That was a line that one of his friends had come out with once, when the teacher had asked a barrage of questions. Toby didn't know what it meant but the comment had riled the teacher.

'Fine.'

'Ready for the performance?'

It was an effort to answer. 'Yeah.'

'Yes.' Bill spat the word. 'If your mother was here now.'

'Yeah, yeah, I know. She'd correct me for my sloppy speech.'

Toby looked out of the window. What a drag his dad was. And tonight they were going to be stuck in together. He wished he was back in Lucy's company, hanging out on that cosy sofa of hers, listening to music, going through her vast record collection, sharing jokes and chatting.

Glancing at the wing mirror he noticed the window cleaner's van was still behind them. He was probably heading into town and his next client, but then when Bill turned into their lane, the man indicated too and followed into the lane. Bill's truck turned to the left and along a bumpy track that led to their cottage. Toby kept watching to see what the man was doing. He'd stopped. He wasn't heading down to the school. He was stationary and was watching the truck. Bill swung the vehicle round, parking it in front of the bank of bracken that flanked a wooded area to the side of the cottage. Toby jumped out and walked back a short way into the lane to get a better view of the man's van, but it had gone. He stood there for a few moments, wondering what had just happened. It was odd, as if the man had been deliberately following them.

'What's up?' Bill asked. 'You look like you've seen a ghost.'

'There was a window cleaner at Lucy's. He was dead creepy. I'm sure he was watching us play our guitars. He spent ages on the windows and whenever I looked up, he'd look away. I think he's just followed us home. He came halfway down the lane and stopped. Seemed a bit weird that's all.'

'What did he look like?'

'Long nose, greasy hair, acne marks all over his face. Ugly. I've seen him around, somewhere, not sure where.'

'Come on, let's go inside, get the tea on.'

∽

As Bill opened a can of beans and poured it into a saucepan to heat up, all he could think about was the window cleaner. Maybe it was nothing. Bill's sixth sense told him something wasn't right. He poured the beans over toast on two plates, then took the saucepan to the sink. As water splashed over the pan he stared out of the window and up the track to where Toby had been looking. Was the man out there watching the cottage? Before putting the plates on the table, he quickly went round closing all the curtains.

Much later, when Toby had gone upstairs, Bill picked up the phone to ring Jasper.

After chatting for a few moments, Bill's voice fell to a whisper. 'The reason I'm phoning is because I've been thinking about what you said the other day in the wood, about being followed.'

'That's what Steadman told me, whether it's true or not. You didn't seem too worried.'

145

'It's probably nothing but there was a window cleaner at Lucy's while Toby was over there practising for Town Week. It sounds far-fetched but Toby reckons he followed us home and hovered at the end of the track before turning to go.'

'Did he go down to the school?'

'No, that's the thing, he didn't. And I'm the caretaker, I'd know if we'd taken on a new window cleaner.'

'That's odd. Keep your wits about you, Bill.'

'Toby thinks he's seen the bloke around. He isn't sure where.'

'Ask him tomorrow, see if he remembers.'

'No, I'd rather just forget it.'

20

Pregnancy had deepened Sandy's love for Jasper. After the loss of their first baby, she was looking forward to the sight of her husband holding their newborn and being filled with love. As the big day approached, her preparations were in full swing. She just wanted everything to be right.

During the week, Sandy had gone for a walk with Lisa, a friend who'd recently given birth. They'd met at an antenatal class. Sandy had joined the class to get to know other expectant mums. She didn't really like groups, and walking into the community centre, she'd known right away that it wasn't going to be her thing. Thank God for Lisa, the only one that Sandy had really gelled with.

Lisa had a brand new Maclaren three-in-one pram buggy. The carrycot could be taken out to put in the car and even used as a cot around the house. The frame folded up and there was a basket for shopping. It was so much lighter and more modern than the cumbersome old coach-built Silver Cross prams. Sandy had tested it out on their walks together. She wanted this latest model, in the same way that some men desired a particular car.

Today, being a Saturday, seemed like the perfect opportunity to pop over to the Army & Navy store in Guildford, view their collection and put a deposit down. Jasper had just been paid.

'What's up, darling? You've been staring out at the garden for the past ten minutes,' Sandy asked Jasper.

Jasper was sitting at the kitchen table cradling his coffee. She put a plate of hot buttered toast in front of him and took a slice for herself. He'd seemed so distant of late and not his usual self. On a few occasions she'd caught him with a worried expression on his face, but when she'd asked him what was wrong, he'd said that his broken arm was hurting or that work was stressful. He was hard to reach, keeping his worries bottled inside. If work was making him feel down, she hoped it wasn't anything serious.

When he didn't answer her, his eyes still distant, the toast untouched, she tried another tack. Preparing for the baby's arrival would cheer him. After all, he'd enjoyed decorating the nursery. 'Shall we buy the pram today?' She sat down at the table next to him, her words having an instant effect on him because he turned to face her with a frown on his face which changed to a smile. But it wasn't a natural smile. She wished he'd tell her what was bothering him.

'We can have a look, I suppose,' he said flatly.

'Just a look?'

'We don't want to rush into it.'

'Why not? The baby will be here in a few weeks. And it could arrive early.'

'There's still plenty of time.'

And then the penny dropped. He was anxious about the birth and things going wrong. How insensitive of her to think that only she had a monopoly over such worries. 'It's going to be fine,' she said, patting his hand. 'I've got a good feeling.'

'I thought you said your mother might be buying us one as a gift.'

She stared at him, incredulous. 'My mother, buy us a pram?

What on earth gave you that idea? Since when have my parents been generous?'

'Well, if your mum asks, maybe suggest a pram.'

'Don't be ridiculous. It's not going to happen. Unless this is your idea of a joke.'

'Nope, I was being deadly serious.'

'Mum's a mean old cow. Always has been. You know that.'

'All right, calm down, I was just saying that's all.'

'Well, it has to be the stupidest thing you've said in a long time. Honestly, Jasper.'

'Forget I said it.'

'What's got into you lately? You're not yourself.'

'I'm fine.'

It wasn't like Jasper to be so snappy.

'Nothing's wrong.' He glanced at his watch. 'Goodness, is that the time? Jim asked us to pop along to the church hall this morning.' Jasper and Jim first met on the train into London several years back and had become friends, sharing the daily commute ever since. Sandy had never met him or his wife.

'Why?'

'I don't know. Won't take five minutes. There's a jumble sale on this morning.'

'What the bloody hell do you want to go to a jumble sale for?'

'We're only dropping by.'

'I THINK I'll stay here. You know how much I hate jumble sales.' She got up from the table and put her cup in the washing-up bowl. 'All those whiffy old clothes piled high on tables. I don't mind dropping in on our way into Guildford though,' she added cheerfully. She'd soon pull him out of the doldrums. Lunch in town would perk him up. A look round the nursery section of the Army & Navy or Mothercare wouldn't do any harm. He'd soon soften. She smiled to herself. Having that pram in her possession, it would feel like Christmas and birthday had come at once.

∽

JASPER WENT UPSTAIRS to get ready. Brushing his teeth more vigorously than normal, he silently cursed his reflection in the bathroom mirror. He couldn't afford to buy her a new pram and that's what she was expecting—not the second-hand one they were due to pick up from his friend at the jumble sale. He'd planned to surprise her, but now she was talking about looking at new ones. Shit, yet again he'd ballsed up. He should have told her over breakfast. He was really going to get it in the neck.

He rinsed his mouth and headed downstairs, joining her in the hall where she stood smiling up at him. She looked so beautiful. None of this was her fault. If only he could buy her what she wanted. He'd never denied her a thing, not once. He loved splashing out, it was what men were supposed to do and it made her happy. It made him happy to see her happy. She'd given up working at the school at the start of her pregnancy, so she was now totally reliant on him.

He'd got himself into an unfathomable mess and still couldn't believe it. He shuddered as he remembered handing over crisp notes to Steadman in an alleyway near work. And already the bastard wanted more. Steadman was scum, but despite Bill's complacency, Jasper was scared. There would have been trouble if he hadn't coughed up.

At the church hall there was a bustle of people diving into heaps of old clothes and long-forgotten treasures. Occasionally somebody let out a delighted gasp, slinging items over their shoulders, delving into their purses for coins. Jasper smiled sarcastically. He craned his neck to find the lady he was looking for. He was taking a huge risk, knowing how much Sandy hated cast-offs.

'Jasper,' Jim's wife, Mrs Linton called. She waved at Jasper and Sandy from the back of the hall. 'I've saved it for you, it's locked away in the back room.'

'What's she talking about?' Sandy muttered as they approached the buxom, red-faced woman.

'Her husband mentioned they had a pram we could have. If you don't like, just say no.'

'Jasper, I want a new pram, like Lisa's,' Sandy whispered as they followed the woman to the back of the noisy hall.

'I'm so glad it's going to a good home.' The woman led the way along the corridor. 'How lovely to see you both.' She smiled at Jasper, then turned to Sandy. 'And nice to meet you, Sandy, I've heard all about you.'

Mrs Linton turned to unlock a cupboard door and behind her back Sandy glared at Jasper and mouthed something.

∽

MRS LINTON PULLED out a navy Silver Cross from the cupboard, sending a few coats flying from pegs. Sandy could see that one of the poppers on the cover had broken. She gritted her teeth and smiled. Jasper had always known how she felt about second-hand equipment for their child. She'd told him enough times and couldn't have made it clearer. It would be different if they'd been poor, or he'd lost his job.

She couldn't possibly refuse the pram. It would be really rude of her and she'd come across as ungrateful. Mrs Linton seemed like a nice lady and it was kind of her to think of them. After all, she could easily have sold it for a good price.

'This is so sweet of you, Mrs Linton, but...'

'Not at all, dear, not at all.' The woman beamed at Sandy through caring eyes, and Sandy quietly cringed and chastised herself at how unappreciative she felt.

'We were going to buy a new one from the Army & Navy,'

Sandy said. Jasper earned well. They really didn't need this hand-me-down.

'Why would you want to do that?' Mrs Linton looked horrified. 'No point in paying good money. The baby won't be in it for long.'

'My thoughts exactly,' Jasper muttered.

'These old coach-built Silver Cross prams are the best and built to last. I wouldn't trust a new pram. This is a baby chariot fit for a prince or princess. And to think, Silver Cross carried the Queen herself. These carriages are real beauties. Out in the sunshine, the chrome gleams and it glides effortlessly along the pavement. Here, push it down the corridor, you'll see for yourself. Feel the bouncing suspension.'

Sandy stared at the pram, her heart quietly breaking. After her dreadful experience first time around, losing a baby, she just wanted everything to be perfect and for nothing to go wrong. Was it so bad to want everything to be fresh and new? Part of the whole experience of having a baby was buying exactly what she wanted.

As Sandy pushed it along the corridor, Mrs Linton prattled on. 'It's been sitting in our garage for possibly ten years, now I come to think of it. My son had it and his two cousins. You're doing me a huge favour. I'm trying to have a sort out and it's taking up room.' It had clearly done the rounds and it felt as if Mrs Linton was just dumping it on them. Sandy wished she could say no.

Was that a whiff of damp she could smell? She'd heard about cot death. Little babies dying in their sleep. What if old equipment was one of the causes of these unexplained deaths? Babies lying in prams and cots that were damp from having been stored for years in garages, sheds, and lofts.

Thank God they'd already bought a cot. She'd be offering one of those next.

'There's also a cot in the loft if you're interested.'

'We already have one but thank you for the offer.'

'What do you want for the pram?' Jasper asked.

Sandy's stomach knotted. Her head was filling with images of beautiful new prams all lined up in the department store, smelling divine and wrapped in cellophane.

'Nothing, my dears. As I say, you're doing me a favour. I can get Jim to drop it round after six this evening. How's that sound?'

'Wonderful,' Jasper said.

Back in the car, it was a few minutes before Sandy spoke. She was still angry but needed to choose her words carefully. She didn't want to come across as selfish and ungrateful.

'I thought we'd agreed to buy a new pram,' she said.

Jasper was upbeat. 'Mrs Linton saved us a lot of money.'

'We don't struggle for money though, darling, do we? You earn well.'

'It's a good pram. Very sturdy.'

'It would have been nice if we'd discussed it first rather than you spring it on me like that.'

'I'm sorry, but I think she's right. The baby won't be in it for long.'

He'd ignored her question about money. It was his thrift that concerned her more. Lately she found he was always grumbling about the price of things and working out how to cut back on household expenses. It was odd because he'd always spent money so freely, making the point he hated to watch the pennies.

21

Toby and Lucy were in Hyde Park for the Queen concert. It was another glorious day. Wispy clouds brush-stroked against a deep blue sky. Finding somewhere to sit, they collapsed onto the grass. Unfortunately, they were a long way back from the stage, but Toby didn't mind. Any nearer, it would be too loud. He didn't tell Lucy that thought. Didn't want her to think him a wimp. He guessed she was already thinking that by the look on her face when she saw he'd brought cans of coke and lemonade with him. She intended to get tipsy, having smuggled vodka and beer from her parents' stash.

The park was filling up. Toby looked at the sea of faces, the crowd stretching as far as his eyes could see. There were people in the trees as well, which made him smile. He'd never been to such a large event before, never seen so many people gathered in one place. This was massive. He found it overwhelming, but buzzy at the same time. With more and more people filling every available space, Lucy pressed closer to him.

Toby had a soft spot for Kiki, and her poster adorned the wall behind his bed. He was excited when she came onto the stage.

The crowd sang, laughed, celebrating together. Lucy swayed

into him, their hips connecting. Such great sense of camaraderie Toby would never forget.

When Kiki strode onstage, the crowd cheered loudly. But everybody had been expecting Elton John too. Instead, she was carrying a life-size cardboard Elton figure and the audience were expected to sing the Elton parts with her.

After the support acts had finished, Bob Harris introduced Queen. 'This is one of the finest moments I've seen in many a year.' The crowd screamed.

Lucy whistled, leaning towards Toby, stretching her neck to glimpse Freddie Mercury bursting onto the stage, his arms outstretched like an eagle's wings as he greeted his many fans. 'Welcome to our picnic by the Serpentine,' his voice boomed. And the crowd screamed even louder.

Lucy was swigging a bottle of beer, her second one. She hadn't touched the vodka yet. Toby hoped she'd forget about it and just enjoy the music, but maybe that was wishful thinking. How on earth could she hold it all in without needing the loo? He'd spotted a row of portaloos with long snaking queues. If one of them disappeared to the loo, they could lose each other.

'What's he wearing?' Toby shouted at Lucy above the din, but from where they were sitting, Freddie Mercury was a tiny white figure shining across the massive sea of people. Toby could just make out his ridiculous outfit. It looked like a white leotard with a huge gap at the front displaying his hairy chest.

'Don't be a prude, he's a popstar, they wear crazy costumes. Would be strange if they didn't.'

Toby felt the sting of her words, it was a mean comment and made him feel small. She laughed and swigged her beer. Worried about going to the loo, Toby had barely drunk anything.

'I'm going to buy their new album,' he said.

'Oh God,' Lucy shrieked. 'The front row. They're standing up. What the hell? Now we can't see.' Angrily, she rose onto her tiptoes at the same time others were starting to make disgruntled noises.

Enthralled, Toby dropped his jaw as Queen played their opening song—the first half of the overture on their new album, *A Day at the Races* leading into 'Bohemian Rhapsody'. They went on to play songs from the new album. Listening to the music, taking in the scene around him, Toby felt on top of the world, it was almost an out-of-body experience—so compelling.

Music filled the air, hijacking Toby's whole being, the lyrics swimming in his head like a wakeful dream, the lively beat whipping up a sense of togetherness around him–something he'd not experienced before outside the disabled community. It was uplifting, almost surreal. With Lucy beside him, jigging, their bodies close and in sync, so close he could almost taste her sweat. They were in their own little bubble of fun as the music pumped.

'Incredible,' Lucy shouted in Toby's ear. 'Makes me tingle.'

'Know what you mean,' Toby said, shaking his head to the beat. There was something about the vibration, the way the sound travelled and seemed to bounce across the crowd, like liquid energy. But the fans near the front were getting angry and shouting at those next to the stage who were still obscuring their view. It was getting nasty. Luckily Toby and Lucy were nowhere near them because cans and bottles were being hurled around.

A few songs in, Freddie shouted, 'I have been requested by the constabulary for you not to throw things around, tin cans, whatever. So, make this a peaceful event, okay? Sit on your arses and listen.'

Lucy, having finished both bottles of beer, had started on the vodka.

Toby's legs were starting to ache. He'd heard that Queen were known for their long encores and he was beginning to worry about getting out of the park, through all the people and back to the station.

When the last song was over, the crowd started chanting, 'Why are we waiting?' even though it was clear the show was over.

Without warning, the park plunged into darkness.

'Police must have turned the power off,' people shouted. There were swear words and screams.

'They should have started earlier,' Toby said. 'Then they could have played for longer.'

'No, you, wally.' She burped, slurring her words. How much vodka had she drunk? 'It wouldn't have been dark enough. They had to delay the show as long as possible so that it was dark enough for the lighting and stage effects.'

Why hadn't he thought of that? Yet again, he'd made a fool of himself. He wished he could come out with a witty comment to impress her, but he couldn't think of one. He wasn't good enough for her. But right now that wasn't his main concern. It was dark, they were in the middle of a dense crowd of people. He had no idea how they were going to make their way out of the park and Lucy was staggering on her feet, wobbly like a newborn foal. There was nothing he could do to steady her. He was utterly helpless. He couldn't grab her hand, couldn't put an arm around her shoulder or waist to guide her out of the park and down to the tube. If only they'd come in a group. He needed help. He glanced around him, hoping somebody would offer.

'You okay?' Her eyes were swimming. He should have stopped her from drinking so much, but would she have taken any notice?

He couldn't see the appeal of alcohol, after watching its ruinous effects on his dad, drinking to oblivion night after night—a crutch to blot out the loss of his wife, in the months after her death. Thank God his dad no longer drank to excess.

Lucy swayed, giggling, oblivious to their problem. He needed to take control.

'Put your arm round me,' he ordered. 'I don't want you

falling over or getting lost in the crowd. You need to get with it, otherwise we'll be stuck here all night.'

'Love it when you get all bossy.' She giggled and put her arm round him. But after several staggering paces, she doubled over, retching, vomit spraying his new jeans. How disgusting. He'd wanted to act the perfect gentleman, but she made him feel revolted.

'Here, take this.' He bent his head towards a pocket in his shirt and with his teeth yanked out a tissue and waved it front of her face.

'Thanks,' she slurred, taking it from him and mopping her mouth. 'Being with you is like being with my mum.' She burped and he hoped she wasn't going to be sick again.

'Cheers for that.'

'Is okay. I love my mummy,' she said in an exaggerated babyish voice, turning to look at him with pouted lips. 'Oh God, I so need a piss.'

Why did she have to be so uncouth?

'Over here.' He steered her to a line of portaloos.

After they'd been to the loo, Toby focused on shepherding her through the crowd. They nearly stumbled several times before finally reaching the edge of the park. They'd got this far but it had been a huge effort battling through so many people and trying to stop Lucy falling over. That prospect terrified him— she'd get trampled on. Every time she loosened her grip on his shoulder, he reminded her to keep it there. The towering marble structure of the arch loomed ahead of them. Lucy rushed over and collapsed in a heap on a park bench. Oh God. He'd never get her up now. They were going to miss the train. What on earth was he going to do?

'I want to stay here and watch the sun come up in the morning.'

'We can't do that,' he said, sinking onto the bench next to her.

'Why not?' She sounded whiny.

'We just can't.'

'Why don't we get a hotel room then?' Her eyes were sparking with excitement.

'Don't be silly.'

'Where's your sense of adventure?' She was still slurring her words. How long would it take her to sober up?

'I don't have any money. Anyway, they'll be worried if we don't get back.'

'Your dad might be. Mine won't. They never worry about me.' She stretched her arms.

'I'm sure they do.'

'Oh, Toby,' she said, turning to look at him through drunken eyes. 'In your world everything's so black and white.' Another dig. He just wanted to get home. This wasn't fun anymore but before he had the chance to defend himself, she leaned in taking him by surprise, and clasping the sides of his face, gave him a big lip-slapping drunken kiss. He could smell the harsh scent of drink and vomit, and pulled away, shocked. This wasn't how his first kiss was supposed to be. That was more like a facial collision. He stood up with a sudden plan.

'Come on, you, I can see a phone box. We can phone my dad. He'll pick us up.'

'Boring, do we have to?' She laughed but this time it was loud and cackling. Heads were turning. And in that moment, with physical exhaustion taking hold; for the first time all evening, he felt ashamed to be with her. What was his dad going to say when he saw the state she was in?

22

Bill couldn't concentrate. He hated driving in London and usually avoided it at all costs. There were too many manic, rude drivers. He was trying to manoeuvre the truck into the traffic hurtling along Park Lane, but it was hard to concentrate because he was so concerned about Lucy, who'd been slumped on the pavement looking a right mess when he'd arrived to pick them up. And Toby, standing beside her, panic across his face. Now, the three of them were sitting along the bench of the truck: Toby in the middle, Lucy flopped against the window mumbling to herself.

As he braked furiously at traffic lights, Lucy jerked forward, burped and retched. What had the kid been drinking? This was all he needed at two in the bloody morning. As he made a jerky gear change at a set of traffic lights, a ghastly smell of food and drink that had been fermenting in her stomach, spewed out, splattering the dashboard like a child's nursery painting.

Toby looked at Bill apologetically. 'Dad, I'm really sorry. I tried to stop her drinking.'

'I don't feel well,' Lucy moaned, turning white and clutching her stomach. He was going to have to navigate across the road and pull over.

He swerved across two lanes and swung the wheel onto the pavement, hastily applying the brake. Poor parking, illegal, he didn't care. Just get the girl out. He climbed down, went round, opening the passenger door and delicately, taking care not to get vomit on himself, guided her out towards the nearest drain.

He held her head over the drain while more vomit spilled as if he'd just turned on a tap. Yuck, it stank.

Bill glanced up and yelled, 'Tissues, Toby, open the glove compartment.'

Toby lifted his leg and hooked his toe around the lever to open the glove compartment. With both feet he grabbed a packet of tissues and threw it towards Bill where it landed on the pavement right in the pool of sick.

Bill stared at him, struggling not to lose his rag. After all Toby couldn't help it, but at times like this Bill felt frustrated with him. And if he felt this way, a girlfriend would feel this way too. How could the lad ever lead a normal life? He'd always need support.

'For God's sake, Toby?' Bill's heart sank. He shouldn't have said that. 'I'm sorry, I didn't mean that.'

Once he'd helped Lucy back into the truck, they were on their way. Lucy fell asleep, her head slumped on Toby's shoulder.

This was all Jasper's fault—leading Toby astray. Giving him ideas. Making him believe that he could overcome anything and lead a normal life. Jasper didn't understand the barriers Toby faced, the hurdles he'd have to overcome. He hadn't lived with the boy these past fifteen years.

Life had been simpler before Jasper had swept onto the scene, worming his way into Toby's head, and filling it with nonsense. They'd coped well enough. But now—Bill was no longer in control. Toby was slipping away. It was as if they now orbited different planets. Did his son even love him anymore? He'd seen that contempt in his eyes. The barbed comments. The stark contrast—the admiration that Toby had for Jasper. It left Bill lost, broken.

Lucy had sobered up by the time they reached her road. Chaperoning her to the front door, Bill felt saddened to think that Toby should have been doing this, but as usual it was quicker to do it himself. Like everything in their lives.

Bill waited while she found her key and unlocked the door, before he returned to the truck.

'Dad, *I* could have helped her.'

'I just thought it would be quicker if I got out.'

'Fine,' Toby said stroppily. 'You seem like you're in a bad mood because I got you out of bed. Sorry, but it wasn't my fault.'

'I don't think you should be getting involved with her.' As soon as the words were out of his mouth, Bill winced, knowing how Toby would react. No teenager liked being told who they should and shouldn't see. 'This is all Jasper's fault. Introducing you to her. I think she's a bad influence.'

Toby put his feet up on the dashboard defiantly. 'You can't tell me who I can and can't see. I'm nearly sixteen.'

'She's leading you astray. How much had she drunk?' Bill leaned towards Toby and pushed his feet from the dashboard.

'How should I know?'

'You were there.' Bill batted his hand towards Toby. 'You didn't try and stop her from making a spectacle of herself?'

'Oh yeah, right, like I'm going to stop her. Lucy's eighteen, she can do what she likes.' Toby put his feet back on the dashboard and Bill huffed.

'She should have been more responsible.'

'Why?'

'Because…' He stuttered and again couldn't stop the words tumbling from his mouth. 'She was with *you*.'

'Me?'

'Yes. If she was drunk, how could she look after you?'

'I can't believe you've just said that. I don't need her to look after me.'

'I didn't mean it like that.' Bill realised his words couldn't be retracted. But the fact remained, she wasn't a suitable girlfriend for his handicapped son.

'You're a hypocrite, Dad.' Toby liked that word. Had learned it in English. It had Greek origins. 'Remember when you used to drink every night when I was younger? That wasn't very responsible of you.'

'All right, stop your cheek. She's very beautiful but I just think you need to be wary—of her.' Worried how Toby would react to this comment, Bill felt his body stiffen in his seat and he gripped the steering wheel tightly.

'I don't need you worrying about me. I can make my own decisions.'

How wearing this all was. Sometimes he wondered how Rona would have coped with Toby the teenager. Would she have backed him up, or taken Toby's side?

'I only want the best for you.' Bill glanced at Toby and patted him on the shoulder. 'I am proud of you, I hope you know that.'

'I like Lucy. She drank too much today, but we were at a concert. Everyone was drinking.'

'I hope you weren't.'

'I had a couple of cans of cola. And so what if I had been? I bet you started drinking at my age.'

Bill ignored him and kept his eyes on the road. 'I'm worried about Town Week. Everybody staring at you, making fun.'

Toby stared at Bill, a look of annoyance on his face. 'You always have to be negative. I'm sick of it. Jasper's not like that.'

'And he lets you wade into these things without thinking of the risks. I'm more cautious. That's not a bad thing. And I've

163

been thinking of when you're sat on that stage. You could wear a poncho to cover your arms.'

'What?'

Bill was concentrating on navigating down the dark lane towards their cottage, but he felt Toby's eyes bore into him.

Bill indicated to turn into their lane. 'It would look trendy. One of those Peruvian ponchos.'

'You've got to be kidding me?'

The truck jolted over potholes and loose gravel. 'It'll stop people focusing on your arms.'

'They'll be listening to the music.'

'I know they will be, and you play the guitar so well, but adults can be as cruel as kids.'

'Let them stare,' he said as if he didn't care two hoots, but Bill knew otherwise.

'You don't mean that.'

'I'm not wearing a stupid poncho,' Toby scoffed.

'Calm down, keep your hair on.' Bill pulled up in front of the cottage.

'Well, you don't have to come and watch.'

Shocked, Bill stared at Toby. 'Of course, I'm going to be there.'

'Didn't think you'd want to,' Toby muttered.

'Of course I do.' Was Toby just being difficult? Or did he really think his dad wasn't interested in his life?

Bill found it hard to express emotion, particularly pride. What a useless parent he was. He couldn't do anything right.

23

It was mid-morning and Saturday of Town Week. Despite the blue sky and warmth in the air, Toby could feel and smell autumn calling. There was a stillness and freshness about the day he recognised from previous years, everything gearing down to the quietness of winter.

A drummer, bass guitarist, harpist and saxophonist were setting up their equipment as Toby and Lucy climbed the steps of the makeshift stage, erected at the top of the park where the land was flat.

There was a low hum of chatter across the field; the odd snort or whoop from a drinker, people embracing each other, laughing, and catching up on gossip as they wandered between stalls. Toby wasn't bothered about looking at cakes under cellophane, hand-knitted teddy bears and baby blankets and the bizarre array of hobbies that occupied people's time, like the growing of gigantic turnips. He didn't enjoy watching others try their luck at the coconut shy, Hook a Duck, Ball in Bucket, or Fairground Striker. He'd taken a dislike to fetes years ago, mainly because he couldn't play any of those games and it was frustrating to watch others have fun.

A girl sat at a grand piano in the corner of the stage tinkling various tunes, warming up. But Toby was more interested in watching the saxophonist working on his instrument and getting into shape with his sounds. Toby was also keen to watch the other musicians, particularly the drummer.

'Come on.' Lucy was standing behind Toby. 'We've got ages to hang around, we're not performing till two-thirty, let's have some fun. What's your favourite ride?' She was looking beyond the cakes and toys, the coconut shy, the hoopla and other games, to the fairground rides at the far end of the field. He took a moment to study her. She looked so beautiful, wearing thick black mascara which accentuated her features, her eyelids lightly dusted with a green powder, and lips shiny. Standing next to her made his brain buzz and without answering her he headed down the steps of the stage, glancing back with a smile as he led the way towards the queue for Devil's Tower, adrenaline spiking as he watched legs dangle from the top of the tower as the seats shot halfway down to Australia and back up again.

'The tower? You daredevil, Toby. But will you be able to hold on?'

'Why not? Look,' he said pointing, 'the bar clamps so close to the body I won't need hands to hold the bar and they harness you around the waist.' It worried Toby that he wouldn't be allowed on the ride. He'd be gutted.

She smiled at him and in that moment despite his fear of the unknown—he'd never been on a high impact ride before—he knew he had to prove something to her. Bravery, strength.

As they drew closer to the action, the noise from the rides fought with the music. A crazy concoction of Elvis Presley, Status Quo, and Chris Spedding. But underneath was a bass beat, thump, thump, thump, like the thump of Toby's own heart.

'Motor Biking' was playing at full pelt. Lucy punched the air, swivelled round, and bounced on her feet, head nodding, hair lifting. Toby smiled. She was nutty. Batty. Out there. But he loved it. She didn't care who was watching, who was judging her.

'I love this song, it puts fire in my blood, makes me want to climb on a motorbike, rev the engine, full throttle.' She moved her shoulders and hips and then with arms extended looked as if she was starting a mower and pushing it across the lawn. Then she raised her left hand behind her head, moving her arm in a series of quick jerks as if starting a water sprinkler and firing it at the lawn.

'Wow'.

'If I die, I hope the angels sing 'Motor Biking.'' She twirled, raising her hands. He liked Lucy the rebel. He looked up at the sky. Maybe his mother was looking down from heaven. *That girl's a breath of fresh air.* That's what she'd say.

Lucy laughed and looked at Toby. 'What's so funny?'

'Nothing.'

'Don't you ever dance? It's good for the soul.'

He felt heat rising to his face. 'I'm rubbish at dancing.'

She sniffed the air, wrinkling her nose. 'I smell hot dogs and fried onion,' she said excitedly, her arm wrapping around Toby's shoulder. She let her nose guide them to the burger and hot dog van where they joined the queue and ordered sausages in baps.

He felt pathetic for not having any money on him, but she was quick to hand over some coins.

'Here,' she said, offering him a bite of his bap. She'd squirted mustard and ketchup on. A 'T' on hers and an 'L' on his. He should have told her he hated mustard, but it was an 'L' for Lucy, like she was offering herself to him. He felt his brain cells glow and grinned at the hot dog seller, a woman in a queue, anybody. He was in heaven and his brain had gone all fuzzy. But he stared at the mustard as she pushed the bap towards his mouth. He was going to have to suffer the yellow gloop—for her. The spongy bread stuck to the roof of his mouth, and he forced himself to swallow, the mustard slipping down his throat, burning his insides. His gut twitched, ready to retaliate. Lucy was looking at him as she fed him, as if she somehow knew, so he took another bite, a large one this time, trying not to pull a face of disapproval. Mustard was for real men. Everybody knew that.

Toby scanned the crowds imagining those idiots on his football course seeing him now. He played it out in his head. They'd swagger off the dodgems or the Octopus and catch sight of him and Lucy, their mouths dropping open in shock. He willed it to happen, felt his heart race in anticipation. It was shallow of him, pathetic even, but Lucy turned heads. She made him feel alive and he just wanted the world to see them together. But he was never going to tell her that. She'd laugh and tell him she had a boyfriend already and he'd feel that crushing sense of defeat, like a beetle underfoot.

'Dodgems,' she shrieked, pulling Toby towards them.

'We've just eaten.'

'So what? Come on.' She pushed his shoulder, coaxing him.

Saying no wasn't an option, but the thought of throwing up yellow mess all over her blouse filled him with horror.

Lucy handed blue tokens to the dodgem attendant, and they went through. She pressed herself to the side of the car and took control of the steering wheel as Toby stepped inside, their bodies touching.

'Here we go,' she squealed. The dodgem car shot across the floor and the ride disappeared in a blur of screams and jolts, blood pumping through his head as if it was about to burst. And that mustard. Rising, rising, rising. They banged into other bumper cars. His stomach jolted. He wanted to throw up. Then the car stopped, and the session was over. Toby swallowed hard, willing himself not to throw up as Lucy checked her watch, alarm on her face. It was time to get back to the stage.

They dashed across the field, out of breath by the time they reached the stage, clambering up the steps to the corner where Toby had left his guitar.

Except that it wasn't there.

He looked at Lucy, hoping she'd tucked it somewhere out of view.

'Don't look so worried, Toby, it'll be here somewhere.' Lucy swept her fingers through her hair, frantically spinning round, her eyes searching every available space. 'Have you seen his guitar?' she asked the drummer, then the saxophonist.

'No, but check under those coats, it can't be far away.'

They went to the back of the stage, pulling up the flaps of the canvas covering the stage along all three sides, but the guitar was nowhere in sight.

'Has anyone been on the stage, other than us musicians?' Toby asked the harpist.

The drummer shrugged.

The saxophonist was eating a sandwich. He put it down on his lap, looking thoughtfully at Toby. 'There was some geezer who came onto the stage, said he was checking cables at the back. To be honest I didn't take much notice.'

Toby and Lucy frowned at each other. 'What did he look like?'

The drummer had a blank expression on his face. 'Sorry, I didn't take much notice of him.'

'What are we going to do now?' Toby heart was sinking. All those hours of practice. For nothing.

Toby berated himself; this was his fault, he should have made sure his guitar was safe. He was sure he'd hidden it under a pile of coats.

'You do realise we've been put back by an hour? Plenty of time to borrow one,' the drummer said.

Lucy stared at the drummer. 'You could have said.' Then turning to Toby, she said with urgency, 'We need to find my dad. You can borrow my guitar. I thought you played better on mine anyway.'

She dashed off across the field leaving Toby staring after her, wondering why on earth she couldn't have told him that before. He slumped onto the step.

Toby's brain was bombarded by blind panic. What if she didn't find Henry?

Finally, he saw her lumbering over the field, panting, reaching him, flinging the guitar on the grass, putting her arms around him as if their lives depended on this one short performance. Extraordinary. *She* was quite extraordinary.

'You have no idea the hassle I had. Dad refused to drive me home. Said he was busy managing the event.' She dipped her head to get her breath back. 'I dashed round like a mad thing trying to find someone who'd help. Jasper's wife, Sandy, took me. Thank God. Nice woman.'

'I didn't know you knew each other.'

'We don't. But she was with Jasper. He's in a bad way, broken arm, bruising on his face.'

'Yeah, I know, he's lucky to be alive.'

Just then the fairground rides slowed to a halt and the music faded out, a signal that their performance would soon begin. They dashed up the steps and onto the stage, taking up position. Ten minutes later the first musician, the saxophonist began. Toby had already seen the programme sheet, knew the saxophonist would be playing an old and timeless piece, a jazz standard by Johnny Green called 'Body and Soul'. He made it look so easy, but Toby knew it couldn't possibly be. So much puff needed. Within a minute Toby was captivated. Such a mesmerising, smooth and moving piece and played so incredibly well. It made Toby think he was in New York late at night, the rear lights of yellow cabs gliding along. He glanced at Lucy and they both smiled. Her eyes were sparkling, lost in the shared moment as the calming melodic notes filled the air.

Next up was the drummer, Pete, playing 'Honky Tonk Woman' by the Rolling Stones. Toby had chatted with the drummer earlier in the day when he'd watched him setting up his drums and cymbals. Intrigued, Toby had learned that young drummers often practised playing this song because it required them to play different patterns at the same time with hands and feet working independently. 'What are you doing?' he'd asked when he saw Pete tape tea-towels around the side of the drums. 'To get a muffled sound at the end of the notes,' Pete had replied.

With a burst of ruthless force, Pete crashed his cymbals over the rumble of audience chatter. Men and women were swaying, children dancing round their parents' feet, dogs tugging on leads. Toby caught Lucy's excited face, a fiery energy crackling between them. It was intense, feverish, hypnotic even. Each beat travelled down his throat, vibrated in his chest as he watched Lucy gyrate, her eyes fixed on him. For a moment he thought she was about to lean in and kiss him and he quickly looked away, confused, swept along in the beat like the crash of waves on shore.

Then it was their turn. Toby felt surprisingly underwhelmed as he sat on his chair, guitar on the floor in front of him, Lucy at his side holding the microphone. He put on his poker face. As long as there was no pinkness in his cheeks to betray him, he'd be fine. This was about survival. Retreat would be a disaster, a show of weakness. It wasn't an option. He let his mind and toes do what they knew how to do. His toe striking the first chord, the will for adventure took over from the shy sense of vulnerability he'd always felt at school concerts. He stole a quick glance at the crowd before looking down to concentrate.

Nothing could have prepared Toby for what happened afterwards when he and Lucy stepped forward to bow. The crowd erupted, wild with applause, a few people whistling, punching the air. It was bizarre; the previous performers had less fanfare. Each second, each minute they clapped, felt like an eternity. But as Toby looked out at the sea of faces with increasing anxiety, horrified, he noticed that Lucy was no longer next to him, waving at the crowd, but had slipped behind him so that he now had the full limelight and was patting him on the back as if he was the hero of the afternoon. Two women rushed over and speaking from the side of the stage they called to Lucy, 'Well done, love, for giving him this chance and your singing was great too, but I'm sure you already know that.' And the other woman agreed, adding, 'You made his day.'

One man in the crowd looked out of place.

He wasn't clapping. Equally unnerving, he just stared at Toby as if he was a museum exhibit.

It was the creepy window cleaner.

The glow and euphoria Toby had felt strumming his guitar disappeared. Like a rainbow washed to grey, the experience cheapened by weird excessive clapping. It was well-intentioned but he could read their faces. 'However bad my life is, it could be worse, I could be him.' This was their feel-good moment, but it wasn't making him feel good. He wanted to shout at the crowd, 'I'm not your inspiration, thank you very much.'

He was a spectacle, one of those poor unfortunate children damaged by thalidomide.

Something in him cracked. All he could do was flee to the back of the stage, pushing through the gap in the canvas, jumping down onto the grass and running along the side of the park until he reached the high street and beyond. He kept on running until he was out of breath and beyond the high street saw a bench and stopped. He slumped onto it, unable to hold back the hot angry tears.

24

With his head bent low, Toby's misty eyes fixed on his feet as he tried to calm down and collect his thoughts.

He'd been sitting on the bench for maybe fifteen minutes when he felt it dip. Someone had plonked themselves beside him and he sensed they were about to speak.

'All right?'

Toby lifted his head and stared into the cold, hard eyes of Lucy's window cleaner. What was he doing here?

'I've got to get home,' Toby said nervily, getting up and moving away.

'Why d'you run off just then?'

There was something about this man that made him feel uneasy. 'I'd had enough.'

'But they were cheering.'

Toby shrugged. 'I don't like all that attention.'

Before the man could reply, there was a beep and Toby was relieved to see Sandy and Jasper pulling over.

'Looks like Daddy's come to pick you up.' There was a spiteful edge to his words.

'He's not my dad,' Toby called over his shoulder as he rushed to the car.

'Really? He looks just like you.'

Weirdo. Creep. After the ordeal in the park, he wasn't going to let this arsehole wind him up.

He dipped his head to get in the backseat. Sandy was driving and looked gorgeous in a yellow cheesecloth dress, her hair loose and flowing.

As they pulled away from the pavement, Jasper turned to look at Toby. 'What happened, mate?'

'I bottled it—sorry.' Running had helped to release the tension, but now that he was talking, he was wound up again. 'Anyone else, they wouldn't have got hysterical. I'm never doing anything like that again.'

'They were only showing their appreciation. You were both brilliant,' Sandy said, indicating to overtake a car now that they were away from the town.

'But the focus was all on me. And Lucy stepped aside to let them applaud me. I don't know why she did that.'

'I thought that was really sweet of her,' Sandy said. 'She seems like a nice girl, putting you before herself.'

'I wish she hadn't. It felt patronising.'

'You're being oversensitive,' Sandy said, sighing and rubbing her forehead. He was surprised that she was even bothering to comment.

'Come on, Toby. You were in a school concert a few months back, why's this any different?' Jasper asked, shifting in his seat.

'You weren't on that stage. You don't know what it felt like. Individual performers aren't singled out for special praise at school concerts. Have you seen my dad?'

'He's gone home. But I said we'd drive round to see if you were about and drop you back.'

Toby stared sulkily out of the window. 'I don't want to go home yet. Can I come over to yours?'

'Don't you want to go to the barn dance in the village hall this evening?' Jasper asked.

'To watch people prancing across the floor, hand in hand with a stranger?'

'It's just a bit of fun, no one takes it seriously.'

'I'm not going,' Toby said, emitting powerful leave-me-alone vibes while thinking what a daft suggestion it was, given his handicap.

'Not even if Lucy was going? Go on,' Jasper coaxed, 'I know you like her.'

'She's probably got a boyfriend.'

'I don't think she has,' Sandy said, turning into their driveway.

'She said something about meeting her friends for a few more rides at the fair.'

'You could have gone too,' Jasper said.

'She didn't invite me.'

'You could have invited yourself.' Sandy parked the car, taking the key from the ignition as she turned to wink at Toby. 'You just need to be more assertive, pet. You'll get there, it just takes time.' Her kind words took him by surprise and suddenly in that moment as she smiled at him, he missed his mum. Maybe he'd misjudged Sandy. She was actually okay. Sometimes. When she wasn't talking about the dog in that cringey voice of hers. 'Maybe ask her out to the cinema sometime. *Logan's Run* is on.'

'Hark at you, Sandy, giving the lad advice on courting.' Jasper laughed.

As they got out of the car, Toby felt embarrassed by where the conversation was heading and suddenly wanted to be on his own. 'Actually, I've changed my mind, I think I'll walk home.'

'Do you want a lift?' Sandy asked.

'No, I'm fine thanks.'

'Don't let today get to you, sunshine,' Jasper smiled, walking with him to the verge beyond the drive, his hand on Toby's shoulder. 'I think it was very encouraging. You should be proud of yourself, and you know what?'

'What?' Toby was itching to get away and didn't want another lecture about life.

'Henry said if you wanted to, you could pitch up in the shopping street on a Saturday morning and make yourself some money.'

Toby had noticed the odd busker, but he didn't have the confidence for that, and if today was anything to go by, it would be pure torture.

'It's one way of earning some pocket money.'

'No, I don't think so.'

After saying goodbye, Toby headed out of their close and onto the pavement leading back towards the town. He felt hot and clammy, sweat trickling down his back. The day had been warm and sticky. Then ten minutes into his walk, out of nowhere, the sky darkened like a bruise, sucking colour from the day. The air smelt different—musky and sweet.

Ahead, was a bus shelter with a wooden bench. Feeling the first drops of rain, Toby dashed towards it to avoid the deluge, wishing he'd taken Sandy up on the offer of a lift. He'd be at home now, running a nice warm bath with lots of bubbles. Then he'd shut himself in his bedroom, put an LP on and curl up with the book he was currently reading, *The Midwich Cuckoos* by John Wyndham. He was enjoying the story which was about a village waking up to find all its women pregnant. They gave birth to children who were all identical with golden eyes, silvery skin and with super psychic powers. How odd it was, Toby thought, that the villagers were so accepting of this strange phenomenon, just going about their lives normally. Reading the story had made him think of the birth of thalidomide babies like himself, baffling doctors, the medical profession and their parents. Until they'd discovered what was causing so many babies to be born with deformities, it must have felt the stuff of science fiction movies.

From the cover of the bus shelter, Toby stood peering out, his gaze falling to a puddle swelling in size as raindrops hit like bullets, carrying him away into a trance and emptying his mind of everything that had happened that day. He didn't notice Lucy pull up on her moped, until the front tyre spliced through the puddle, spraying him with water and making a ribbon effect as she twisted the moped to a halt.

'There you are,' she said, getting off the bike and dashing into the shelter. She took her helmet off and put it on the bench. Toby stood to one side, watching her. He thought she looked even more beautiful with wet hair and he imagined her fresh out of the shower. She bent over, gathering her hair up, twisting it into a ponytail to squeeze the water out. 'I've been looking everywhere for you.'

'Why? Weren't you supposed to be meeting your mates afterwards?' He turned away from her so that she couldn't see the resentment on his face. He would have liked to meet her college friends—but hadn't been invited.

'You rushed off. They were in the middle of the applause.' She stepped in front of him, forcing him to meet her eyes. Her expression was one of bewilderment. He stared at her before looking away.

He plonked himself on the bench. Taking deep breaths helped him control his emotions. He hadn't a clue what to say. He didn't know why he'd run off.

She joined him on the bench, her damp trousers touching his. If she reached out now to embrace him, it would be the hug a mother would give her son after he'd fallen from his bicycle, or a kiss of pity.

'Doesn't look like it's going to clear any time soon,' she said, peering up at the clouds.

'No.'

'You were great today. The crowd were only showing their appreciation. Better that being booed at.' She smiled, gave a half laugh.

Perhaps he should explain. 'I found it too much.'

'They loved you.'

He turned to face her. She looked cute, like a drowned rat. He got up and went to lean against the side of the shelter. 'They clapped because they saw a handicapped person doing what they thought was extraordinary, but underneath their smiles and their whistles they were thinking, if I was him, I'd want to kill myself, what an awful life he's got. How brave is he? And oh look, he can play a bloody guitar with his feet. How bloody amazing is that?' Toby rarely swore, especially not in front of a girl—particularly one he wanted to impress. But he couldn't help it, he was so worked up and she just wasn't getting it.

'I thought you wanted to do it?'

'Yeah. I was looking forward to it. But it was like a freak show,' he said in a sullen tone.

'Then I don't get it. People are going to clap. Would you rather they booed instead? Was it just stage fright? Your guitar disappearing?'

'Did my guitar turn up? Dad's going to kill me for losing it.'

'You didn't lose it. It went missing. Stolen.'

'It was a mean thing to do. Who would do that?'

'I don't know. You can have my guitar.'

He looked at her, saw kindness in her brown eyes, as if she'd do anything for him. But he was torn. He wished she'd stop helping.

Her kindness felt patronising because it was way over the top. 'Thanks, but it's yours.' He sounded flat and ungrateful and hated himself for that.

'Please, I want you to have it. I can buy another. I've got a job.' It was easy patter, but what she was really telling him was, 'I feel sorry for you because I'm lucky, I can work, I can save up for all the things I want. Look at me, I'm normal, but you, you're one of the poor unfortunate ones.'

He wanted to make out that his dad would buy him another, but he'd be lying. And it sounded pathetic to be reliant on parents. At his age, most lads had a paper round.

'My dad says you could play on a Saturday morning in the shopping centre. He was impressed.' She laughed. 'Takes a lot to impress the old geezer.' She was too posh to call her dad an old geezer. Toby found it funny and smiled.

'Nah, I don't think so.'

'You'd earn loads.'

'Too stressful.'

She poked her head out of the shelter. 'Rain's stopped. I guess I better be off. You walking home?'

He felt breathless as panic set in, watching her mount the bike, suddenly realising he wouldn't be seeing her again. He wasn't even sure she'd want to, especially after today. With her helmet on and the key in the ignition, it was now or never.

'I'll be seeing you then,' she said, turning her head and smiling at him.

Then he remembered Jasper's suggestion. 'Do you fancy going to the pictures sometime?' he blurted. '*Logan's Run* will be on.'

'Really sorry. Pete's asked me to see that with him.'

Her words hit and he felt his chest tighten. 'Who's Pete?' She hadn't mentioned a Pete in all the hours they'd spent together.

'A guy at college.'

Toby wasn't going to pry further—it was none of his business. He'd been wondering if she had a boyfriend and now it was clear she did.

All he could do was stand and watch her ride off, cutting across the road, picking up speed, disappearing from sight and from his life.

25

'What's Mummy got?'

Kneeling, Sandy waved a titbit of chicken at Tibs, who was lying in his basket beside the radiator. The dog lifted his head, regarding Sandy through sorrowful eyes, then went back to sleep. Worried, she turned to Jasper, sitting in his armchair by the lounge window reading the Sunday papers and sipping coffee. 'Did you see that? He's not interested. Hasn't eaten all day.'

Jasper folded the newspaper he'd been reading and put it on the arm of his chair. 'You fuss too much. Probably just lost his appetite.' He shook his head. 'After all this time, I still don't know why you called him Tibs. It's a cat's name.'

Sandy stroked the dog and kissed her head. 'You're not well, are you?' She always adopted a baby voice when talking to the dog. 'Maybe he'll perk up. It's just that I read something in a magazine. It said if your dog won't eat it could have developed anorexia.'

Jasper laughed. 'Don't believe everything you read.'

'Says a journalist.'

'Exactly.' He smiled at her. 'You should be worried about our baby, not the dog.'

Sandy did worry, but it was going to be different this time around. She hadn't taken thalidomide. She'd been so careful and had followed all the advice. Not even so much as a drop of alcohol or paracetamol had passed her lips. This time she was going to have a happy, healthy, beautiful baby.

'Only ten days now. Not long,' Jasper said.

Sandy had made a checklist. She was very organised and wanted everything to go smoothly and for there to be no last-minute hitches. The phone number for the taxi was beside the telephone. Her hospital bag was packed and sitting by the front door ready. Toby and Bill had agreed to look after the dog.

She headed to the kitchen to make herself a coffee. Babies were so tiny and fragile, would she instinctively know what to do? Giving birth all those years ago she'd not had the chance to test her motherly instincts. She imagined staring into the baby's eyes and whispering, 'I can't do this'. She had to remind herself for the umpteenth time, things were going to be all right this time. Her doctor had given her lots of reassurance and every test available.

She took a mug from the cupboard, switched the kettle on and waited for it to boil. Now that the birth was so close, she felt daunted. She'd soon find out if she was up to it, and she had Jasper. They were in this together. Her worst fear though was him being called away on business, Sam asking him to go to Northern Ireland to report on the Troubles. She didn't want Jasper caught up in the violence. He'd nearly lost his life at a carnival; she wasn't going to let him go to Belfast.

She sipped her coffee as she stared out of the window. The garden usually made her think about life and hope, watching flowers grow, the colours change. But with the leaves a soggy mess on the lawn, and the sun hidden behind a blanket of white cloud, it looked sad and forlorn. She turned and made her way upstairs to the nursery. Jasper had spent a couple of days decorating the room and it looked both beautiful and functional.

They'd decided on a Noah's Ark theme. The wallpaper, cot sheets, curtains and even the rug carried the same motif. As the child grew and acquired soft toy animals, they would be displayed on the shelves that Bill had kindly put up. Sandy sat in the pine rocking chair and looked at the brand new cot they'd bought. It had cute pictures of reindeer and bunnies at either end. It was hard to imagine that in a matter of weeks, a baby would be sleeping there.

Soon she'd be woken in the night to feed the baby. But that was all right. Sandy was a night person.

Was this baby for Jasper more than for herself? Was she doing it to stop him spending so much time of his free time with Toby? Jasper worked crazily hard. All she wanted was more of him—a proper husband. One that put her first, family first.

Getting up from the rocking chair, Sandy felt a twitch in her abdomen. She'd had a grumpy tummy since the previous afternoon. Maybe it was the bread she'd made. The yeast caused bloating and a gassy stomach, but it was so delicious, she'd eaten three doorstep-sized slices. Thinking about it, she'd given the dog some bread too, fresh from the oven.

Sandy stood at the side of the cot, feeling like a space hopper on legs, more belly than person. About to lean down to smooth the bedding, she felt a trickling sensation between her legs.

It couldn't be, could it?

She'd expected a Niagara Falls-type gush, but nevertheless it was just enough to catch her attention and let her know something was happening. Popping to the loo confirmed that the baby was on its way. At the top of the stairs, she took several nerve-steadying breaths, telling herself not to panic, before heading downstairs to tell Jasper.

Jasper was in the study bashing away at his typewriter with his back to her.

She said, 'I think my waters have broken.'

He stopped typing and swung round. 'Oh shit. You sure?

Why couldn't the little bugger have waited until its due date? Then my plaster would be off and I could drive you.'

'I haven't felt a contraction yet.'

'Sit down. Take it easy. Don't move. I'm ringing for a taxi.' Flustered, Jasper dashed into the hall. 'Won't be long, darling,' he called through as soon as he was off the phone. 'They'll be five minutes. I'm going to ring Bill now, ask them to look after the dog.'

Back in the study he perched next to her on the settee and touched her belly. It looked as if it had been pumped up like a ball, the skin stretched like a drum.

'I'll be so glad when this is all over,' she said, tears rolling down her cheeks.

He kissed her forehead. 'It's going to be fine, darling, I'm here. There's nothing to worry about.'

She patted her belly. 'Oh God,' she puffed. 'I just felt a contraction.'

He rubbed her back vigorously. 'What can I do?'

She looked at him. 'You sure you want to watch the birth? It'll be messy.'

'You bet. I'm a modern man.'

Other women might not give two hoots about their husband seeing them with their legs wide apart and screaming for England. But not Sandy. She cared very much about how she looked. Suddenly anxious, she didn't want Jasper to see all that blood and sweat, her hair wild and unkempt. It was just so undignified. 'If things get complicated, they'll only shove you in the corridor.'

'I don't care. I'm coming with you.'

'Oh God, another contraction,' she screamed, leaning forward. 'Where's the taxi?'

∼

Toby didn't know what the problem had been with the dog. He'd been at Sandy and Jasper's for about an hour and Tibs seemed fine. Toby tipped meaty chunks into his bowl and the dog wolfed it down as if he'd not eaten in days. Sandy worried too much about Tibs. Mollycoddling, Bill had called it. Sandy acted as though the dog was a fragile baby to be tended to every second of every day.

Toby wandered into Jasper's study and flopped onto the settee to stare at all the books adorning the shelves. This was a treat, having his favourite room all to himself, scanning the rows and yanking out anything he fancied taking a gander at. He felt like a kid in a sweetie shop—where was he going to begin? Each book held its own world of wonders.

As he was tilting his head to read the titles on the spine, there was a knock at the door. It would be his dad, but then he remembered that Bill had a key. He went into the hall and opened the door. To his astonishment, it was Lucy.

26

As he beamed at Lucy, Toby's spirits rose.

'What the hell are you doing here?' she said, stepping inside.

'Looking after the dog.' Toby was about to ask if Jasper had sent for her. He wouldn't have put it past Jasper to connive to get them together.

'Where are they? I popped round to ask if they'll need a babysitter once the baby's born.'

'They're at the hospital. Sandy's gone into labour.'

'Wow, really?' Lucy said.

'I'll tell them you called.' It wasn't really his place to invite her in, but he couldn't stop himself. 'Do you want to stay a bit and hang out?'

'Go on then, I've nothing better to do.'

'Come and see the dog,' Toby said, heading towards the kitchen. 'It's a Tibetan spaniel, quite cute. Doesn't bite. I was going to let him out into the back garden, but now you're here we could take him for a walk.'

Lucy glanced up the stairs, her hand on the newel post. 'Can I have a sneaky peek upstairs?' She had a cheeky glint in her eyes.

She was kicking her shoes off, preparing to climb the cream-carpeted stairs. He could read her like a book and knew that mischievous streak. Mostly it was appealing, but not now when Jasper and Sandy could return at any moment. Toby knew all about birth from his mum. As a midwife, Rona had plied him with many stories. Sometimes pregnant women arrived at hospital too soon only to be sent home to wait until their contractions were more frequent. Or they were told it was a false alarm.

'Come on,' he said, coaxing her in an up-beat tone. 'I'll show you Jasper's books. He won't mind.'

'I'm not interested in books, Toby, or dogs.' Halfway up the stairs, she looked down at him and laughed mockingly. 'I bet they've got a continental quilt. Come on, I want a nose.'

Toby bombed up, stepping in front of her on the landing. 'It's not right, Lucy, please come down.'

'You're such a goody two shoes. You need to let your hair down. Let's try the bed out.' She grinned at him, throwing a flirty, come-hither look. Rooted to the spot, heat rising to his face and neck, he just wanted her to stop. But she'd noticed the bedroom door, wide open. She pushed past him and headed in.

He stood at the doorway watching her.

'I was right. A luxurious continental quilt, probably filled with goose feathers.' It was only bedding, who cared? She flung herself onto the bed spreading her arms and legs like a snow angel, then rolled around giggling. Anywhere else, he'd let his guard down, rush over, join her, jump up and down, then have a pillow fight. Would they kiss? The thought made him tingle. He hesitated, on the brink of throwing caution to the wind. But the last thing he wanted was to abuse Sandy and Jasper's trust.

He turned his back on her and padded to the stairs, calling out an excuse, 'I can hear something. Better go down.' If she wanted to snoop, be it on her head.

'You're no fun.'

Returning to the study, he plonked himself on the settee

while he waited for her. This was a chance to show off Jasper's book collection. He glanced at the shelves and wondered if there were any she'd read and could recommend.

He heard her come down. It sounded as if she'd found the lounge. He got up and went into the hall.

'Lucy, I'm here.'

'Wow, alcohol,' she gasped.

Toby's heart sank. This was all he needed. But it was pointless to ask her not to touch it, she'd ignore him.

As he walked into the lounge, she was bending down, about to open the corner display cabinet.

'Fancy a drop of Martini?' she asked him, as if she owned the place.

'No,' he said firmly.

She laughed. 'You're funny, Toby.'

'What do you do when you go babysitting? Surely you don't swig their drink?'

'No. But I do raid the biscuit barrel if there's anything nice going.'

She got up and walked towards him. 'I was just teasing you.' She tickled his neck. 'You're easy to wind up.' She squeezed his chin and laughed. 'Come on, show me these books then.'

'One day I'd like a room like this, a smaller room but with books crammed onto every shelf. Sometimes I think it would be nice to work in a library. I'd walk between the rows of books thinking of all that knowledge in one place,' he said after taking her into the study and sitting down.

'You've got to be kidding. The staff are frumpy old women with stern faces and no sense of humour. Too quiet for me. You can't even hear a pin drop in our library. I'd be bored out of my brain.'

'Are there any books here that you've read?'

Despite her obvious reluctance, he was glad when she got up to take a better look. '*The Great Gatsby*. One of my favourites,' she said, pulling it from the shelf. 'The Roaring Twenties. What an exciting era. I've got a photo of my gran in a flapper dress. Everybody says she looks like me, but I can't see it.'

'A few weeks back someone made the mistake of thinking Jasper was my dad.'

'I must admit, when I first met you both, I thought he was too.'

'Well, he's most definitely not,' Toby said. 'I asked Jasper if he had any photos of himself at my age. I wanted to see if we looked alike as teenagers.'

Silent, they gazed around the room. Lucy got up and looked along the shelves. She pulled out a black box. 'These look like photos.'

'I hope they don't come back,' Toby said anxiously. 'I'll check the front window.' Toby went into the hall to check, then darted back.

As they sat together on the floor, Lucy tipped the contents of the box onto the carpet. The photos were sepia. People of all ages. But with no dates or names written on the back they could have been anybody and they didn't know if the pictures were Jasper's family or Sandy's.

'There's nothing here,' Lucy said, now on her hands and knees, shovelling up the mess. Suddenly it didn't feel right. What were they doing, sitting among all these pictures that had nothing to do with them?

But hang on, Toby thought. A photo caught his eye and he pushed it aside with his toe. Lucy picked it up, squinted and examined it close up. She rose to her feet and took it to the window where the light was better. Toby went to join her. Standing close to her, he could feel her breath on the side of his face. This felt good, they were a team, on a mission.

'I think this is him.' A teenage boy was standing in a field, but he was too far away to see the details of his face and because the photo had been taken so long ago, it wasn't a clear shot.

Toby peered at it. 'Can't see much. Maybe there are better ones.'

Lucy turned to the shelves. 'Here we are, these look promising,' she said, pulling several down and untying the ribbon of a large black book. Inside, each photo had been slotted in and labelled. Some of the labels were peeling and the writing had faded. Kneeling, she laid it on the carpet and carefully turned the cardboard pages, giving a running commentary as Toby peered over her shoulder.

'Weddings, more weddings, beaches.' She sounded bored.

'Studio photos,' Toby said, a few pages later. 'These must be very old.' He gazed at a picture of a group of people sitting on cane furniture with stiff expressions on their faces posing against a painted backdrop.

And then, near the end of the album as she turned the next page, Toby wasn't prepared for the shock that gripped him when he found himself staring down at a pair of eyes that looked uncannily familiar. It was a large black and white photo of a boy's head and shoulders.

Jasper. At about the same age Toby was now.

He stared at the photo and froze. The resemblance was both unmistakable and striking. All of Jasper's features: the crease in his left cheek, the shadows under his wide-set eyes, his thin lips, the shape of his forehead, even a mole to the right side of his mouth. But it was more than that. It was the expression on Jasper's face. It was as if Toby was looking in a mirror and seeing himself.

It was a coincidence. Had to be. A fluke of nature. It happened all the time. Everybody had a double somewhere in the world. They were called doppelgängers. But what were the chances, Toby considered, of someone coming across a doppelgänger of themselves?

Lucy frowned. 'Are you sure you're not related?'

'It's just a coincidence. We better put this lot away.' Toby was so shocked at the likeness he didn't want to talk about it and needed her to go so that he could be on his own to think.

Something didn't feel right, and the more Toby thought about it, the more unnerved he was. Was Jasper a relative—Bill's brother? That had to be the most likely explanation but even that was far-fetched. Bill had three brothers and Toby had only met two of them. As far as Toby knew, the family had fallen out with the other brother. They hadn't spoken with him in years. Toby didn't know what the falling out was over, and come to think of it, he couldn't even remember the man's name. He'd never met him, and nobody talked about him. Just supposing Jasper was this estranged brother. Maybe Bill was the only one in the family who'd been happy to take him back into their lives.

But then surely his dad would have introduced Jasper as his uncle.

'I don't mean to get rid of you, Lucy, it's been nice seeing you, but...'

'You want me to go.'

'I think you'd better.' Toby wished they were going to see *Logan's Run* together. How was he going to suggest meeting again? 'Be great to see you sometime,' he said.

'Yeah, that would be cool.'

After she left, Toby sat on the bottom stair in the hallway with the dog at his heels, staring out of the window onto the driveway, waiting for news of Sandy. They'd been gone for more than two hours so it looked likely that it hadn't been a false alarm. In which case he expected Bill to drop over to pick him and the dog up and take them back to the cottage.

Toby thought he knew his parents well, but did he actually? It was scary to doubt them. It made him feel uncertain about himself. He turned to lean against the wall, closing his eyes as he tried to process the thought that Jasper could be related to him.

And then a new thought popped into his head unannounced, taking him by surprise and making his heart thump in his chest.

What if his mother and Jasper had had an affair? If affairs could happen in novels and films, then they happened in real life too. But he couldn't for one minute see Jasper being attracted to his mother.

It seemed odd that Jasper appeared one day, interviewed them for his feature on the thalidomide families, and from that day on had remained in their lives.

Did he honestly believe that his mother had slept with Jasper?

It was absurd. His parents had loved each other. She'd been devoted to Bill. Several years later and his dad was still devastated by her death, which was why he'd not gone on to meet anyone else.

And yet—nothing made sense.

27

All those weeks watching her belly grow bigger and bigger. Now they were here, in the hospital's delivery suite. It was finally happening—they were having a baby.

His wife's face was red, all that panting, all that effort, the sheer exhaustion of it all. Beads of sweat glistening under the humming strip light that winked overhead, the bulb needing to be replaced. The stuffiness of the small room, no windows, no air, hot. It was bad enough for Jasper, sitting in an uncomfortable chair, the vinyl sticking to his bottom, pins and needles in his legs–, so numb, he shook them violently. But pins and needles were nothing. What Sandy must be going through–, he couldn't possibly imagine. Just wanted her to be all right, the baby safe, healthy. When would it be over? *Please God let it be soon.*

Sandy screamed, 'How much longer?'

'You're doing brilliantly,' Jasper said, trying to sound calm despite the nerves jangling inside him. He'd been trying not to focus on the clock ever since they'd arrived at the hospital hours ago. It wasn't helpful, he didn't want her to worry, best to be vague and take all references to time out of his vocabulary. Keep her nice and relaxed. Huh! Was that even possible?

There was nothing he could do to stop the pain. He'd rubbed her back till his palms were sore. She'd had gas and air, pethidine, surely there was something more they could do? Something to stop her agony.

How useless am I? He might as well be a goldfish in a bowl, swimming round aimlessly, no purpose, taking up space on someone's shelf, peering out through the murky waters at the drama unfolding before his very eyes.

Bloody hell, men had it easy. He'd never appreciated that until now. How could that be fair? A picture of Adam and Eve popped into his head. A woman had eaten the fruit in the Garden of Eden. And ever since then, women had been paying the price. God's punishment. But he didn't believe in the Bible; the story was twaddle. He'd been given the minor role, the fun part, the fumble in the sack. Blink and you'd miss his appearance. Like every father who'd walked the planet. Did they all feel the same?

He looked at her, feeling helpless. Her hair, wild, damp, splayed out across the pillow. He'd never seen her look such a mess. But the rawness of her—she was still beautiful.

Get up, Jasper, you twat, she needs her face mopped. His eyes darted around the room. What had he done with the cloth? The midwife, Jenny, smiled at him knowingly, passing him a damp cloth before putting a cuff on Sandy's arm to check her blood pressure. The midwife was amazing. So young, yet so experienced. All these professionals, including those nurses who had cared for him and the coppers injured at the carnival back in August; they were young but their care was incredible.

His wife's life was held in the balance. If her blood pressure shot up it would put additional stress on her heart and kidneys. *Shit.* Women died in childbirth. The sudden thought made his heart pound in his chest. *Please, God, let her be okay.* What if the baby's head was so big that it tore her? She'd be in agony.

Think positive.

Holding Sandy's clammy hand, he gently patted her forehead

with the cloth as another wave of pain rolled over her. Whatever he did, it wasn't enough. He was a cocktail parasol in a rainstorm. It was frustrating being here making no difference. He was out of his depth—like everything else lately. This was the culmination of everything that had happened these past few weeks. The office weasel forcing him to sell his Jag. Pressure from Bill not to tell Sandy the truth. What a good-for-nothing he was. But Sandy, she was amazing. She had a superpower, could grow babies from seed, with no instructions needed. Wow. How clever was that? It was like leaving a load of ingredients in the kitchen and coming home to a baked cake.

The cake wasn't always perfect. Babies weren't either. Occasionally someone opened the oven too soon, the cake flopped. At some point Toby's development had gone wrong, the cells failing to divide correctly at a specific point in the pregnancy. A quick error that would affect his life forever. And all down to that bloody tablet. Distaval.

What if there was something wrong with this baby too? Life was unpredictable. Shit happened.

Another contraction. Would this be it, the final push? Sandy panted, blowing out air like a puffa fish. 'I can't do it, can't do it, can't do it,' she yelled. 'Help me.'

'Beautiful, keep it going, keep it going, keep it going,' coaxed the midwife.

'You can do it, darling, you can.' He got up, suddenly light-headed.

'Can't do it, can't do, I'm all stingy below,' she cried.

Jasper rubbed her arm, her cheeks were blotchy and bloated.

'Push past the stinging when you feel it,' the midwife instructed as she leaned over Sandy.

'Can't do it. Can't get it out.' Her voice terrified him. Shrill, she sounded like a hyena, or some other wild animal.

Jasper sat, then promptly got up again. When had he last eaten or had a glass of water? There was ringing in his ears, his vision was all blurry, soft around the edges, then nothing. He felt the hard floor, the rattle of a metal trolley. Yelped in pain, his side hurting. *Jesus, I'm on the floor.*

Voices—Sandy. 'My husband's passed out.'

The midwife calling to someone, 'Dad's passed out.'

His head was fuzzy, their voices were merging. The midwife said, 'Stay on the floor, sweetheart. Just getting a nurse to help you.'

A wave of sickness washed over him. He tried to get up, but a hand gently pushed him back. 'Don't get up.' He felt sick, needed to throw up. The outline of a nurse swam into view, her blue outfit a blur. She was holding a paper bowl and he leaned over and emptied his stomach. What a wimp. He'd just fainted. 'Better?' the nurse asked, easing his head onto a cushion.

'Can't do it,' Sandy cried again.

'Push into your bottom, push again, you're so close now,' the midwife encouraged.

'Yes you can, darling, yes you can,' Jasper gasped from the floor straining to pull himself up. 'Nearly there, darling.'

'Stay there,' the nurse told him. 'Jenny's taking good care of your wife. Have some water, you're dehydrated,' she said, offering him a cup of water. He took a few sips. Yes that was what he'd needed.

Sandy gave a blood-curdling scream. 'Help me.' He lifted his arm—so heavy. His whole body—heavy. He tried to get up. Couldn't. The nurse put her hand under his arm and helped him up.

'Baby's crowning,' the midwife said urgently.

What on earth did that mean? So much terminology.

'Keep it coming. I can see baby.'

'What's happening?' Jasper yelled. He was missing the crucial moment. His head was fuzzy. He was missing the birth of their baby. He'd failed her. Yet again.

One almighty last scream from Sandy.

And then, the baby's first cry.

'It's a girl,' the midwife announced as Jasper staggered to his feet, clutching the side of the bed for support.

Sandy looked exhausted. He leaned down and kissed her cheek, feeling the heat radiating from her face. 'You've done it, you clever thing.'

Sandy was still lying on her back with her knees bent and spread apart as if not daring to move. The midwife pushed the sheet from the lower half of her body. The baby, lying on the sheet came into view in a pool of mucky fluid. Blueish, covered in blood and a creamy substance. Looking like she'd just been in a fist-fight.

An intense rush of love jolted through him like a shot of heroin. He stroked Sandy's head and they watched in amazement as the midwife cut the grey cord. Jasper remembered that they'd decided only yesterday to call the baby after Sandy's grandma.

'Hello, Angela, welcome to the world.'

28

'Let's go to the Wimpy to celebrate Angela's birth,' Toby suggested excitedly. 'And can Lucy come too?'

Bill had finished work early for a change and this was as good an excuse as any to treat the lad to a slap-up meal. Making Toby eat with the boarders on the frequent evenings he worked late pricked Bill's conscience. Prison slop, was how Toby described school dinners. *Food you wouldn't serve your pet pig.* Grisly meat, watery custard, overdone broccoli. He was exaggerating, but nevertheless Bill felt guilty.

The cheerful red seating and bright lighting lifted Bill's mood as they slid into a booth at the back of the restaurant, Lucy grabbing the laminate menu, declaring she'd have a Brown Derby for dessert.

Bill smiled. Such an impetuous lass. 'Let's order drinks first,' he said, eyeing the waitress as she approached their table.

After they'd ordered, Lucy nudged Toby and said, 'Go on, tell ya dad what we found in Sandy and Jasper's house.' She had a devious look on her face that made Bill wary of her. The girl was trouble. He'd seen it from the start, but what could he do? The boy was smitten. He hadn't forgotten that dreadful night when he'd picked them up from Hyde Park after the concert. The shock at seeing Lucy splayed across the pavement. The state she'd been in. Puking up in his van. It had taken Bill the best part of several weeks to rid the interior of the smell. Aside from her looks—and she was a little beauty for sure—Bill didn't know what Toby saw in her.

Before Toby had the chance to reply, the waitress was back with their coke floats and a mug of tea for Bill.

Toby and Lucy blew through their straws, giggling and creating foamy bubbles peaking to the top of their glasses.

'Pack it in,' Bill snapped. 'You're acting like a pair of toddlers.' He waited for them to stop before prompting, 'You found something at Jasper and Sandy's?' He looked sternly at Toby. 'I thought you were there alone?'

'I just dropped round. Toby invited me in,' Lucy answered, sitting up straight, clearly the master here. She glanced down at Toby as if waiting for him to let her off the hook. If their friendship developed into a relationship, he'd be the shadow, at her beck and call. It was hopeless, the boy was infatuated.

Toby threw Bill a sheepish look, his face pinking.

'Just tell him, Toby,' Lucy urged.

Toby looked mortified, didn't want to answer, Bill could see that. But Lucy was determined to override his silence. 'We were looking at photos of Jasper when he was young.'

'I find that very disrespectful, Lucy.' Bill grabbed the tomato-shaped ketchup bottle, using it as a stress ball. 'You were there to look after the dog, not snoop through their stuff.'

'We weren't.' Lucy was quite obviously lying. She flung her hands on the table with a huff.

What a rude girl she was. This was the last time he'd invite her along. She was doing her best to ruin the occasion. It rattled Bill; he didn't take Toby out very often and this was supposed to be special. Little rich kid. Her parents probably took her out all the time.

'Put the bottle down, Dad, you're going to have an accident and squirt everyone.'

Bill pushed the bottle aside and smiled. 'The lid was on.' He paused. 'You were obviously snooping. That was bang out of order.' He frowned at Lucy. She needed to be put in her place.

'We just looked through some albums that were on the shelf in Jasper's study. He doesn't mind me looking at his books. If anything, he encourages it. He wants me to learn,' Toby said.

Bill eyed him, trying to gauge if there was any criticism of himself behind Toby's words.

'Photo albums aren't books. They're more private. Personal.'

Their mixed grills arrived, and Bill cut Toby's dinner into small pieces so that he could feed himself, knowing the lad would be embarrassed if his dad helped him to eat.

'We came across a photo of Jasper when he was about Toby's age,' Lucy said after she'd eaten a mouthful of burger.

Bill's heart skipped a beat. Lucy was putting him off the delicious bacon he was savouring in his mouth. He stared at her, sensing what was coming.

Toby looked straight at him, his confidence back. 'We looked identical. Almost like twins.'

How uncanny. What Toby must have felt on seeing the likeness, Bill couldn't imagine. Must have really unnerved him. But Bill couldn't rise to it and give the game away. What the bloody hell was he supposed to say? Act casual. Carry on eating. But he'd gone off his meal and his stomach was cramping. They weren't going to let this drop.

Maybe he should go along with it, sound interested. 'Really? What's the chances of that happening, I wonder? But I guess it does.' Bill hated himself. The lies. How much longer could he continue to hide behind this cloak of deception? If it came out, what about Lucy? He didn't trust her. She wasn't the sort to keep a secret. She'd blurt it out to her parents. And they were upstanding members of the community. Her dad was the bloody mayor, for God's sake. Half the town's police officers were probably good friends of his. No doubt he was a Mason too. Jesus, he felt backed into a corner.

'Go on, Toby.' Lucy nudged him. 'Ask your dad. The thing that's most on your mind.'

'Give me a chance.' Toby looked disgruntled and took a swig of his drink. 'I'll ask him later, not here.'

'Fire away,' Bill said with reluctance through a forced smile. He put his knife and fork down and stared at them.

Toby, looking increasingly uncomfortable, glanced from Lucy to Bill. He stuttered before blurting his words out. 'Did Mum have an affair with Jasper? Is that why I look like him?'

Bill burst out laughing. 'Your mum, have an affair? Can you honestly see your mum having an affair with someone like Jasper? They're about as mismatched as a saucepan and a toothbrush. For goodness sake, Toby.'

The lad looked embarrassed. 'Well yeah, there is that.'

Lucy was laughing hysterically. She was enjoying this. Bill loathed her even more.

'We didn't meet Jasper until after your mum died.' Bill daubed his food with more ketchup, realising his nerves were making him squirt-happy.

'That's what I thought.' Toby frowned.

'It's the daftest thing I've heard in a long time,' Bill said, stabbing a sausage.

'Is there something you're not telling me?' Toby asked, a serious expression on his face.

Bill felt a powerful judder shoot through his body, as if he'd walked into a lamp post.

'Like what?' His question sounded weak and pathetic.

Toby spoke through a mouthful of food. 'I dunno.' He shrugged. 'Is Jasper my uncle?'

Bill looked at Toby through wide eyes, incredulous.

Toby laughed. 'He is, I thought so. Why didn't you say?'

'No, don't be daft. Course he's not your uncle. You do have an uncle that you've never met though. Ricky.'

God, Ricky, how long had it been? Bill stared off into the distance, his mind floating back to childhood. Bill's parents had died a few years back, but he had three brothers who still lived in Blackpool. Since moving south, he hadn't been back to visit them. He should have made time to stay in touch. But work had ruled his life. And then there was Ricky. His youngest brother who ran off to Scotland with a girl after getting her up the duff. Nobody had seen or heard from him since. They'd long stopped talking about him.

'Who's Ricky?' Toby was asking, but Bill, oblivious, was engrossed in his thoughts.

'He left home when he was about fourteen. Nobody knows where he is,' Bill said, going on to explain how Ricky had disappeared.

'You don't think Jasper is Ricky? He could have changed his name as a disguise to come back into your life.'

'No, that's just ridiculous, Toby. Jasper isn't related to us. It's just a fluke that you look alike. Sometimes people do. Might be some scientific reason for it, but hey, I'm not a scientist. Let's just drop it, shall we? I'm tired of this conversation.'

Toby raised his eyebrows at Bill, looking unconvinced. 'For now, I guess,' he said slowly. And then in the next breath asked, 'Can we order dessert now? Lucy wants a Brown Derby and I'm having a Knickerbocker Glory.'

Their desserts arrived and they tucked in. 'Love it in here. Did you know, Mr Murphy, that lots of people walk out without paying and the waitresses don't even notice?' Lucy said.

'I hope you've never done that,' Bill said pushing his plate away. He wanted to go.

Little madam, she'd finished her dessert and was now hiding behind the menu laughing. It felt deliberate. Like she was trying to wind him up.

Bill picked up his keys. 'Come on, I've got an early start tomorrow, let's pay up and go.'

On the way home, Bill realised the weight around his neck wasn't going away. It was preying on Toby's mind. He was bound to bring it up again. Maybe not today, but certainly some other day. How would Bill handle it? This was the second occasion that he'd dismissed Toby's questions about his likeness to Jasper. It was as if a door, long fastened and secure, was being forced ajar and it was now just a matter of time before the truth finally found its way out.

He couldn't spin this out for much longer. The enormity of it all it was sucking him under. But if Toby knew the truth, he'd turn on him. Their relationship over, he'd end up alone, a miserable old git who'd failed his boy. Or worse. He'd be thrown in jail. Never work again. Who would employ him with a criminal record?

29

Sandy settled Angela to sleep in the pram out on the patio where she could keep a watchful eye, while folding laundry at the kitchen table. It was Monday, a week after coming out of hospital. She headed upstairs to put the clothes away. On her way back she glanced through the open doorway of Jasper's study where he was bashing away on his typewriter, to ask if he needed a refill of coffee.

He turned to smile at her. 'I could get used to this working from home lark.'

'Back to the office tomorrow?'

'Sadly, yes.' Standing up, he stepped towards her and lifted her chin. 'Am I wrong in thinking this is domestic bliss?'

'Maybe not at two in the morning, darling, when Angela's screaming at full pelt.'

Jasper laughed, just as the doorbell rang. Sandy went into the hall. They weren't expecting anybody and most of their friends knew better than to just arrive on the doorstep and risk waking the baby. Probably just the postman with yet another parcel—more presents to welcome Angela into the world.

She could see the outline of a woman through the bevelled

glass of the front door. If she wasn't mistaken, it looked very much like her mother. Surely not. Her mother never went anywhere unless it was to her local shopping parade near to her parents' North London home. She couldn't drive and moaned about public transport, avoiding it at all costs. Sandy glanced over her shoulder at Jasper in the study doorway and threw him a worried look. He fell against the doorframe, pent-up breath escaping from his lips, his eyes rolling to the ceiling. He knew. They both did.

Gathering her wits, Sandy hesitated, waited for the caller to press the doorbell again, more urgently this time before opening it.

Sandy's brain stuttered for a moment, a sudden coldness hitting her core as every part of her went on pause. She stared open-mouthed at the familiar figure dressed in that hideous old grey coat and her hair scraped back into a tight bun. She was the woman Sandy called Mum, but mum was just a name. They weren't close, never had been. Sandy had always felt uncomfortable around her mother and had never been able to put her finger on quite why that was. Seeing less of her had helped her to cope, but their relationship remained strained and difficult. If Sandy could liken her to an inanimate object, she'd choose a barbed-wire fence; her mother's purpose had always been to deter anyone from getting close. Not even her make-up or her smile softened her features. She wore a sour-puss expression, and bitterness was moulded into her bones.

'Well come on then. What are you waiting for? Are you going to let your mother in?'

Sandy hated her sharp icy tone, but stepped aside to let her in. 'What are you doing, Mum? Where's Dad?' She peered into the driveway expecting her dad to leap out from behind a bush and surprise her. Then her gaze fell to the ground. Between her mother's frumpy black shoes sat her battered brown suitcase.

She didn't plan to stay? Maybe the case contained presents for the baby. Unlikely, Sandy thought.

'I got the bus over. Left him at home. About time he learned to cope on his own.' She barged past Sandy and dropped her case at the foot of the stairs. 'Hello, Jasper,' she said curtly. 'What are you doing at home, thought you'd be in the office?'

'I'm working from home for a few days, spending time with Sandy and the baby.' In a silky tone, he added, 'And how are you, Irene? Nice of you to pop over.' Jasper was always charming to everyone. It took a lot to rattle his cage and people often told him that he had the patience of a saint.

Irene looked at him with a hard face, and in an officious tone without the trace of humour said, 'Well you can go back, now that I'm here to man the ship.'

Jasper raised his eyebrows to Sandy as if asking her to explain what was going on. But she was just as confused as he was.

'What's in the suitcase, Mum?'

Sandy prayed she wasn't staying. She had a good routine going with housework, the baby and sleep, and Irene would ruin all that. It wasn't as if she was pleasant company. She'd be nothing but a hindrance.

Sandy pulled a face at Jasper to confirm that she was as much in the dark as he was.

'You weren't going to invite me, so I've invited myself.' Irene laughed but it was a laugh laced with sarcasm and she sounded like a witch. 'I'm sure you need the help.'

Sandy headed to the kitchen to put the kettle on. She could put up with her for a few hours, but beyond that it would be tough.

Following Sandy into the kitchen, Irene cast her eyes around, her gaze falling to the area near the cooker where a few peas had been trodden in. 'Place could do with a clean.'

Sandy turned her back on her mother as she popped teabags

into cups and made fresh coffee for Jasper, pulling a face at the wall.

'He's still drinking that posh coffee then?'

'Yes, likes his coffee, does Jasper.'

'Tastes like grit. Must keep him awake all night.'

'He's fine, he's a grown-up.'

'How are you feeding the baby?' she asked, untying her scarf from her head.

Her parents had visited the hospital the day after the birth, but nevertheless Sandy would have expected her mother to rush out onto the patio to peek at her new grandchild. But why be surprised? She wasn't going to be the doting grandma. A cold fish, she was motivated more by duty than love.

'With formula.' As soon as the words were out, Sandy knew it was the wrong answer, but whatever she told her mother, she'd criticise. She could never win and that was how it had been for as long as Sandy could remember. Sometimes she wondered how her dad had coped all these years, and whether it had crossed his mind to leave her. Sandy wouldn't have blamed him if he had.

Irene gaped at Sandy in horror. 'Whatever is wrong with the equipment God gave you? Breast is best. Always has been.' She tutted and put her handbag on the table with a thud.

Sandy clenched her jaw. It was her baby and she'd do what she thought was best. 'Not that old slogan. Formula milk is packed with everything the baby needs.'

'Honestly, Sandra,' she said in a patronising tone, removing her glasses to polish them with her sleeve. 'You were never one for listening to advice.' She wagged her finger and in a stern voice said, 'I know why you won't breastfeed. You're worried about getting saggy boobs and stretchmarks.' She huffed and rolled her eyes to the ceiling. 'Worried about that precious figure of yours. Nothing changes there.'

Sandy squeezed the teabag firmly against the cup watching the water darken, her annoyance mounting by the minute. Why was her mother always so negative and horrible? What had she done to be treated this way?

About to pull a chair out, Irene focused her gaze on the patio. 'I had to get three buses to get over here to see my granddaughter. You weren't going to bring her to us. Mrs Hemmings next door wants to see her. She's made a matinee jacket.' She headed to the glass door and opened it.

'No, Mum, please, let her sleep. It took ages to settle her.' Sandy slammed the mugs on the table and bolted over to the door to stop her.

'Don't be an old grump. She's got to wake at some point. It's not good to let them sleep all day.'

Sandy flinched. Suddenly light-headed, the last thing she wanted today was her mother's vile company. The gall of her, turning up uninvited.

Her stomach muscles were cramping. That was the effect her mother had on her. As a child Sandy had experienced the same abdominal pain that she now reckoned had been caused by nerves.

'Mum, I said no. She's just been fed, I'm exhausted. You wake her and I'll have her crying all day.' *Wish she'd go*, her head screamed.

'Don't be silly, Sandra.' She pulled the door across and a blast of cold October air entered the kitchen. Ignoring Sandy's wishes she leaned over the pram cooing. She picked Angela up, and cradling her in her arms, brought her back inside. Still asleep, thankfully the baby didn't stir. Sandy was grateful for that, at least. Sitting down at the table her mother smiled down at her grandchild—a smile Sandy had not seen before. She stared at her mother, captivated by the warmth of her disarming smile, so genuine, so unlike her. Pulling the pink blanket from Angela's tiny body, Irene chuckled. 'Not a monster this time. Everything appears to be perfect—just as it should be. What a blessing it was that your first died.' Her eyes met Sandy's and she had a serious expression on her face. 'You know that, don't you?'

'Don't let Jasper hear you say that.' Sandy sipped her tea, her stomach knotting with tension.

'I'm sure he'd agree with me. It would have changed your lives. What a burden that child would have been. And who would have adopted him in that state? You would have been lumbered.'

'You mean, *you* would have been lumbered.'

'I didn't say that.'

'But that's what you meant.'

'Things happen for a reason. Somehow, I couldn't see you raising a handicapped child, Sandra.'

'I know you've never been that interested in my life, Mother, but in case you've forgotten, I've spent the past few years helping out at St Bede's and raising money for the Thalidomide Trust.'

Irene gave an exaggerated huff. 'That was just an excuse to dress up and pose in front of the cameras. You, interested in fundraising for charity?'

'I loved working at St Bede's, helping those poor unfortunate children. And we've befriended the caretaker and his disabled son, Toby, who has no arms. His mother took thalidomide.'

Irene raised her eyebrows and sniffed. 'I can't see Jasper having much in common with a school caretaker.' She glanced down and smiled at Angela.

'He's very close to Toby, loves the lad,' Sandy said.

There was something not right about her mother. Sandy had always known that her mother's childhood had been tough, her own mother dying when she was just eight years old. As Sandy grew older, she found herself dwelling on how hard that must have been, but it was a closed subject. Sandy knew better than to ask. 'The past often affects the present and shapes who we are.' She glanced at Irene for a reaction, hoping that maybe she'd open up, but all she saw was fragility in her pale eyes. 'I remember you telling me about the handicapped boy who lived next door when you were a child. He was affected by polio and couldn't walk.'

'Horrible little boy. Couldn't stand him.' Her sour expression looked like it could curdle milk.

Sandy hoped she wasn't planning to stay long because if so, she'd meet Toby. After his ordeal at Town Week, Sandy felt strangely protective towards him. Poor boy had been so upset, which had been such a shame given his outstanding performance on stage.

Sandy wanted to ask her why she was always so negative, but a part of her feared her mother. She never had a nice word to say about anybody. It had become wearing, soul-destroying, and embarrassing, but at least she was predictable. When somebody was unpredictable you didn't know where you stood.

'How will Dad cope if you're away, Mum?'

'It's about time he learned to cope.'

'I suppose he won't mind if it's just a day or two.'

She sneered. 'If I want to stay longer, then I will do. He'll have to cope.'

AFTER ANGELA'S FEED, Sandy prepared soup and bread for lunch which they ate at the kitchen table. The atmosphere was tense, even Jasper was quiet. She could see that he wasn't happy about her mother's arrival. Sandy silently seethed. Damn woman, turning up to wreck those precious moments that she'd so looked forward to—having Jasper to herself and sharing their new experience together as a family.

'Why don't you two go for a nice walk? I can look after the baby and do some cleaning.'

There had to be an ulterior motive. When had her mother ever been helpful? She glanced at Jasper, who seemed to like the idea. It would be nice, Sandy thought, just to get out of the house and away from the old bat. But Sandy was still sore, after her stitches. They wouldn't be walking far. They could find a bench to sit on and decide how they were going to tactfully get rid of Irene.

'That's a nice idea. I could do with a break from the office,' Jasper said, smiling at Sandy and touching her hand.

'Okay, but we'll take Angela, we've not been out with her yet.'

'Suit yourself. You don't trust me to look after her.' Why did she always do this, trying to pick fights?

'It's not like that, Mum.'

'I've got a question to ask you,' she said, looking serious. 'I didn't want to ask you over the phone or when we visited the hospital.'

Jasper and Sandy glanced at each other. This sounded ominous.

'Why did you call her Angela?' Her tone was icy.

'After grandma. Your mother.'

'You've never met your grandmother.'

'All the more reason to name the baby after her.' Sandy got up, collected the bowls and carried them to the sink.

'Have you registered the name yet?'

'Yes.'

'Why didn't you check with me first?'

'Why would we? We thought we'd surprise you,' Jasper said. He leaned back in his chair, his arms folded, his eyes wide with shock.

'I thought you'd be touched.' Fighting tears, Sandy turned away from her mother. She could feel herself shaking. Yet again she'd done the wrong thing in her mother's eyes, when all she'd ever wanted was to please her.

She returned to the table just as her mother's fist connected with it. Angela, now cradled in Jasper's arms, woke yelling. He got up and rocked the baby.

Irene's face had twisted into an ugly expression, every line around her eyes deeper and darker. 'Change it,' she screeched. 'Go back to the registrar first thing in the morning.'

'We can't,' Sandy said, cowering. Why was she angry? It was a pretty name.

'If you don't, then I want nothing to do with my granddaughter.'

Sandy gaped at her in horror. She hated her mother's emotional games and temper tantrums. What was the big deal? Sandy knew exactly what was coming: silent treatment, guilt, blame, manipulation in order to get what she wanted.

'That's a massive overreaction.'

'Come on, Sandy, let's go for a walk.' Jasper smiled warily at his mother-in-law. 'Give you a chance to calm down, Mrs Lambert.' Putting Angela in her pram, hurriedly throwing a blanket over her, he joined Sandy in the hall where she was hastily putting on her coat and reaching for the door handle.

30

'You look shell-shocked, darling,' Jasper said when they reached the end of the drive.

'What on earth is wrong with my mother?' Still shaking, Sandy was shivering with shock. 'There's a screw loose somewhere.'

'Let's find the nearest bench.' Jasper picked up speed, steering the pram to the kerb as he prepared to cross the road.

Within ten minutes they found a wooden bench by a bus stop on the main road into town. Sitting down they laughed at how ridiculous this was—escaping from the toxic, overbearing mother-in-law who'd pitched up in their home, about to suck all the joy out of their lives. She was a parasite that fed on misery and left Sandy feeling both powerless and miserable. And as for her staying over, Sandy couldn't let that happen. But did she have the guts to turf her out and send her packing? No. She was too polite. Too respectful, even though her mother had never shown *her* any respect.

'I can't bear it,' she said, 'she's soul-sucking and seems to feed on misery. Her mother died when she was small, I thought it would be a nice gesture to name Angela after her.'

'I know you did, pet. You've a kind heart, but for some reason she's taken great offence to it. We'd better choose a different name.'

'But she thinks we've registered the birth.'

'Maybe we could call her Jane Angela rather than Angela Jane.'

'Doesn't have the same ring and Jane's more of a middle name than a first name.'

'We don't have to rush to register her. Why don't you try talking to her about her own mother's death?'

Sandy turned to him, aghast. 'I can't do that. It's a taboo subject.'

'There are plenty of other names to choose from. She was beside herself. Did you see her face? It was boiling with rage.'

'But why give in to her? She's completely self-centred. It's all about her. She's a spiteful woman, always has been. And if we choose another name, she'll find fault with that too.'

Jasper sighed. 'How long is she staying?'

'I don't know.'

He looked at her, jerking his head back. 'You didn't ask?'

'Well, no,' she stuttered. 'I didn't like to.'

'Oh, for goodness sake, Sandy. Stop being so timid. We need to know.'

'When I tried asking, she was dismissive.'

'Toby's coming round later. In all this time I've not had a chance to talk to the lad about Town Week. And school. I was going to see if he wanted to stay for dinner too, as long as you didn't mind.'

'Really?' Sandy stared at him, incredulous. 'Don't we have enough going on at the moment?'

'You want me to cancel him?' Jasper asked in a weary voice.

She shook her head. 'It's not exactly convenient, is it?' She didn't like to see him disappointed, knowing how important

Toby was to him, but sometimes didn't it make sense to let Toby and Bill get on with their lives?

'I'll cancel him then.'

'Don't do that.' She touched his hand. She admired his kindness and patience. Perhaps Toby's presence might diffuse the atmosphere. It would do her mother good to meet him, after her spiteful comments about their first baby. Although Sandy would have to feed Toby, because if he ate with his feet it would be awkward. She felt herself blush, wincing as she imagined the horror on Irene's face.

'I think you need to give your mum clear boundaries. She can't just turn up out of the blue, it's not convenient.'

'Easier said than done.'

'Sometimes it's best to be firm, even though it's hard.'

After a short walk round the block, they returned home just as it started to drizzle.

'Sandy bumped the pram over the threshold and into the hall, half expecting to be greeted by the drone of the hoover or the sight of her mother dressed in a pinny with a feather duster in hand.

'Mum,' she called out. Then she heard it. Crying, coming from upstairs.

∼

JASPER LOOKED AT SANDY. 'You better go up, see what's wrong,' He lifted the baby from the pram, took her into his study, lowering her onto a nest of blankets on the carpet so that he could resume work. At his desk, he slid open the top drawer, fumbling for his stapler.

The letter was gone.

He yanked the drawer right out. Maybe it was caught at the back, or in another drawer. His heart pounded. Fuck, it wasn't there. Collapsing onto his knees he rummaged through every drawer, swiped papers from his desk, collapsed back into his chair with a huge sigh clasping his pounding head. *Why the hell did I write that letter, what was I thinking?* One of them had it, which one—Sandy or her mother? Or Toby? He'd been in the house alone.

Every part of his body went on pause and his insides felt as if there was nothing there. He sat there, completely numb, not even daring to think about the huge consequences. What a fool he'd been. Frantically he began searching again, hoping it was there somewhere.

∼

SANDY HUNG her coat on a peg. Puzzled, she stood at the bottom of the stairs for a moment wondering how she was going to tackle the thorny issue of the baby's name. She'd hoped they'd return from the walk to find her calmer, more accepting and even cheerful, but that would be hoping for too much. Her mother could never just let things be. She had to persist in getting what she wanted and became obsessed about small things. Her dad was fond of saying, 'Your mother's got another bee in her bonnet.'

Sandy went halfway up the stairs and called out. When there was no reply, she headed up and reaching the landing paused, listening to her mother's faint sobs. They were coming from the baby's room. What on earth was she doing in there? The door was closed so Sandy hovered outside. Her first thought was that her parents had fallen out and she'd conveniently used the excuse that she'd come here to help.

'Mum,' she said softly, knocking at the door. Hearing whimpering, she turned the handle and went in, stopping short to gasp when she saw her slumped on the floor clutching one of Angela's teddy bears, which she quickly dropped when she saw Sandy in the doorway. She looked pitiful and vulnerable and hurriedly adjusted her face with a sniff and a dab of her eyes. Irene was much too dignified to cry in front of others, but although she'd kick up a fuss, have a tantrum, tears were never shed. She wouldn't dream of letting others see her in this state. Something was wrong. This wasn't just about the baby's name.

Sandy sat on the floor close to her mum and tried to take her hand to comfort her. Irene quickly pulled it away and threw her a sour look.

Sandy noticed an envelope which had been opened, and it was tucked in her cardigan pocket. Had she received bad news?

'Angela.' She gave Sandy a frosty glare.

Sandy felt as if she'd been slapped around the face.

'You seem to enjoy upsetting me. Getting yourself in the family way all those years ago while living under my roof, now this. Rubbing my nose in the past.' Her nails were digging into her palms. Her pain seemed irrational, out of proportion, and this puzzled Sandy.

'I'm sorry. If we'd known the name was going to upset you, we would have chosen a different one. We could use her middle name, Jane. It's just as pretty.' What was she agreeing to? She didn't want to call the baby Jane. She'd spent her life giving in and pandering to her mother. She was used to it. Damn it, no, why should she change her name? 'Actually, Mum, no, I don't want to call her Jane. She's Angela.'

'Just look at me, slumped here. Like my own mother, the last time I saw her.'

Sandy spoke softly, careful not to rile her. 'How did she die, Mum? You've never talked about her.'

'She didn't die.' The words were spat like bullets. 'She walked out on us. There one minute, gone the next. Happy now?'

Sandy's hand flew to her chest. A tingling sensation swept through her and instinctively she grabbed her mother's arm. 'You would never have told me?'

With a flick of her wrist, Irene brushed her daughter's hand away and inched along the carpet curling her feet under her bottom. She'd never been a tactile woman. In a pained voice she said, 'The past is best forgotten.' Her whole body was trembling as she reached out and gripped a cot bar.

'I don't believe for one moment you've forgotten her. That's a huge thing to happen, Mum. You've carried the sorrow in your heart for years. You poor thing.'

'Don't be all soppy and sentimental,' she said with contempt.

'I can't believe it.' Sandy was stunned. 'I could have a grandma out there somewhere. Haven't you tried to find her?'

'No. You just learn to get on with life.'

'And have you? I don't think so. Otherwise, you wouldn't be sitting here crying. It's turned you into a bitter and twisted woman because you've not dealt with it, you've not faced it full on.'

She flinched. 'How dare you. We've never got on, you and me. You always preferred your father.'

'I loved you both.'

'Don't lie to me, Sandra. I may as well have left when you were young. You two were as thick as thieves, the pair of you. I was invisible half the time.'

'You... invisible?' That was so not true. Her mother was the dominant partner in the marriage, the leader. Her father was under the thumb.

'Would you like me to make dinner later?' Sandy was taken aback at the sudden change in conversation. The portcullis had come down. Her mum was unwilling to open up and so for now, the matter was closed.

'If you want to. Toby's coming for dinner.'

'Ah, Toby,' she said in a strange, almost mocking tone of voice, her eyebrows raised. 'And will his caretaker dad be coming, too?'

'He's not a caretaker dad, but he is a caretaker. Toby's coming alone. He's popping over to spend time with Jasper.'

Irene stared at Sandy, her body tensing. 'Why?'

'I think Jasper's helping with his homework.'

'You said Jasper sees a lot of him.'

'Yes.'

Squinting, she had a peculiar expression on her face that was hard to read. 'And you don't find that strange, Sandra?'

Thoughtful, Sandy fiddled with her necklace. Any other mother and she would have opened up, told her how Toby made her think of the child she'd lost. 'Should I be?'

She narrowed her eyes and held Sandy's gaze. 'That's what you'll have to ask yourself.'

Sandy wasn't rising to these enigmatic statements. With a flourish she headed for the door. 'I best see to Baby.' While her mother was here, Baby it was.

∼

TRYING to help Toby with his math's homework, Jasper found it hard to concentrate. All he could think about was the missing letter. Who had taken it? Sandy, Mrs Lambert or Toby? Falling into any of their hands was terrible, but he wasn't sure which was worse. It was much more likely to be Sandy, but she never went into his study other than to offer him coffee. She considered it to be out-of-bounds, respected his privacy and she wasn't interested in any of the books on the shelves. His mother-in-law had barely been in the house for five minutes and for what reason would she snoop through his drawers? Maybe she'd been looking for something to write on or a stamp to send a letter of her own. He felt sick to the core. Writing it had been a terrible mistake. Ever since the altercation with Ronny Steadman, he'd vowed to tell Sandy the truth. But weeks had passed. He had no guts about him, but in truth there hadn't been an ideal moment to tell her. Would there ever be? He'd always find excuses, there would never be a perfect time. Now that the birth was out the way, he was running out of excuses to delay.

'You're miles away,' Toby said. 'Has the baby turned your brains to mush? Mum used to tell me that babies do that to their mums. Not sure it's the same for dads.'

'Sorry, sunshine. Brain's a bit addled. It's all the broken nights.'

'It's okay, I think I understand it now. I'll finish the rest at home.'

'I'm like a walking zombie. I didn't realise how hard a baby would be. She's hijacked my sleep for nights on end.'

'I don't like our new maths teacher. He doesn't explain things very well.'

'Well anytime you don't understand something, I'm only a phone call away.'

He gave him a sympathetic smile. 'Have you reflected much on Town Week? You were pretty upset.'

'I wasn't upset,' Toby snapped.

Jasper knew he was fibbing. His legs were jiggling and his eyes downcast—they were all giveaways.

'I was angry.'

'Go on... explain.' Jasper's tone was calm, but as he observed Toby with curiosity, he wanted to understand what made his son tick. What was it like to live through his eyes?

'It was nerve-racking.'

'I can remember the first time I spoke in front of an audience. I was young, but not as young as you. I'd just finished National Service and the local Methodist church asked me to give a talk on Cyprus. The church hall was packed, mainly with older ladies. Someone told me to imagine that everybody in the audience was naked. I never understood that advice. I think it was supposed to make me feel less nervous. Can't say it worked though.'

'Have you had to stand up in front of big audiences since?'

'I've done lots of public speaking.' Jasper smiled. 'I love it.'

Toby stared at him. 'How can you love it? It's terrifying.'

'It can be, but adrenaline pumps through your body to calm your nerves. I like the thrill of it.'

Toby shook his head. 'The crowd wasn't interested in my musical skills. When they saw my arms, their jaws dropped open. He looks weird, they were thinking. I saw them whispering. Look at his body. Poor boy, he'll never make it.'

'You might have been their first experience of handicap.'

Toby was hunched over. 'You mean they've never seen a body that's unfinished, hands that are the work of the devil.' His tone was bitter. 'That's what people say about us Flids.'

'Sit up. Let's see your face.' Jasper waited. 'That's better.' He smiled at him. 'Now stand.' Sullen and with reluctance, Toby did as asked. 'Pull your shoulders back. Good. Now look at the bookcase and imagine each book is a person. Hundreds, all looking at you. Look out there at the sea of faces, look up with confidence. They're waiting to hear you.' He paused for impact. 'They're waiting to hear what you, Toby Murphy, have to say. Everything that comes from your mouth, or in your case the guitar.'

Toby giggled. 'I get your point, can I sit down now?'

'Breathe deeply. Feel confident, Toby. You have so much to give. Don't get a reputation.'

He frowned. 'What reputation?'

'A reputation for being disabled and difficult.'

'I'm not difficult.'

'I know you're not, but you've got to try and imagine how *they* see you.'

Sandy came in, stepped over the sleeping dog and gathered up empty mugs. 'How's the homework going?' She glanced at Toby's exercise book, open on the coffee table.

Jasper noticed a chill in her voice. Had she found and read the letter or was she just stressed because of her mother? They'd not been able to speak alone since getting in from their walk and he still didn't know how long the ghastly Mrs Lambert intended to stay. He wouldn't find out until they were in bed later on. 'We're practising body language in front of an audience. The books are the audience.' Jasper swept his arm towards the bookcase. 'Town Week left him feeling deflated.'

'I'm okay,' Toby said.

'I'm the one with the experience,' Sandy jested. 'All those catwalks I've strutted along, scantily clad. They could blindfold me and still I'd find my way.'

Her experience was completely different to Toby's, but she was trying to help.

She waggled a finger at Toby and chuckled. 'Models are conscious of their bodies too. No, let's correct that. We all are. I used to be so insecure about my weight. Mum will tell you.' She looked down at her stomach. 'Now that I've had a baby, I'm going to have to accept that a saggy belly might be here forever, but what does it matter? We weren't put on this earth to be visually pleasing. Be proud of yourself, Toby, you don't know what you can achieve.'

The phone rang, startling them all. Jasper reached to pick it up, glancing at Sandy and Toby, a finger to his lips to indicate for them to be quiet.

'Cooper,' came Steadman's smarmy voice.

'Can I help you?'

Angry, Jasper just wanted to swear at him. But Sandy was standing close by, watching him, as if waiting to know who it was. He turned his back on her, hoping she'd leave the room and take Toby.

'That's very polite of you. Is wifey in the room? Caught you at a bad time?'

Jasper wasn't going to rise to the bastard's sarcasm.

'You owe me more money. We had an agreement.'

'Sorry, I can't hear you, you need speak up.' He ended the call and raised his eyebrows to Sandy. 'Bad line.'

He wanted to pull the lead from the phone but couldn't while she was in the room. He hadn't heard from Steadman since the baby's birth. Had even dared to hope he'd given up his campaign. Now that he'd phoned, smelled Jasper's fear, he'd keep calling. Maybe even in the middle of the night. And Mrs Lambert was here. An added complication. There was no end to this. He had to get on with it, had to tell Sandy. As soon as Mrs Lambert had left.

'I just came in to tell you both that dinner will be ready in twenty minutes.'

'I'm really sorry, Mrs Cooper, I should have said, I'm going to the cinema with Lucy. Her dad's picking me up from here, soon.'

'A date with the lovely Lucy?'

Toby blushed. 'We're seeing *Logan's Run*. She told me a couple of weeks ago that she was seeing it with a bloke called Pete from college. But last night she called to ask if I still wanted to see it.'

'Maybe she's blown him out,' Sandy suggested.

'Or he's blown her out,' Jasper added.

'Or she's already seen it with him and is just being polite in asking me. Feels sorry for me, thinks I've got no one to go with.'

'That's not true, sunshine.'

'I hope you have a lovely evening, Toby.'

31

Vince had been following the boy. He now knew a great deal about his life. Where he lived, where he went to school, his strengths on the football pitch. He'd even watched him play the guitar with that new girlfriend of his. It was useful being a window cleaner. All he'd needed to get started was a set of ladders, sponge, and bucket. And for that he got to see into people's homes. Into their lives.

Toby's life.

Window cleaning wasn't the sort of work he expected to be doing, but after the trauma of his job at the hospital and what it had done to his mind, anything was better. The nightmares still disturbed his sleep and he'd never be able to erase the horrific images that continued to haunt him.

He could make a difference. Stop it happening. Get one of the big papers to take his story seriously and call the local health authority to account. Money to help the affected families.

It would be headline news. Everything he'd witnessed. He'd always wondered, did this go on in every hospital across the country?

It was a late Saturday afternoon and Vince had just been into

Dunn's for a pair of socks, then he dashed into Woolies for a selection of his favourite sweets, Black Jacks and Fruit Salads from the Pick N Mix. With the shops now closing, he wondered what to do with his evening. Fancying a swift half, he nipped into the White Horse Hotel. It was a comfortable place to pass time. He wandered up to the bar, with its chessboard design now speckled with baked-in beer stains. He pulled out one of the high stools to sit at. Twenty minutes later and with his thirst quenched, he drained the last dregs. About to consider another half, he noticed a young girl slip into the bar and head straight for the toilets. He could have sworn it was the girlfriend of the thalidomide kid. Swiping a newspaper on the bar in front of him, he quickly hid his face. Should he wait for her to use the loo, then get up and follow her, see where she was going? Maybe she was out with Toby for the evening, and he was waiting outside for her. He pretended to read the paper and when the barman came to ask him if he needed a refill, he shook his head, letting him take the glass away. A few moments later Lucy emerged from the loo, her eyes focused on the swing doors leading into a porch area and the main door. He put the paper down. She didn't notice him slipping down from his stool, inching his way in the same direction.

Out on the street, Vince glanced in both directions and caught sight of the pair of them heading up the hill. Keeping a safe distance, he was intrigued to find out where they were going.

They stopped at the cinema and Vince watched from afar as they read each board. He could see that *Logan's Run* was showing. It wasn't Vince's type of film, he preferred horror, but he knew teenagers were rushing to see it. He held back, watching them join the queue.

Dashing into the nearest phone box, Vince dialled Ronny's number.

'What do you want?' Grumpy sod. He sounded half-asleep.

'The boy's about to go into the cinema. I'm going to follow him in.'

'And do what exactly?' came his brother's weary voice.

'I'm not sure yet. I don't have a plan.' Everything Vince did was impulsive. He never planned.

'You prat. This has gone too far. It was fun watching Jasper squirm. But I couldn't give a shit about the guy's private life. I was surprised he coughed up as much as he did.'

'He's scared you'll tell everyone his dark secret.'

'Drop it, Vince. I'd give you a cut of the money, but you were always nicking off me when we were kids.'

'I'm not interested in money. I'd rather my story was out there.'

'Sam's big muckers with the hospital's chief. Think they went to the same public school. I can tell you right now, he won't be interested. It's all about protecting the old boys' network. There's enough nasty stuff going on, especially with the IRA, without overloading people's brains with more tragedy and wrongdoing.'

'If it bleeds, it leads. You should know that. But you don't want to help me. You never have done.'

'Fuck off.'

'That's not a nice way to speak to your bruv. When the boy goes missing, they'll come knocking at your door. You may as well tell your journalist friend what this is about. It's not difficult, just get him to publish the story.' Vince slammed the phone down and walked over to the cinema to buy his ticket, before heading into the auditorium.

∽

WHILE THEY WAITED in the queue, Toby and Lucy chatted about the TV programmes they liked watching.

'I love coming to the cinema. That big screen. I always feel as if I'm inside the film living what they're living.'

'What's your favourite TV programme?' Lucy asked.

'*Steptoe & Son.*' Toby couldn't help it. He had to do an impression of Harold saying to Albert, 'you dirty old man,' which he repeated several times, because it was so hard not to.

Lucy laughed. 'That's a great impression. You dirty, dirty old man. It's not the same when I do it. You can do it better.'

'Do you like *Some Mothers Do 'Ave 'Em?*'

'That's the most annoying programme I've ever watched. Frank Spencer, he's such an idiot and his eyes are always popping out.'

'Ooooh, Betty.' Toby laughed. 'My dad likes it more than I do. He's a telly addict.'

'Have you got a colour TV? We have.'

'Lucky you. First time I saw colour was at our neighbour's house when we all watched Princess Anne's wedding together. The wedding was boring. All I wanted was to see her new TV. The colours were so bright. Everyone's skin looked orange, and it looked like they were wearing bright pink lipstick, men an' all.'

After buying their tickets they wandered through to Screen One. Toby's eyes adjusted to the dim lighting as they looked for seats. He wished he'd led the way so that he could steer her to the back row, but she was in front. He'd been wondering all day if he was going to get a snog. Grandmothers aside, he'd never kissed a girl but longed to kiss Lucy and kept imagining what it would feel like. It would be a proper kiss this time and not that drunken, slobbery smack on the lips she'd given him in London. But how to kiss? Did people instinctively know what to do or did they get instruction from watching actors on films?

And what he'd give to touch those beautiful breasts.

Two years older than Toby, Lucy was probably used to boys with tons of experience. There was zero chance for him. He'd look an idiot to even try.

Toby could but dream, but knew his nerves would prevent him.

'What about nearer the back?' he suggested. 'We'll get boggle-eyed right in front of the screen.'

'Okay,' she said, looking round at the rows.

They took a couple of seats at the end of an aisle nearer the back and opposite the fire exit. Toby stared ahead, his eyes fixed on the red velvet curtains, trying to figure out whether Lucy was now his girlfriend. Was this a date or just an evening out with a mate? He'd feel so proud to call her his girlfriend. The thought made him go all warm and fuzzy. She seemed to like his company. He wondered what had happened to Pete. Had she blown him out? Toby considered being direct, just coming out with it. How hard would that be, to ask her if she'd be his girlfriend? He just wanted to know where he stood and if he was in with a chance. He didn't want to make an idiot of himself by assuming they were boyfriend and girlfriend.

The curtains parted and the adverts started. A woman's face filled the screen, the camera zooming in to her deliciously plump lips as she unwrapped a Cadbury's Flake. Toby sneakily glanced at Lucy, checking her lips out. *'Only the crumbliest, flakiest chocolate tastes like chocolate never tasted before,'* came the music. He'd like to taste Lucy's lips. *'Feather-like flakes, crumbly chocolate.'* He found himself imagining feeding Lucy a Cadbury's Flake, the pair of them laughing, the crumbly flakes spilling down her top, between her breasts. On impulse Toby turned to Lucy, hoping she'd feel the same. As their eyes connected, his heart raced. This was the moment. *Now or never. Lean in, you idiot, do it.*

Lucy rubbed his shoulder and smiled, but the vibes weren't coming, her eyes were guarded, the moment lost. And now the screen was filled with royal blue, the theme tune for Pearl & Dean playing, signifying the start of the film. Lucy swayed her shoulders, glanced at Toby and together they hummed along. 'Ba ba, ba, ba, ba.' As she folded her arms and inched further from him, his heart sank. How he wished she'd rest a hand on his lap. Some intimacy, togetherness, how nice that would be.

∼

THE FILM HAD ALREADY STARTED when Vince slid through the swing doors and into the auditorium, quickly surveying the rows before the attendant appeared, waving her torch. Where were they? The place was crowded. He scanned the whole room. This was hopeless. What a stupid idea to come here. And then, a flash of light from the screen illuminated the silhouette sea of figures and just in that second, he glimpsed the boy. What a stroke of luck. And incredibly, there was a vacant seat in the row behind them. Vince hurried over, hoping that neither the boy nor his girlfriend would notice him.

Twenty minutes later and it was hard for Vince not to be drawn into the film. The actors were good, Jenny Agutter, Farrah Fawcett and Peter Ustinov, the story action-packed. But while he watched, he tried to work out what to do. The fire exit was adjacent. He could grab the boy, but how? Or he could just pass him a note asking him to meet in the foyer afterwards. But to say what? He'd work that out when it came to it.

Suddenly the film stopped, and they were plunged into darkness. Was there a power failure? This was his moment. It was now or never. Another minute passed, then the attendant came in with her torch and made an announcement. 'Ladies and gentlemen. We're very sorry, there's a problem but we are trying to sort it. If you could bear with us. Your patience would be appreciated.'

The sound came back on, but there was still no picture. No sign of Lucy either. She'd be back, any moment, then he'd miss the opportunity. He'd have to be quick. Stop dithering. Now. He leaned forward, touched the boy's shoulder.

'Toby, quick, come with me. We'll find your girlfriend. I think there's been a bomb scare.'

~

TOBY GLANCED ROUND, felt someone close behind him, but the lighting was poor and he couldn't see. He couldn't make out who it was, but he recognised the voice. Maybe a teacher from school. He went to get up, stepped away from his seat. Then felt an arm around him. With light coming from the fire exit sign, he saw who it was and panicked.

'It's okay, don't be frightened.' Toby felt dazed and flustered, didn't know what was happening. Lucy, where was she? If a bomb was about to go off, she could get killed, maimed, trapped. The Guildford pub bombing—it could happen again. The man was strong and forceful and almost pushed Toby towards the fire exit and out and along the corridor, down a flight of clanky metal stairs. Could he smell smoke? Or was it just stale cigarette smoke? Any minute he expected to hear a loud bang, but Lucy, he had to find her.

Toby felt sheer blinding panic. 'My girlfriend, I can't leave her behind.'

'She'll be fine. Let's go down the stairs,' the man ordered. He did as he was told as if on automatic pilot. What was this about? The man was trouble. Toby had seen that, the minute he'd clapped eyes on him at Lucy's house. He had a mean face and a harsh voice. Please God, somebody come so that he could escape, now before they were outside. But the stairwell was silent, nobody was there and then they were outside, and the man was still gripping his shoulder tightly. What should he do, make a run for it? Nerves had taken over, his brain had frozen. He couldn't fight, he had no strength inside him.

'I need to speak to you. About something important. I'm not going to hurt you, not unless you do something stupid.' They carried on walking to the end of the street. Where was he taking him? And if only the streets weren't so empty, he could yell, get someone's attention, but would he when fear had taken over and he felt paralysed?

Lucy, she'd be worried. Would wonder what the heck had happened to him.

Stopping at a car, Vince opened the passenger door and clamping the back of Toby's neck with a big rough hand, pushed him down and into the car. 'Stay there and don't even think about running away. I'll easily outrun you. You hear me?' The man's face was close to him. He meant business. Toby smelt sweets, maybe Black Jacks, masking rancid breath. His teeth were yellow, rotten, hideous. For the first time since Blackpool, when he was bullied in the school woods, Toby was terrified. He tried to push the morbid thoughts hitting him at once and focus on one thing—how was he going to escape?

The car stank of curry. He hated curry. Spices. Yuk.

Vince swerved the car jerkily out into the road, rammed the gear stick into second, then third, picking up speed. Where was he taking him? What was this about? Was he going to die? He tried to force back the tears, great heaving gulps rising in his throat. *Got to stay calm.* Jasper's words came back to him in a flash. *Don't be afraid to face fear. Don't give up hope.* He bit his lip, silently prayed he'd get out of this. He felt sick, sick to the pit of his stomach and the man's stinky aftershave mingled with curry made Toby want to throw up.

They drove out of Guildford, the city bleeding into the countryside and darkness. Fear coursed through him, but Toby had his wits about him, trying to memorise the names of the villages they passed through, any road signs. But his heart was pounding, and it was so dark.

Vince indicated and turned into a lane leading to a cottage with fields on either side. There were no other houses.

Toby's chest was too tight to cry. 'Where am I?'

'We're here.'

The man got out and came round to open Toby's door, grabbing him by the shoulder. Toby sobbed, 'I want to go home.'

'Just get out,' he yelled. The man's eyes were travelling over him. Trembling, bursting for a wee, Toby couldn't move. His legs, heavy weights.

Out of the car, underfoot it was stony. Shuffling forward, he was frightened he'd stumble. He was pushed towards a flight of steps, tall weeds either side of a path, a door ahead with roses rambling around it. The man reached forward to open the door and flick a switch. Light flooded a single room from a bare lightbulb.

The air was damp, musty, unlived in, but he must live here—curry. A table in the corner was littered with packaging and foil containers—leftover curry, globules of yellow dotting a dirty tablecloth. Shards of poppadum had spilled onto bare floorboards. A spoon standing in a jar of mango chutney. He wasn't hungry but was his next meal leftover cold curry? Bile rose in his throat.

'I want to go home. Please, let me go home.'

From behind him, Toby heard the key in the door as the man turned it, locking them in. A soft clunk as he took it from the keyhole. He was trapped. A prison. There was a door ahead. And another to the right—perhaps a toilet with a window. A means of escape?

A faint glimmer of hope; they'd be out looking for him by now. They'd never find him. They were in the middle of nowhere. Wouldn't know to look here. Who would hear him, who would raise the alarm? The cows in the field?

'Sit down, over there,' Vince shouted. Toby looked at where he was pointing—to a dark area under the stairs. Too frightened to argue, he did as he was told. He hated the idea of being penned in. When he didn't move, Vince prodded him in the back. Toby dipped his head as he stepped forward, crouching, then dropped to his knees. Spiders. There were always spiders in dark crevices. Tears sprang to his eyes, great sobbing gulps. He curled up tightly feeling the warmth of his own body against the chilly air.

'I won't kill you,' Vince said in a gruff voice. 'I won't, okay?' Toby looked at him and saw a trickle of sweat travel down his hairline. How could he be hot? The room was cold. And he badly needed a wee. Didn't dare ask for the loo.

His tears were heavier now, big plops. He didn't believe the man. His life was in danger. This was it. He was here to die. He wanted to kill himself, better than waiting for this horrible creature to do it. He looked like a kidnapper, everything Toby would have imagined, from the man's raven eyes to the size of his nose, to the blueish shadows under his eyes. Why had he brought him here? What did he want?

'Don't cry.'

'Let me go home.'

The man knelt, inched closer to Toby, blocking his exit route, his eyes drinking Toby in. He felt a warm trickle escape down his legs. Couldn't hold himself any longer. He wished he had the strength to lash out, kick him. He was good with his feet. His legs were normally strong, but not now. They were wobbly, like jelly.

'Where am I?'

'You'll find out, I suppose, eventually.'

Snot trailed down Toby's face. He needed a hanky. He tried to wipe his nose on his sleeve. Vince pulled a tissue from his own pocket and leant over to help Toby blow his nose, a kinder, caring expression on his face that took Toby by surprise.

At least he wasn't tying him up—yet. The baddies in films always tied their victims to bedposts.

'I've been watching you play football. You're good. Very agile. I've always wanted this.' He paused, a smile flitting across his face. But there was a sinister glint in his eyes. Did he plan to hurt Toby, finish him off? 'To get you on your own, find out more about you.'

Toby's heartbeat was racing, nearly exploding. And between his legs, warm, wet.

He remembered. He'd seen the man watch him play football.

'You're special, did you know that?' The man had a look in his eyes, as though he wanted something from Toby and had wanted it for a long time. No one had ever looked at him like that before, with such intensity, it was so unnerving and through dark, powerful, hungry eyes. A lump rose in Toby's throat.

'You're one of the lucky ones. You got to live.'

What was he talking about?

'Thousands of you weren't so lucky. Mothers miscarried, many babies were stillborn, or much worse, they died at the hands of the doctors because they were born with no genitals, no anus, missing organs. Yes, sounds horrible, doesn't it? So deformed, their lives weren't worth living. Do you know what those doctors did in cases like that?'

Mute, Toby shook his head.

'They snuffed out those little lives.' He clicked his fingers and a smile played on his lips.

Is that what this monster intended to do to him? He couldn't die. His life, it had barely begun. And Lucy, lovely Lucy. He just wanted to get out of here, but how? If only he could think, but his brain had seized up.

'State infanticide, that's what it's called. But you won't read about that. It's not been reported. The public don't want to hear the grotesque truth, so I'm told. Bet they don't tell you about those horrors at that school of yours. And I don't expect that journalist fella, Jasper, talks about it. He's only ever reported half the truth.'

'I want to go home.'

'Not yet. I need you to do something for me, but we'll come to that later.'

What was he talking about? Why was he here?

'I've seen it, enough to know what was going on in every hospital right across the country. Doctors, so disgusted at what they saw, crying out, praying to let God take those babies, then ordering the midwife to put them on a windowsill without any clothes, the window open.' He clicked his fingers. 'They slipped away. What do you think of that, young Toby? What if that had been you? Left to die. How many tablets did your mother take?'

The man leaned towards him, waiting for Toby's reply.

'I don't know.' His sentence was a strangled croak.

'I'll tell you what happened to those dead babies, shall I?'

Toby's gaze fell to the dusty floor. Spiders were now the least of his worries. He didn't want to hear any more.

'Parents weren't consulted about their wishes, only told that their babies were cremated, but they had no idea that hospitals were burning their babies' remains in incinerators alongside other waste which generated power to heat the hospitals. They were treated like any other organic waste, like a tumour or clump of cancerous cells.' Toby looked at him in horror. Was he talking about thalidomide babies? His face was twisting, there was a tightness around his eyes. 'Those babies had no rights. You must have learned about the Nazis in history lessons?'

Toby didn't reply, didn't want to hear any more.

'Remind you of the Holocaust?'

Toby spoke in a careful, neutral voice, not wanting to rile his captor. 'It happened a long time ago.'

Vince gasped, looked shocked. 'But, Toby, it still goes on. We still treat human life in the same callous way. Babies, torn from the womb every hour of every day, then incinerated. Hospitals are fuelled by the remains of those aborted foetuses. I worked at a large hospital. I saw it all. I had to incinerate those bodies. I had to assemble body parts of thalidomide babies before scooping them up for incineration.'

'Stop,' Toby screamed, surprising himself.

The man had a faraway look in his eyes. He stared over at the fireplace as if something was about to descend from it. His mind was a million miles away, hypnotised.

This was Toby's chance to escape. There was a gap beside him large enough to squeeze through. He shuffled his bottom, but the man was fast. His evil eyes snapped back to Toby, his hands clamping his legs, stopping him from moving.

He let out a sob. 'It's horrible, but I can't do anything about that, I just want to go home, please, my dad will be wondering where I am.' He whimpered. 'Who do you blame? I don't know what you want.'

'I don't know who I blame. I'm haunted by the remains of those babies.' Vince pulled a packet out of his pocket, lit a cigarette, and took a deep puff. 'It's dark outside. Think of all the things that they'll think has happened to you.'

They'd be worried sick.

Everything I've told you—it needs to be in the papers. You agree?'

'Yes.' Toby didn't understand, but instinct told him to agree.

'You're going do something for me. Understand?' His voice was sharp.

Toby nodded. Had no idea what he was agreeing to.

'You know Jasper's phone number?'

'I think so.' Toby's voice was shaky.

'You're going to tell him to get in his car and meet us over at Bourne Lake. And he mustn't bring the police. If he brings the police, his secret is out. And your life's in danger.'

'What secret?'

'It's not for me to say.'

Toby had no idea what he was on about, but at least he'd not been hurt—yet.

'Right, get up, we're going to find the nearest phone box.'

32

Jasper was tired of his sour-faced mother-in-law. All she'd done all day was complain, little digs here and there, nothing was ever right. Her strange behaviour, it masked something deeper, it had to. Relieved when she said she'd head up to bed, Jasper was desperate to talk to Sandy, find out what was going on, what Mrs Lambert's temper tantrum had been about.

Jasper closed the lounge door and joined Sandy on the sofa. She was already in her nightdress, her feet curled under her, as she focused on feeding the baby. The dog lay sprawled beside the warm radiator.

Jasper turned the TV off. 'What's going on with your mother?'

Sandy looked suddenly upset, as if tears were threatening. She winded the baby then put her back in the carrycot beside the settee. 'She dropped a massive bombshell.'

'She's leaving him?' Jasper was flabbergasted.

'No, but that wouldn't surprise me. Any sane man wouldn't put up with her as long as Dad has.' She paused and took a deep breath. 'She told me that my grandma didn't die. She walked out when Mum was small.'

'What?' Jasper stared at her, then at the door, as if his mother-in-law was lurking beyond it, listening in.

'I don't think Mum had any intention of ever telling me. Naming the baby after Grandma has dragged this up. I'm so shocked, Jasper.' Her eyes were filling with tears. 'It's as if I don't really know my mother at all.'

Jasper put his arm around her and gently brushed the tears from her cheeks. 'What she must have gone through all these years. It's no wonder...' He didn't need to finish the sentence. They could see the damage it had done to Irene. Jasper had never liked Sandy's mother but now he almost felt sorry for the woman. Could he find it in himself to forgive her, for her behaviour over the years? Most of all for the harsh way she'd treated Sandy all that time ago. Threatening her nineteen-year-old pregnant daughter, have your baby adopted, or leave.

'I like the name Angela. We could keep the peace and call her Baby till she's gone, but I don't see why we should.'

'Me neither.'

'After she told me, she clammed up. Typical Mum. I'm hoping she might tell me more, but I'm not going to pry. It'll have to be when she's ready. She was pretty upset earlier. Never seen her like that before.'

From above, a bedroom door slammed.

Jasper looked at Sandy. 'What now?'

Feet pounded on the stairs.

'Brace yourself. I think she's had some news. She was nursing an envelope in her pocket earlier,' Sandy warned.

The envelope. He felt himself go cold.

Irene burst into the lounge waving a piece of paper. Ignoring Sandy, she stormed straight to Jasper, her face red, her eyes cold, hard, flinty.

His day of reckoning—it wasn't supposed to be like this. Not in the scenarios he'd played in his head. His stomach hardened as he jerked away from Irene. He suddenly felt light-headed, as if floating above the unfolding scene.

∼

'Mum, whatever's the matter?'

Her mother was waving a piece of paper, her face thunder. A petition for divorce?

'I bet you had no idea, Sandra. I never wanted you to marry him.' She pointed at Jasper. 'I can always sense a wrong 'un and my intuition is never wrong. You've married a liar.' She spat the words with venom.

Sandy should have seen this coming. Her mother didn't look well. All that stuff about her childhood, it was making her loopy. Was she having a nervous breakdown?

'Why were you going through my bureau? You had no right to open that letter. It wasn't addressed to you,' Jasper snapped.

'I was looking for a stamp. If you didn't want my daughter to discover the truth, why leave it there for her to find?'

'Letter? Mum, Jasper, one of you explain. You're scaring me.'

Jasper went to stand by the window, his face solemn.

'The handicapped boy, Toby. He's your son. Here, read it.' Irene thrust the letter at Sandy.

A fog swept over her. Total confusion. 'What?'

The envelope in Jasper's drawer. A declaration of love. That's what she'd imagined. She swallowed hard. 'Mum, what did you just say?'

'Toby's your son.'

Her mother's words spliced through the air. Everything around her went on pause, as if she was floating in space. She glanced at Jasper. His head was tipped back, jaw clenched as he stared at the ceiling.

∼

'Read the letter, Sandra.'

Jasper, quietly cringing by the window, watched as his confused wife read the letter. How on earth was he going to explain the inexplicable and defend himself? His legs about to give way, he sank onto the seat in the bay, heart banging in his chest.

When she'd finished, there was silence. Watching the crushing shock plastered across Sandy's face made him loathe every fibre of his being. He hadn't a clue what to say. How to make it up to her. She stared ahead for several moments, then dipped her head as if praying. He knew she wasn't. The only faith she had was in their marriage and that was now called into question.

Unable to discern his fate, he watched as she suddenly swung round to face him.

∼

Sandy was aware of a deafening buzz ringing through her ears. Everything around her went on silent. Her brain stuttered with the devastating shock bearing down on her. It was easier to pretend she was floating, in a dream. Far less shocking than the alternative.

She made an inarticulate noise then folded the letter, ripped it twice, threw it into the air and watched it flutter to the carpet.

If this was a joke, it was sick. 'Our baby died,' she said emphatically. When neither of them spoke, she stared from one to the other and in a louder voice, said, 'Our baby died.'

'No, Sandy, he didn't die. He's alive. He's Toby. The dates, place of birth, it all tallies.' Jasper's voice was soft, but she wasn't registering what he was saying. All she felt was utter confusion.

'Mum, tell him,' Sandy screeched, her voice shaking. 'You were there, Mum. This isn't true. The doctor told me he'd died. Doctors don't lie. Doctors are good people.'

Sandy felt disconnected. In the space of ten minutes her life had changed.

Jasper got up and went to sit beside her, putting his hand on her back and pressing his fingers gently into the soft fabric of her dressing gown. She knew he was trying to reach her, but it was as if she'd just woken from a nightmare, disorientating and disconcerting.

'I'm sorry, Sandy. Bill told me not long after I met him and Toby. I've known for about three years. I shouldn't have kept it to myself, but I did. I didn't know how you'd react. Bill was scared in case you went to the police. We thought it best to keep it a secret.'

His voice came to her like the distant crackle of a broken radio in another room.

'I can't take this in. Please, one of you, tell me this isn't true?' She felt herself collapse inside and go cold, as if the temperature in the room had suddenly dropped.

'I'm afraid it is true,' Jasper said, still rubbing her back. 'Bill should have taken him back. But his wife was desperate for a baby. They'd been trying for years.'

She looked at Jasper as though viewing him through an early morning fog. His words were floating, he seemed spectral.

'How can it be?' she snapped, turning to face him, refusing to believe it. Something rose inside her like a thundercloud—raw and fearsome. She shouted, 'A midwife wouldn't take a baby. A doctor falsifying a certificate, and me, the mother, kept in the dark. And Bill, he would have brought my baby back. He's a good man. He wouldn't have let that happen.' This was the worst kind of nightmare, the one you don't wake up from, the one that turns out to be true. Was it true?

'Dreadful things did happen. Some thalidomide babies were

put in cold rooms to die. You know that happened. Stop being so ignorant, Sandra. They didn't expect them to live,' Irene said.

Sandy hated her mother's spiky words. Her mind zoomed back to her pregnancy and birth. Those missing moments, when she'd been asleep on the hospital ward, recovering and groggy on pain relief, out of action. That must have been when they'd made decisions about her baby. Her baby. 'Mum, did you know?'

Irene shrugged. It was as if she'd just been asked what she wanted for dinner. 'No, I didn't know any of this. I'm as completely in the dark as you are.'

She didn't trust her mother. She must have known. 'Did you help arrange this, Mum? Don't lie to me,' she said in a sharp voice.

'What's wrong with you, girl, don't you believe me?'

'How is it possible for someone to steal a newborn baby and bring it up as their own? And without arousing suspicion?' She covered her face in total disbelief.

She was living through a car crash, rocking from one soul-jarring impact headlong into the next. But now the crash had come to settle. As if she was taking stock after the impact.

She looked up at Jasper and thought, *he is my husband.*
He does not lie.
He's never lied.
He wouldn't lie to me. I trust him. Implicitly. I'd trust him with my life.

'Jasper, you lied to me.'

Jasper covered his face with his hands. 'I'm sorry, Sandy. I was wrong to keep it from you.' He uncovered his face and stared at her through bulging wet eyes.

She got up on shaky legs. 'You let me believe our baby was dead,' she said coldly, pausing to dab her eyes with the baby's muslin which had been draped over her shoulder. 'How could you, Jasper? How could you be that cruel?' Her face crumpled and she let out a sob. Jasper's head was bowed. In shame, she hoped. He glanced up at her and despite the self-loathing and remorse written on his face, she felt nothing but bitterness towards him. 'After everything I went through. This is how you treat me.' What he'd done, it was treacherous. 'You're downright deceitful, Jasper. You can say sorry all you like, till you're blue in the face. This has changed everything. I'll never forgive you. You put Bill's feelings first. All that time you spent playing happy families, just the three of you. Shutting me out. As if I didn't matter. And alone with Toby, having him all to yourself, building that bond.' She stared at him, struggling to comprehend the enormity of it all. 'Did you ever stop to consider me? Keeping this to yourself. Our child.' She banged her chest. 'All that time, not to share it with me.' She sobbed.

How would she be able to function after tonight? Sharing a bed with Jasper. She no longer knew who she was married to.

'I'm sorry.' His voice was weak.

Intense hatred rose and overwhelmed her. Every emotion, every hormone collided. She reached out, slapped him hard across the face. She'd never slapped anyone. 'Sorry?' she spat. 'Sorry doesn't begin to make up for what you've done, Jasper.'

～

DESPITE THE SHOCK coursing through him, he knew he'd deserved it. He flinched, reeled, feeling the sting burn across his face. Just then the phone started ringing. The baby yelled. Irene rushed to pick her up.

Jasper glanced at the carriage clock on the mantelpiece. It was getting late, had gone eleven. It wouldn't be work-related because he wasn't on call.

'Who's this ringing so late? Don't tell me you're cheating as well, because that would just about finish me off,' Sandy spat.

Still dazed, Jasper rose unsteadily to his feet. This could only be one person. Steadman.

In the hallway he picked up the receiver, glanced up to see his mother-in-law standing halfway up the stairs peering down at him, cradling the baby. He wished she'd just go. Cow. All she'd done was cause trouble. He turned his back on her, but through the open doorway to the lounge he could see Sandy, crying, broken.

'Bill, what's up?'

Thank God it wasn't Steadman. But Jasper knew his reprieve was temporary. It wouldn't be long before Sandy knew about the blackmailing.

'Toby's gone missing.'

For a few seconds, Jasper's brain had trouble firing, as if it was playing catch-up. 'Missing? What do you mean?'

'He was at the cinema with Lucy. There was a power failure that lasted about ten minutes and when it came back on, Toby wasn't there. I've rung the cinema, nobody's seen him. I'm worried shitless, Jasper, it's been two hours now, no word from him. I'm going to have to ring the police.'

Time seemed to slow. He couldn't process what Bill was saying. 'Say that again, what's happened?'

Bill repeated himself. Toby was missing. When Bill had gone to pick them both up, Toby hadn't been there. Bill went quiet. Jasper heard him sniff and let out a sob. 'What if someone's got him?' His voice was cracking.

Light-headed, blood draining from him, Jasper lowered himself onto the hall chair. 'It's okay, stay calm, he'll be fine.' His words were a sacred mantra, more for his own reassurance than for Bill's.

'How can you say that, after what's happened?'

'Have you had an argument with him? Any reason he might have gone off? You know what teenagers are like.'

Bill was struggling to speak. All that came out were little gasping sounds, then clear words. 'I love that boy, I'd go to the ends of the earth for him. Can I come over, pick you up, we need to go out and look for him, please, Jasper?'

Jasper was aware now of his mother-in-law's presence close by, her eyes boring into him, lingering there like the ghost of Christmas past, a hint of contempt in the curl of her mouth.

The panic in Bill's voice. He couldn't bear it. They had to get out there, start looking.

'Get over here at once,' he stammered before putting down the phone.

Everything was too much. He was trapped down a mineshaft and didn't know how to claw his way out.

'What's the matter?' Sandy and her mother asked at the same time.

'It's Toby, he's missing.'

His stomach twisted. Was it possible that someone had taken him? Toby might be a capable boy, but without arms he was vulnerable, wouldn't be able to get out of a situation easily.

'Dear God,' Irene said, peering down at him like a high court judge. 'There's only one reason kids go missing. A bust-up with their parents. There's more to this, something else you're not telling us, Jasper. And don't you dare fob us off with more lies. My daughter deserves to know the truth.'

Something shifted in Jasper's brain, a wall of tolerance towards his mother-in-law finally breached, his belligerence waiting to burst. 'You don't know the first thing about Toby,' he snapped. 'And don't pretend to care about your daughter.'

'Stop it, Jasper,' Sandy snapped.

'This is difficult enough,' Jasper said.

'Difficult?' Sandy's voice was shrill. The sudden rise in volume, the raw emotion in her voice made him recoil. 'What did you expect?'

∼

SANDY STOOD BACK against the wall, her heart beating as fast as if she'd just run up several flights of stairs. She turned and went back into the lounge so that he couldn't see a new wall of anger building inside, her brick by brick. She had to calm herself, for the baby's sake. Jasper had turned their world upside down and now her ability to be a good mother was in jeopardy.

∽

JASPER COULDN'T LOOK at Sandy. Every part of him felt wretched. He went straight to the lounge, collapsed on the sofa. His head throbbed and his whole body felt sick.

'Does Toby know the truth? Is that why he's gone?' Sandy asked.

'No.'

She tugged at his arm and shouted, 'He deserves to know who his real parents are.'

Jasper looked at her, horrified. 'Think what it would do to Toby.'

'Think? Don't you dare lecture me, Jasper. Thinking is not your strength.'

'I've screwed up big time.'

'Don't assume I'll be staying with you, not after this,' she said icily.

'Bill spent years covering up for his wife's crime. Trying to bring Toby up the best he could.'

'Defending him,' she said with sarcasm. 'Go and live with him. You think more of that man than you do your own wife.'

'Don't be ridiculous.'

'You don't know what loyalty means. I wish I'd never married you,' she hissed.

The doorbell rang. Jasper turned to the door as if staring towards hell.

As Bill rushed into the hall, Jasper grabbed his jacket from the hook on the wall.

'Where have you looked?' Jasper asked him in an urgent tone.

Sandy got up from the settee and staggered towards the lounge door. She needed to lie down. Every part of her body ached and creaked. Exhausted, she needed to sleep before the next feed, but how could she after this? Angela had been keeping her awake at night. Her sore and bruised personal area, torn during the birth, had needed stitches, and was dragging and uncomfortable.

Panic was flaring in Bill's eyes. His face—ashen, stricken.

'I've driven all round Guildford at least three times and we've searched by the river. I've only just dropped Lucy off. She's as worried sick as I am.'

Toby was her son. She was supposed to love him, protect him like a mother should. He was vulnerable and his life could be in danger. Yet she felt numb. They were related and yet it didn't feel like it.

'Bill,' Jasper said. 'Sandy knows.'

'Come in here,' Sandy ordered Bill, pointing to the lounge. 'I need answers.'

'We need to find Toby. Then I promise I'll come back,' Bill pleaded.

She was shaking, wobbly. 'Get in here, sit down. You've got some explaining to do.'

'Sandy, I'm sorry, I'm so sorry, I know you're angry, but please, we need to find Toby.'

'Ten minutes. Sit. You owe me that much.'

Bill perched on a chair.

'What you and your wife did, it was unforgiveable.' She was shaking.

'But the doctor was going to let him die. And you wanted him adopted.'

Sandy thought the pain would swallow her whole. 'My baby, my decision. Not yours, not anyone else's.'

'I'm sorry. I was caught up in it all.'

'You could have taken him back. You didn't. You stole the most precious thing from me.' She stabbed her chest.

'Calm down, Sandy,' Jasper said, reaching to put an arm on her shoulder.

'Get off me.' She pushed him away. Then turning again to Bill, she shouted, 'You're not getting away with this. You should be locked up and the key thrown away. Your wife was out of her mind, but you went along with it. You're just as guilty. I'll make sure you pay for what you've done.'

'Sandy, please, I know you're angry, but if you go to the police, what would it achieve, other than to upset Toby? I may not be his natural father, but I've done my very best.'

'And I'm supposed to be grateful to you?' she hissed.

'I can't make things right.'

'I'm his mother, I had a right to know. And Toby should be told who his real parents are.'

Irene came into the room. 'I think I'd better take the baby upstairs with me. I'll give her the next feed. You need to rest, Sandra.'

Sandy didn't protest, barely noticing the baby leaving the room with her mother.

'We never meant to keep it from you,' Bill said in a weak voice.

'You're as big a liar as Jasper is.'

Just then the phone rang. Toby? Sandy was rigid as stone, still traumatised, as Jasper answered it.

∼

JASPER ANSWERED THE PHONE, relief washing over him when he heard Toby's voice.

'Toby, thank God, where are you?'

Bill rushed over and grabbed the phone. 'Stay where you are, son, we're coming for you.'

Jasper heard Toby say that he needed to speak to Jasper. It was important.

'What is it?' Jasper asked. 'Is something wrong?'

A man's voice came onto the line. He sounded cold, harsh. 'Right, you listen to me. If you want to see the boy again, you'll do as I say.'

'Who are you?'

'I'm Ronny's brother. You're not to ring the police. If you do, I'll make sure they find out what Bill did. I knew the doctor who helped Bill's wife abduct your baby. I worked at that hospital. The doctor, a Doctor Gerard, broke down to me and confessed it all. I never went to the police. There were far worse things happening in that hospital.'

'What are you talking about? Why have you got Toby? Where are you?'

'Meet me in the carpark by Bourne Lake. You know it?'

'Yes.'

'And, Cooper. Don't bring the police.'

Jasper came off the phone shaking.

'What the hell's going on, Jasper?' Sandy asked.

'I've been blackmailed. That's why I sold the car. Someone at work knows about Toby.'

'Oh my God,' she shrieked. 'How much worse can this get? Has somebody got Toby? Tell me what the bloody hell is going on?'

'When we get back, I promise. Bill and I need to go. Toby's life could be in danger.'

33

As soon as they were in the truck, Jasper told Bill about the man holding Toby.

'He's Ronny's brother, Vince. He spent a few years in a mental home following a breakdown. Could be dangerous.' When Ronny talked about his brother, he always referred to him as the family nutter.

'Shit. If he hurts Toby, I'll kill the bastard.' Bill tightened his grip on the steering wheel and drove faster. Tall hedgerows sped past them in the beam of the truck headlights.

Jasper was restless, his legs twitching.

Bill banged the steering wheel. 'This is a complete nightmare. Toby could get killed.' He stepped up the speed. 'And how the hell did Sandy find out? You promised me you wouldn't tell her.'

'She was bound to find out eventually.' Jasper's chest tightened. Right now, all he could think about was Toby's safety. 'Shut up and drive. We're nearly there,' Jasper said frantically, pointing to the turn off.

They pulled into a pot-holed gravel parking area in front of the lake and with the truck's full beams on they could see a black Ford Capri parked up with two people inside. Jasper recognised Toby's shape in the passenger seat. There were no other cars there.

'It's them. I know this is going to be hard, but you've got to promise me you'll stay here,' Jasper said sternly. 'He thinks I'm alone and we don't know if he's got a weapon. As soon as we've got Toby safe in the truck, belt out of here straight to the police station.'

'I'm coming.' Bill opened his door.

'No.' Jasper grabbed him by the collar, wrenching him back. 'You want to see the boy alive,' he said sternly, glaring at Bill. 'You'll stay here. It's me he wants. We play by his rules, okay? For Toby.'

Jasper reached over Bill's huge, distended belly and slammed the driver door. Pushing the passenger door open against the resistance of a stiff hinge, he swivelled on the worn vinyl seat and planted both feet on the ground, taking in the cold clear air.

'Stay there, don't move,' he reminded Bill. Outside, he inched forward. Waited. Didn't want to approach the car until the man was out.

He heard a click. The door of the Capri was opening. A man stepped out and stared right at Jasper. Nodded. Gestured for him to walk over. There was something menacing about him. Tall, wiry, serpent-like, he didn't look like Ronny, his brother. Jasper inched forward, fear coursing through him, eyes on the enemy. Closer, he was aware of how ugly the man was: greasy hair, large ears, a face marked with acne scars.

'Vince Steadman?'

'Who's that in the truck? I told you to come alone.'

'I can't drive at the moment.' Jasper raised his left arm to show his plaster cast. 'It's Bill with me, Toby's dad.'

The man walked towards him and smirked. 'We both know who the lad's real dad is.'

Panicked, Jasper glanced at the passenger seat. 'You've not told him?' Toby mustn't overhear. Toby turned in his chair, looked terrified. He had to get him out, to safety—but how? He didn't know this man's strength, what he was capable of, didn't know him, had only heard rumours.

Vince laughed, revealing teeth that looked like bomb craters. He was wearing a black leather jacket making him look intimidating and as he reached inside his pocket, Jasper saw something glint.

A knife.

He froze. Stared at the long blade, fear sweeping through him like he'd never experienced before. His body, it seemed to be shrinking, caving in on itself. As if he might melt into the gravel. He'd come totally unprepared, should have brought a weapon.

He wasn't a violent man. Didn't have it in him to harm another human being. But to protect Toby? He'd kill to save his son. Defenceless, he was out of his depth.

'Let the boy go,' Jasper said, suppressing a tremor in his voice.

'Stay back.' He held the knife at arm's length, anchoring his eyes on Jasper as he made feline steps around the car like a leopard watching its prey. Opening the passenger door, to Jasper's horror, he grabbed Toby by the collar, yanked him out, and pushed him to the ground. Toby yelped.

'Stay where you are,' Vince ordered, waving the knife at Toby.

Jasper felt sick to the bone, wanted to rush over, rescue him. From behind, he heard movement, Bill getting out of the truck. His eyes were fixed on Vince—but what was Bill doing? Toby's safety was about to be jeopardised. Vince's eyes flickered to Jasper's right, fearful, calculating.

'Get back in the truck,' Vince screamed.

'Back,' Jasper shouted, waving his arm towards Bill, his eyes still on Vince. *Got to stay calm, placatory. Do nothing that will alarm him*. Pure evil—he could turn, any moment. He had a knife. Could use it. Toby's life—over. *Got to be gentle, careful. Steady.* 'Please, Vince, put the knife down, let's talk.'

Vince lowered the knife as if taken off guard by Jasper's tone. They faced each other in limbo.

'You'll help me?' Confused, Jasper saw a change in his posture, his face.

'We can talk. Just us. If you let the boy go. It's late, he's scared.' Jasper inched closer, his heart in his mouth, his tone soft.

Vince was still holding the knife. One wrong move, he could blow it.

Bill's ragged breath came from somewhere behind him. Movement. *Bill, stay still. You'll screw things up.* Jasper dared not turn, hoped Bill would keep out of it.

'The boy's the bargaining tool,' Vince snarled with venom.

'You don't need to use him. I'm a journalist. I'll listen to you anyway.'

'Think I'll believe that?' His eyes were smouldering.

'Believe what you want to believe.' *Kick the knife from his hand. Do it.*

His voice, cold, mocking, rang into the night air. 'I'll tell the boy the truth.'

Bill cleared his throat. 'Toby.' His voice was shaky. Splintered. 'I'm not your real dad. Jasper is.'

The words snagged in the air like a twig caught in a current. Jasper watched as Toby flinched, as if Bill's words had been hurled across the car park with violence.

Vince dropped the knife and as it clattered to the ground, Jasper lunged forward and wrestled Vince to the ground, twisting his body, searching for the knife in the poor light. Bill was standing near him. A glint of metal, the knife scraping on gravel. Bill grabbed it, hurled it into the dark. A few seconds later a plop as it disappeared into the lake. Relief. Two against one. Bare hands.

'Bill, take Toby home. Go,' Jasper shouted. He just wanted Toby out of harm's way. He'd confront Vince Steadman alone. Bill would send for help. The police would come.

Toby ran to the truck, Bill following. The engine coughed to life, its beams flooding the car park and as it swung round and disappeared, they were shrouded in darkness. He was alone with this unpredictable madman. Would Bill have the sense to go straight to the police?

Toby was safe, but now, miles from any houses, Jasper feared for his own life. A cold sweat formed along his spine. Despite his fear, he needed to understand what was going on. Vince was leaning into his car; finding another weapon? He'd lied. This man wanted to kill him. Jasper had to run, hide. But where? His head was spinning. But as he turned to see what Vince was up to, there was a flicker of light. Vince had grabbed a torch from his car. In a pool of light, he watched him slump to the ground beside his car, bent over. What was he doing? Was this the same man who'd wielded a knife minutes earlier, now bent over? Instead of running for his life, Jasper edged closer, closer still, and towering over him, he bent down, shocked when Vince looked up and in the swathe of light, he could see that he was silently crying. A hard, evil, predator reduced to tears. Either he was acting or genuinely crying. Had to be an act. He'd pounce any minute, pin Jasper to the ground. It wasn't safe. And yet…he was crying.

Jasper's gut reacted—this man's exterior was tough, rough, but inside, he was damaged. Haunted by something, a troubled man.

Caught in a trap of indecision, should he run, get away, or stay, hear him out? Jasper's inquisitive nature kicked in. He knelt.

'There's a bench over there,' Jasper said, pointing. It was starting to rain, they'd get soaked, but this couldn't wait for another day.

Vince got to his feet. In silence they headed towards the wood at the side of the lake and the thick canopy of leaves offering cover from the rain.

34

He was safe. Alive. Free. Could so easily have been a goner. But Jasper, was *he* now in danger? Toby kept his eyes fixed on Jasper as the truck bounced over waterlogged potholes as they left the carpark. Jasper didn't look in imminent danger, they were just talking by the lake. No arguing, no raised arms in anger. He'd be okay, he was tough.

Immersing himself in the almost comforting skanky smell of his dad's messy truck as they belted home, the usual apple cores and crisp packets littering the footwell—everything felt familiar.

Except that it wasn't.

His terrible ordeal had been playing through his mind. But in a split second everything had changed.

The shock of Bill's last words hit.

Jasper—his dad.

Oh my fricking God. His whole body was cold. 'You're not my dad?'

Silence as Bill stared ahead.

A lump had formed in his throat. 'Dad, you're scaring me, talk.'

Bill suddenly swerved into a layby, braked, cut the engine

and turned in his seat to look at Toby. His face was solemn and tinged with grey. Crumbling.

'Rona and me, we aren't your biological parents.'

A buzzing noise penetrated Toby's head. Everything around him stilled as something plummeted inside him.

Then his brain, in gear. 'You adopted me?'

'No.' Bill looked suddenly old and lined. 'I mean yes, sort of.' He shook his head. Confused. Why? 'I've messed up, big time. I need to explain everything, right from the beginning. It'll be hard for you to understand.'

'Was I adopted or not? Why's Jasper my real dad? Did he and Mum…?'

Bill shook his head. 'No, shit, no, nothing like that. I'm sorry. We shouldn't have kept it from you, we always meant to tell you. I didn't want you to find out like this.' Bill thumped the steering wheel.

'You had sixteen years to tell me.' Toby's lip was quivering, eyes filling with tears, stomach collapsing. Helpless, confused, unloved. *Why am I even alive? It would have been easier if I'd died at birth.*

Bill reached out and circled Toby with big strong arms, squeezing him so tightly that Toby felt suffocated. But the hug did nothing to reassure him. There were so many questions hitting him at once.

Toby pulled away and Bill adjusted himself in his seat, looking embarrassed. Hugs and loving words had never come naturally to Bill. But Toby had always accepted that was the way he was. Now, he saw things differently. He wasn't his son. Why would hugging come naturally?

'Rona and I, we'd been trying for a baby for years. I'd always dreamt of having a son to carry on the business. It's what my grandfather always wanted, for the business to be passed down. But I think after a few years I accepted that it wasn't going to happen. But Rona wouldn't accept it. She planned her life around that narrow window of opportunity when a woman is most likely to fall pregnant. Then she started talking about adopting a baby. We rowed about it. I wasn't keen. I bought her a kitten, hoping that would make her happy, but it broke her heart not to be a mother.' Bill looked away.

Mortified, tears clouded Toby's eyes. The sting of Bill not wanting him. Dreaming of a child of their own, a son to carry on his precious business. And now, he couldn't look Toby in the eye, couldn't admit the deep shame, the embarrassment he felt. Toby stared at the floor in disbelief. *Nobody wanted me. Not even the man who adopted me.*

Bill put his arm around Toby and whispered. 'You meant so much to us. You were our miracle. Look at you, look at how far you've come. You survived that evil piece of shit. You're brave. I know you had a bad start in life, and I know this is a massive shock, but at the end of the day, does it matter who your biological parents are? You're your own person. And one day you'll have a family of your own. I'm proud of you.' Bill's voice was breaking. 'You're going to go far in life, Toby. You've got brains. I never had brains.'

'Yes, it does matter,' Toby said forcefully. 'Of course it matters where I came from, my roots, my identity. Who even am I? You didn't want me.' Tears were clouding his vision.

'Not at first, but you don't know what happened. I haven't told you everything yet.'

Toby fidgeted in his seat, a dull ache spreading across his chest. What the hell was he going to find out?

'Your mum, Rona, she worked as a midwife, as you know. Sandy went into labour at the nursing home where Rona worked. Sandy wasn't with Jasper at the time you were born. They'd split up. He had no idea she was pregnant with his baby otherwise he would have been there and supported her.'

His life—it could have taken a completely different course.

'Sandy was young and on her own and her parents pressured

her into having you adopted. But it was what she wanted too. She was desperate to return to her modelling career. When the doctor saw you, he thought either that you would die or that your life wouldn't be worth living because of your deformity. He ordered Rona to put you in the cold room, to let nature take its course. Rona couldn't do it. The doctor thought it was kinder to let you die. Rona thought that God had a purpose for you. To leave you to die, it would have been murder. She refused to let you die. What he was asking her to do, it was inhumane, barbaric. She wasn't having anything to do with it. At some point in their argument, the idea of taking you home, bringing you up as our child, must have come to her.'

'Why would a doctor go along with that? Surely Sandy had a say? I was her baby.' Toby's heart was breaking. His real mother, lying there helpless. But she hadn't wanted him. Her stupid career had been more important. Sandy, Rona, Bill, the doctor. All of them selfish, out for their own ends.

'Rona had the one up on the doctor. He was having an affair with someone at work and Rona knew about it. She threatened to expose their affair unless he created a death certificate to satisfy the authorities.'

'I have a death certificate?' Toby let out a sob. 'I must have a birth certificate.'

'Yes, I'll show you your birth certificate.'

'Where does it say I was born? Whose names are on it?' Toby hollered. Everything, a lie. His life, it was fast unravelling.

'We told our own doctor we hadn't known that Rona was pregnant. We made up a story about you being born on the kitchen floor. We were living in London when you were born, but we moved back to Blackpool days later. We had to. To get as far away as possible. To keep a low profile.' Toby noticed a look of defeat that haunted Bill's face. 'If the police were to find out, I could end up in jail.'

His mother, a kidnapper. That she could have stolen him; it

was unimaginable. She was a good person. Stealing had been something she was totally against. Had condemned shoplifting. Burglary. She was a Christian. Had gone to church. Made sure Toby never missed Sunday school.

If it were true—how could she have done something so wrong? She was gone and now the image he had of her—a good person, had been snatched away.

Oh God, Sandy. His real mother. Did she even like him? Did she know? Was that why she'd been so kind to him after Town Week? He'd thought it odd, now it made sense.

After the shock came anger, bubbling and popping inside him. 'You took a baby. How can you live with yourself? How could you have kept this from me?' What arrogance to think Rona was entitled to him. How dare she treat him like hers for the taking, a toy? Show off what a good mother she was, bringing up a handicapped child. He thought she was his mother. But she was just a good thief!

'If Rona hadn't taken you, you would have died. We saved you,' Bill shrieked.

Toby stared at Bill in horror. 'That time when Jasper came to our old house to interview us, did you know he was my real dad?'

Bill shook his head. 'No, I swear to you, I didn't know. But after we got to know him, it dawned on me who he was. It was like putting together the missing pieces of a puzzle.'

Toby gave an indignant laugh. 'You were keen to tell me the truth about Father Christmas. And I was only young. But you kept this from me. Something of much greater importance. All the time we've spent with Jasper, you both knew. Said nothing. I hate you. I hate you both.' And right in that moment he meant it.

'You would have died if Rona hadn't rescued you.'

'Sandy wasn't given a choice. What if she'd decided to keep me? And if she wanted me adopted, why couldn't you have gone through the proper channels? Rona stole me. That's got to be one of the most serious crimes.' He couldn't bring himself to call her Mum.

'Don't you think I know that?' wailed Bill. 'It was a spur of-the-moment act.'

'Was she avoiding the vetting process? Did you have something to hide, is that it?'

'No, of course not.'

Furious, Toby screamed, 'I'll tell you why she took me. In case Sandy changed her mind. Or you were turned down.'

'If she hadn't rescued you, chances are you would have ended up at St Bede's as an orphan. That's the fact of it.'

Bill turned the engine on and without another word they drove home in silence. A headache was brewing, Toby could hardly see the road ahead through a veil of tears.

Arriving back, Toby looked up at the cottage. It was home but would never feel like home again. It seemed to be saying *you don't belong here.*

Nothing was real anymore. He used to see himself reflected in his parents. Not now. Not ever again. He was stuck with this man who'd pretended to be his dad all this time, but they were made from different clay.

35

As soon as Jasper and Bill had left to go looking for Toby, Sandy rushed upstairs and banged on her mother's door.

Must rescue my baby from Mum's clutches, can't trust her, can't trust anyone with my baby. Especially the professionals. I'll never trust a doctor ever again.

She'd never let Angela out of her sight ever again. Too risky. Too unsafe. *Got to keep her close.*

She was Angela. Her baby. Her property. What was her mother doing, slinking away with her baby, hoping to slip upstairs unnoticed and take over Angela's care? Angela was barely two weeks old. She needed calm, safety, not the chaos of the past hours. She needed the protection and warmth of her mother's embrace.

'Oh God.' It struck her now. For the first time. She was surprised by the intensity of her feelings catching her unawares. All those wasted years when Toby had been denied the love of his real mother. She let out a sob. Every sorrow hit at once. His first smile, first laugh, first steps, she'd missed it all.

'Open the door, Mum, now.'

Bleary-eyed and confused, Irene stared at her daughter.

'Give her back.'

'She's asleep… or was.' Angela woke and started screaming. Sandy rushed over, grabbed the carrycot and hurried downstairs. 'Sandra, where are you going?' Irene was standing on the stairs.

'Where's my car keys?' Sandy shrieked, resting the carrycot on the floor, spinning round, then grabbing the keys from the hall table.

Irene dashed down the stairs and blocked her exit. 'It's the middle of the night. You're not going anywhere.'

'You can't stop me. All my life you've been trying to stop me. Well not this time.'

'Wherever you're going, it can wait till the morning. Do you want me to make you a nice cup of tea?'

'I don't want you to make me anything. Now get out my way.'

The baby was howling. 'You can't take her out in the cold dark night. I won't let you. You can't drive in that state.'

Sandy was hysterical. Like a banshee. Her mind was crumbling. The devastation of everything was all-consuming. 'This is all your doing, and you wonder why I'm in a state?' She pushed her mother out the way and unlocked the door. 'I'm going to the police station.'

'Wait till the morning.'

'Someone's got Toby. I'm his mother. It's up to me to do something, don't you see?' she screamed. All the times when she'd felt irritated because Toby took up so much of her husband's time, and now she felt fiercely protective towards him, just wanted the boy to be safe. Bloody hell, he was her son.

'Stop being a drama queen, so typical of you, Sandra.'

Sandy wanted to hit her. She deserved a swipe. If only she had a different mother. A caring one. She'd melt into her arms. Her mother had a wall of steel around her heart. 'You're a fool, Sandra. Ring the police instead but don't get in the car. Not in that hysterical state.'

Sandy turned to look at the phone and right in that moment it started ringing. News of Toby?

Irene grabbed it and a moment later mouthed to Sandy, 'It's your father.'

They did have marriage problems—Sandy knew it, had suspected all day. This was clear confirmation. Why else would her dad ring in the middle of the night? Her mother had pretended to play the doting grandma while concealing her ulterior motive—to get away from her dad and get her feet firmly under the table at their place. Sandy didn't wait to hear her mother's excuses, she picked up the carrycot, opened the door and walked straight out to the car. Glancing back as she swept from the drive, she could see her mother still on the phone. In the time it had taken Sandy to put the carrycot on the back seat and start the engine, she hadn't dashed out to the car to stop her. As usual there were too many other priorities going on in her mother's life to care. She only loved herself and that was the way it was always going to be.

Out of the drive she paused to look up at the house. The house hadn't changed, but her marriage had. How could she carry on the boring routines of married life, cook his dinner, share a bed after this? She no longer knew who she was married to.

How could she have been so taken in by this liar, so naive? Her chest tightened, squeezing as though it might crush her heart as she sped away, tears rolling down her cheeks, emotions all over the place.

She'd have to return, where else would she go? But to go back, find the motivation to make things right with her mother and with Jasper. She couldn't do it. Not an ounce of her wanted to. They'd let her down. Badly. How could she ever forgive them? She was drained. Physically, mentally, emotionally. She hardly knew who she was anymore.

The motion of the car had settled Angela. She was no longer crying.

Reaching the junction to the main road, she hesitated, unsure which way to go. Her brain was cloudy, she couldn't think clearly, as if a cocktail of chemicals was flooding her synapses. Clarity pushed through, telling her to go back, Angela would soon be due for a feed, she had no milk with her, what was she thinking? Sandy pulled over, reached in the back and gently took the baby in her arms, flinging the driver seat back to give herself more room to cradle the baby. She stroked her hair, the silk of it smooth under her fingers. This baby was the centre of her world. The most precious thing. She had to protect her, nobody else would. She couldn't trust a soul.

Her second child. For years she'd not wanted another, but Jasper had. He'd been broody from the start of their marriage. She'd not been interested. She only changed her mind about having another because she'd felt so crushed with jealousy, all that time Jasper was spending with Bill and Toby. She'd thought by getting pregnant, having this baby, she'd bring him back to her. Create a family unit, just the three of them. Help him to refocus on her. All this time and she'd never known the reason why he'd spent so much time with Bill and Toby. Why couldn't he have shared the news with her? His wife. She was supposed to be the most important person in his life. She was nothing. Unimportant. Why couldn't she have seen the writing on the wall? How stupid of her. Toby was so much like Jasper, yet she hadn't seen it.

She put Angela carefully back in her carrycot and pulled away from the kerb and into the night, still turning the same thoughts round in her head as she drove aimlessly along country roads, eventually finding herself climbing York's Hill on the North Downs. The road cut its way up the hillside, with embankments towering over either side of the narrow lane. What was she doing, where was she going? She hadn't a clue, her brain was still cloudy. The lane made her feel claustrophobic, the hedgerows were crowding in, obscuring the view. She glanced back at the silhouette of her sleeping baby in the rear-view mirror. It was so dark, right out in the country. She could hear her soft, slow breathing and felt a sweet ache for the life she'd created.

It was starting to rain and within minutes it was battering down on the car and bouncing on the tarmac ahead. The wipers were going at maximum speed. She found it tiring to drive up the lanes, her fingers gripped tightly on the steering wheel. She couldn't see much. Trees reached up into the black sky, tall and still, resembling soldiers. Each twist and turn of the road looked the same. She was lost. Alone on this desolate road, the more her confusion about her life and where it was heading, grew. Who could she turn to? Who would understand the turmoil spinning through her head? A fury worse than anything she'd ever experienced, a simmering vat of anger that could explode like a fireball destroying everything in its wake. Fury drove her along, making her step harder on the accelerator. Her legs were weak, her hazy brain clouding her judgement. Oh to feel free as a bird, gliding, sliding.

The wipers swooshed, marking time, like beats of her life. Was that what she would do from now on, just go on, like the ticking hands of a clock? The disappointment, the utter devastation of what he'd done to her, what they'd all done, descended on her like a blanket of fatigue and she rubbed her eyes to banish the weariness. There was no way back to her old life, no way forward either. She'd be stuck in this misery forever.

Then suddenly lights in her eyes, bright white, blinding. A lorry. She couldn't see. She wrested the steering wheel to the side. She couldn't hit it. It would kill them. She swerved the car to the other side of the road. Couldn't get out of the way. The light was blinding, whited out everything. She put her arm up to obscure the light, swinging the wheel, unable to see. Wrenched the wheel round again. Came to a juddering halt by the roadside, her head flopping on the steering wheel. *Shit. What the hell am I doing? I could have careered off the road, killed us both.* All around her there was darkness apart from the beam of the headlights. She sat listening to the thump of her heart in her chest. There was nowhere to go. She couldn't go to the police. Something was stopping her. It didn't feel right. What would that achieve other than to get back at Bill and Jasper? It wasn't the best thing for Toby. And she didn't want the publicity that would come with a court case. She was angry, but her anger was directed not so much at Bill, but at her husband. He was the one who'd let her down. She had to get home. Wait for him. Have it out with him.

Angela stirred. Let out a cry. Sandy lifted her from the carrycot, eased the driver seat back to give herself more room to rock the baby in her arms and switched on the interior light to take a better look at her. Her little face was all creased up. She was perfection. Angelic. To think that Rona had *chosen* to parent a handicapped child. It was an altruistic act. Rona was a selfless woman. It was incredible. That new thought sparked admiration within Sandy. Taking a baby was wrong, but on one level it was a noble act.

Sandy realised she could sit for hours just watching Angela if she wanted to. She was her mother. She knew every part of her body. She was hers. That was something she hadn't been able to do with her first baby. Not to have seen him, smelt him. Those thoughts were once again haunting her. Toby. He had a name. He was alive. And in that moment, she had a desperate urge to sit with him, look at him—really look at him. What colour eyes did he have? She couldn't remember. Did he look like her? Sound like her? What did he think of her? She wanted to hold his hands, touch his face. Heat rushed to her cheeks. She couldn't do that. He was a teenager, not a small child.

How would he respond to the news that she was his mother?

Sandy dreaded to think. She didn't know him at all. He'd only been in their lives for three years and for much of that he'd spent far more time with Jasper than with her. She'd seen him fleetingly, never for long and in truth that suited her. But now she wanted to spend time with him, get to know him properly.

Why though? Out of duty, because she had to? Her head was in turmoil. She couldn't just step from being an outsider in his life to motherhood. Friendship, taken slowly, yes. It was possible.

36

With the rain easing, Jasper and Vince picked their way over the slippery shingle beside the lake. Ahead, the rocky shore had a blueish hue under the dark sky. Jasper stopped and turned to face Ronny's brother.

'What's this all about?' Jasper kept his voice steady. *Mustn't rile him, stay calm.*

Shit. Was he about to be blackmailed? Again.

'How long ago was it that you wrote that feature on the thalidomide scandal? Must be three years ago.' Vince had recovered from his meltdown and the sarcastic tone had crept back into his voice.

Jasper stared across the lake.

'You only report what you want to report. Things that affect you,' Vince snarled.

'That's not true.' Jasper kept his gaze fixed on the lake. Was this about to turn ugly? Where were the police? Had Bill called them?

Aware of Vince staring at him, Jasper wondered what was coming. 'I worked for years at the hospital where Toby was born.'

Jasper's heart flipped. He turned and stared at him.

'I know far more than you think.' He tapped the side of his nose, just like his brother would have done.

'I've pieced it all together. I remember your wife. She was recovering on the ward, oblivious to the fact that she'd given birth to a boy with no arms. I saw her later, leaving the hospital, unaware her baby had been stolen. I've seen her round the village. I know it's her. I never forget a pretty face. I came into the delivery room just after your son was born. Poor blighter. My job would have been to take him away, dispose of him, if he'd died during birth. But he was alive, and the doctor ordered the midwife to put him in the cold room. If he'd died in that cold room, it would have been my job to carry him away.'

So shocked, Jasper couldn't speak.

'The doctor who delivered your baby confessed it all to me late one night when we were alone. The kidnap. I think he thought it would make my job more bearable if I knew someone else was struggling with theirs. Either way, he trusted me with his crime. I overheard the doctor telling your wife she'd lost your son. And I also knew your wife's midwife, the woman who took him. I'm pretty sure I saw her hurrying away from the hospital the night she took him. She was carrying something. I couldn't see what. At your office Christmas party last year when you showed Ronny the picture of Toby, you were drunk. You let it slip. Office parties are dangerous places. Many a secret is revealed at those affairs. You only have yourself to blame.'

He bent and picked up a stone, hurling it into the lake.

Jasper felt sick. He needed to sit. He headed towards a boulder and perched on the edge, feeling the cold and wet seep through his trousers.

Vince stood in front of him a couple of metres away. 'I couldn't handle my job anymore, all that I was being asked to do. I had a breakdown.' He bent, threw another stone into the lake—cathartic perhaps. 'Want to know what my job entailed?'

'I think we should have this conversation another day when we're both calm.'

Vince stared at him through reptilian eyes, anger hardening into his ugly face as his hand came out, grabbing at Jasper's neck, pushing him back. 'You're fobbing me off. It's your job to know what's going on,' he screamed. His eyes were narrow as slits, evil radiating from them. He stabbed a finger at Jasper's arm. Jasper reeled in shock. 'You're a fucking journalist,' he snarled. 'It's time the truth was out. Time the public knew. Thousands of thalidomides were miscarried, hundreds stillborn. So deformed, death was certain. Many had no genitals, no anus, no eyes. It was my job to dispose of those poor wee bodies.' He stepped closer, his face taut, his mouth pinched as he waited for Jasper to react. But all Jasper could do was look at the ground, horrified.

'I want to hear your story. I will hear it. But I need to find out how Toby is. Right at this moment he's my number one concern. Why did you kidnap him? I could go to the police.'

'I wanted to get at you, for telling half the story. The thalidomide babies who died deserve their story told too. Every life has a story. Even those who never got to breathe.'

'All you had to do was pick up the phone and ring the newspapers. It's not hard.'

'You can't turn your back on those children who died. Many slipped away naturally, but others died at the hands of the state. Doctors called them monsters, prayed the Lord would take them. And when their prayers weren't answered, those doctors often suggested infanticide.'

'Look, we're going to sit down and you're going to tell me everything,' Jasper said.

'Can I rely on you?' Vince hissed. Spittle landed on Jasper's face, and he wiped it with the back of his hand.

Vince was broken and would take those horrors to his grave. One screwed-up individual, he'd seen too much.

'It must have affected you badly.'

Vince shook his head, his face looked full of despair. 'I've had psychiatric help and I'm still not over it. It triggered schizophrenia. Jasper, I have a dangerous illness. I'm on medication.'

Now he understood. His bizarre, irrational behaviour—kidnapping a child. It wasn't normal behaviour.

'You've got no idea what's going on in hospitals up and down the country. That place, it's one of London's leading hospitals and when I worked there, I was expected to throw all the aborted babies into the same incinerator they used for the hospital's rubbish. I've not worked there for five years, but I bet it still goes on. To dispose of human remains like they would any other waste product shows what society and our hospitals have come to. You make your living out of other people's misery, so, go on then, report it.'

'Why don't you call me tomorrow? We can set up a meeting.'

'I will do, but I have to say, I hate journalists. You're all the scum of the earth.'

'We're not all brutes like your brother.'

'You two have never got on.'

'Well...' Jasper stared off into the distance. 'We work together. I'm not going to comment, it wouldn't be professional.'

'He's always been a nasty shit, ever since we were kids. He once threw a dead toad into my bed. Among other things.'

'I'm going to go now, okay? Give me a ring Monday morning. We'll talk.'

Jasper turned and walked towards the car park, his shoes wet and squelching. Back in the carpark, nobody was around. No courting couple, no dog walkers. But without a phone box in sight, how was he going to ring Bill or Sandy? Heart banging in his chest, he paused to catch his breath. Just then a sweep of lights illuminated the car park. Jasper shielded his eyes, glancing at the number plate through the blinding light and drizzle. Relief swept through him when he saw it was Bill's truck. He dashed over, yanked the passenger door open and climbed up, panting and unable to speak. 'Let's go,' he gasped.

Before he'd had the chance to close the door, Bill was sweeping the truck round, gravel crunching under the tyres.

They were out onto the road. 'I thought you'd call the police. You could see he was dangerous. He could have killed me.'

Bill ignored him. 'What happened? His car's still there.'

Jasper let out a howl. 'I thought he might be dangerous, but he seemed harmless.'

'I shouldn't have left you alone with him.'

'I wanted you to get Toby home, safe. He definitely has a screw loose though. He worked in the hospital where Toby was born. He knew Simon Gerard, the doctor who falsified Toby's birth certificate. Bill,' he paused, 'he knows everything. He's pieced it all together, but I don't think he's a threat to us. He just wants his story to be heard.'

'What story?'

Jasper told him.

'Christ, I feel sick.'

'Is Toby back at the cottage? How is he?'

'He'll wonder where we are. I've explained everything. Wasn't an easy conversation.'

'Shit. How did he take it?'

Bill turned off the main road, pulled into a layby and killed the engine. He put his head on the steering wheel and let out what sounded like a strangled cry.

'You've no idea what Toby will do. If we don't get back to the cottage soon, he'll panic and call the police.'

Bill cradled his head as he looked up.

'We're losing time.' Jasper leant towards him, trying to make him see sense.

The wipers were squeaking as they sluiced rain from the windscreen.

'I've been through a hell of an evening, with Toby asking question after question as we drove back. I can't take much more. My head's about to explode.' Bill rubbed his temple.

In a calmer voice Jasper said, 'Just head back to the cottage. Let's see how Toby is, I need to speak to him myself, then I must get back to Sandy. Fuck that Steadman guy.'

Bill spoke in a frantic voice. 'Leave the chat with Toby till the morning. I'm dropping you back home.'

Bill tore down country lanes, his tools in the back of the truck rattling when he braked hard at every corner, barely stopping at junctions. Jasper was desperate to get home. Sandy was never going to forgive him. All the trouble he'd caused her. He didn't deserve her.

'Ring me,' Bill said as Jasper got out of the truck and looked up at his house. The lights were still on. Sandy and her mother—they were still up. Despite it being so late.

Tibs rushed into the hallway to greet him, tail wagging, wanting a fuss. Jasper bent to stroke the dog's soft fur. Something wasn't right. The house was silent. Maybe they were in bed but had forgotten to turn the lights off. That wasn't like Sandy. He glanced up to the balcony. The door to the room his mother-in-law was sleeping in was open, the light on. He kicked his shoes off and, about to leave them by the front door, noticed they were covered in pond weed. He stood catching his breath, bracing himself for what lay ahead. He was dreading the conversation he was about to have with his wife. He crept up the stairs.

Where was his mother-in-law? Her room was empty. The bedsheets were ruffled, her bags gone. Had Sandy kicked her out? Surely not. He turned his head to the master bedroom. Seemed to be the one room in the house without a light on. Stepped along the landing and peered in. The bed looked unmade. He switched the light on. She wasn't there.

Panicked, he yelled, 'Sandy, Sandy, where are you?' Getting himself into a steam he dashed into the ensuite, the baby's room, the other spare room, rushing down the stairs, heart hammering, on into the lounge, his study. Where were they? He spun round in the hallway, there was nowhere left. Maybe she'd gone back to her mother's house. Perhaps Sandy's dad had come to fetch them. He glanced at the hall table—had she left a note? He dashed to the kitchen, peering at the table. Sometimes they left notes for each other in the fruit bowl or propped against the kettle. This was maddening. He just wanted to take her in his arms, lie beside her and open his heart to everything that had been going through his head these past three years. She needed to understand. But how was that even going to be possible, now that she was in her mother's clutches? That woman, she was like poison ivy growing round a tree; she'd suffocate and stifle every loving thought her daughter had for him.

Puzzled, Jasper stood at the bottom of the stairs for a moment. Where was she?

37

She'd taken Irene and the baby and driven to her parents' house. He'd lay a bet on it, but it was too late to ring to find out for sure. Jasper didn't want to experience the wrath of his bitch of a mother-in-law down the end of the phone. He'd leave it till the morning. Right now he couldn't think straight. Everything he wanted to say would come out all wrong and garbled. It had been a fraught twenty-four hours.

Jeez, it hadn't taken Irene long to sink her claws into Sandy, poisoning her mind, turning her against him, coaxing her away from him. How was he going to persuade her to come back? He couldn't believe that she'd go off with her mother, after everything she'd done, the cruel things she'd said. But maybe Sandy felt bad about her mother's past and wanted to help her. It was crazy. Was she planning to leave him?

Jasper poured himself a large whisky and stood at the lounge window looking out, half expecting the car to pull onto the drive. Draining the last drop, he headed upstairs and collapsed heavily on the bed, feeling like a whale plunging into the ocean.

He woke from a terrible nightmare. Jerked up in bed, eyes

wide open. For a few seconds he froze there, propped on an elbow, heart hammering in his chest as he remembered.

He started to shove his legs out of bed, but the top sheet fought him. He wrenched it loose from the mattress so that he could force his feet to the ground. With a dull thud in his head making him feel nauseous, he grabbed the glass on his bedside table. Then it came flooding back. Yesterday's events.

He heard a cry. Angela. They were back. His heart soared. Why hadn't he woken when they'd returned? He must have been well out of it. He was surprised he'd slept so well and felt guilty. She'd had a long drive. It was wrong of Sandy's mother to let her drive all that way, and in the state she was in. Whatever had Irene been thinking?

The bedroom door pushed open, and Sandy stood there in a long white nightie. Her face looked drawn, her hair matted and dishevelled. Her eyes, red and swollen. She looked pitiful, vulnerable. He just wanted to reach out and take her in his arms, but her body was rigid. She wouldn't welcome a hug, and anger could bubble from her at any moment. He had to tread carefully. One wrong move, one insensitive word spoken, he'd lose her. They were frail, their marriage as delicate and breakable as a spider's web and it was down to him to fix.

How had he ever considered them to be a solid couple? No marriage was. He could see that now.

'Where have you been?' he whispered.

'I went for a drive. To think.' She was chewing her lips. She was a mess of tics and visible tension.

'Where's Irene?'

'Dad came to pick her up. I think even she realised she couldn't stay and that we needed to sort this out.'

'Can you forgive me?' he ventured.

'It's too soon to ask that of me.'

'Yes, of course.' He stared down at his feet, his body sagging.

'I don't know where we're going, you and me.'

He felt a powerful judder shoot through his body. 'What do you mean?'

'Surely you can see.' She gazed forlornly at him. 'This is supposed to be the happiest moment of our marriage, our newborn. This time around, this is what we chose. To be parents. But you've stolen that joy from me.'

'I lied to you. I deceived you. What I did was unforgiveable. I know that. But I love you, Sandy, I don't expect you to forgive me right now or anytime soon. I want us to be a family. I want that more than anything.'

'It's made me think…how can I ever trust you again?'

A cold chill swept through him. It was a perfectly valid point. But it made him think about how she'd kept her first pregnancy from him. She could have made more effort to find him. She'd planned to have their child adopted and if they hadn't bumped into each other in New York, he would never have known about the pregnancy.

'If Toby had been adopted, my child would be out there somewhere. You deceived me. Yet I trust you.'

Neither spoke, both trapped in their own affront.

Jasper backed down. 'Sandy, please, what are we doing? We have two wonderful children. This is stupid.'

'Stupid.' Her hackles were up.

'Sorry, that was flippant of me. Poor choice of words.' He stood up and went to put his arm across her shoulders.

Shrugging him off, she said, 'I need to feed Angela.'

'Do you want *me* to? You need to rest.'

'Haven't you got work to catch up on?'

He glanced at the phone on the bedside table. 'It's Sunday. I need a break. I must see Toby. With you. Think what he's been through.'

She glared at him. 'Don't you dare tell me that, Jasper, as if I don't already know that. This is about a child having his whole world turned upside down. This is about him, not us.'

She turned to leave the room, obviously wanting a break from the conversation, using Angela as the excuse. He watched her. He felt such an intensity of love towards her. He couldn't lose her. Alone in the bedroom, he realised that something very serious had just happened between him and Sandy. A significant breach had opened up in their relationship. This was about trust. Could trust be rebuilt? He had absolutely no idea. If it couldn't be, would she end up resenting him for the rest of her life? He wondered gloomily how bad things would become. When trust was lost, it never came back. That he believed to be a fact. It was like dropping and smashing a vase. It could be glued back together but could never hold water and flowers again.

As Jasper dressed, he could hear Sandy padding about the house, talking to the baby, the pattern of her routine resumed. There was something about the rhythm of her routine that made him think that from this point on, he would be excluded. Were they simply going to orbit around one another, not speaking, not confronting the issues they faced? A way of life that would be too awful to contemplate. Maybe he was jumping ahead. Perhaps it wasn't going to be like this at all. He'd have to wait and see what happened today when they went round to Bill and Toby's.

He heard the purr of the kettle, the clink of china, the slam of a cupboard door as he headed downstairs to confront the difficulties that lay ahead. Sandy was sitting at the kitchen table, fingers looped through the handle of her teacup, staring vacantly into space. Her face looked gaunt and pale, dark smudges beneath her eyes.

Angela was in her pram on the patio and although she wasn't far away, it felt as if mother and child were a million miles apart, the fine thread connecting them, severed. Sandy locked in her own world. If the pram disappeared, would she even notice she was gone?

Sandy got up and pushed her chair back, robot-like. She went over to the cupboard, took out a mug for him and poured coffee from the percolator before putting it in front of him. He was grateful for this simple act of kindness he normally took for granted. She still cared about his needs, hadn't given up on him, or was she merely going through the motions because what else was she supposed to do?

'When are we going to Bill's?' she asked in a calm tone.

'Sooner the better. Get it over with.'

She stared at him, wide-eyed. 'What?' she snapped. 'This is all about you and how you feel. It'll never be over for Toby. Never be over for me either. Just because you've had three bloody years to come to terms with the shock.'

'You're twisting my words. I'm not proud of myself, Sandy. I would have told you.'

She shook her head, her mouth twisting into a scowl. 'You can do as much explaining as you like. Fact remains, you put that man's wishes first.' She jabbed the table with a finger. 'I'm your wife. Does that mean nothing to you?'

'I know that.' He couldn't think of what else to say.

She hissed through her teeth. 'Do you realise how utterly weak and pathetic you sound?'

'Come on, go and get dressed. This is going to be difficult.'

'What did you expect, Jasper?' She gave him a big sigh and threw him one of her looks.

38

Toby was standing as close as possible to the bathroom mirror, nose to nose with his reflection. He wasn't checking for spots or examining bags under his eyes. He wasn't sure what he was looking for. Recognition of who he was, who he belonged to as he studied all his features: cheeks, chin, forehead. Staring, staring. To be certain he still existed. The rediscovery of himself. A stranger stared back, blinked too. Over the course of a single day and night, the familiar had vanished. Did he still belong here, in this house, to this man he called Dad?

The floor seemed to sway, or maybe it was his body shaking.

Who even was he? *I am does not exist.*

You're still you, he told his reflection.

He wondered what name Sandy and Jasper would have chosen for him. Had Sandy even thought of her baby in terms of a name? After all, she had planned to get rid of him. How could a mother do that?

He frowned. How could he carry on calling Rona and Bill, Mum and Dad? They were the foundation upon which he'd built his life, his history. The past was supposed to be the one certainty. It had happened. It was recorded. Written about. But the future was guesswork.

His past, it was all a lie. They were the people who'd raised him—but they weren't his flesh and blood. They were strangers, like his reflection. His captors. It was a strong word, yet truthful. They were kidnappers—nice ones—but kidnappers all the same. As he stared at himself, letting those thoughts wash over him, he felt a strong sense of guilt. It didn't feel right to think of them, his mum and dad in such a harsh way. They'd loved him. He loved them. That had to count.

He wished he could stop loving them. Somehow it didn't feel right. *Why am I so mixed up? I'm like the sea. One minute a millpond of calm, the next, choppy waves are crashing.*

He looked deep into the reflection of his eyes.

Who am I?

There is no I.

Then his gaze fell to his shoulders. This is how people have always seen me. *I'm not Toby. I am a victim of thalidomide. That's how I will be remembered in years to come. The boy with the short arms. My handicap will define my life.*

A doctor had taken one look at him and decided that he wasn't going to live. A snap decision that changed everything. He'd decided that only the fittest would survive. He'd played God.

Rona had taken him because of, and despite, his handicap. She'd seen beyond his shortened arms, had wanted him to live. Had put her faith in him. If she hadn't taken him, would he have died?

The idea of his own death sent a chill through his body. The concept of no him. No Toby.

Surely, they would have been happier with a child of their own. They took him out of sheer desperation because Rona couldn't conceive. He gave them the chance to be parents. A chance they wouldn't have had.

Did it matter if you didn't have kids? He wondered why it was so important to people.

'Do you want egg?' Bill shouted from the bottom of the stairs, breaking his thoughts. 'You better hurry up and get down here, they'll be round soon.'

Toby stepped onto the landing. 'Not hungry.' He pictured Bill, tea-towel slung over his shoulder, the egg boiled and steaming in his hand, water dripping through his fingers. His dad loved weekend cooked breakfasts and the kitchen was always left in a tip afterwards: eggshells on the worktop, frying pan soaking on the floor—of all places.

'You've gotta eat,' he shouted. He was in one of his stressy moods.

'Not hungry.'

'Great. I've boiled three. I'll have to eat them all then.'

Bill was cutting it fine, cooking so late.

'Can you get down here and help me tidy up?'

Toby headed down the stairs. 'It's only Jasper and Sandy coming.'

'Stop arguing. Just look around you, see what needs doing. It will be the first time that Sandy's come round. She'll think we're right messy buggers,' he snapped.

Toby didn't care what the cottage looked like. Bill was buzzing around plumping cushions, lugging the Hoover out from the under-stairs cupboard, gathering up dirty cups and lobbing them into the sink. He just wanted their visit to be over.

Something hard slammed into him. He was about to see his parents and baby sister.

Half an hour later and with the cottage tidier, Toby heard a car pull up, doors slam, voices, then a knock at the door.

'Don't just stare at the door, open it,' Bill said in a jumpy voice. 'Oh bugger, where are my shoes?' Bill spun round jerkily. Toby glanced at his dad's bare feet, then noticed egg on his t-shirt. What an embarrassment.

After opening the door with his toes, he stood back to let them in. The air became thick sludge, his head foggy. Awkward, majorly.

A waft of Sandy's perfume tickled his nose. Flowery and pungent.

Seeing them here, it was the weirdest feeling in the whole world. A feeling he couldn't describe. What was he supposed to say?

Jasper was his usual self. Relaxed, charming. 'Packet of bickies,' he said, putting them on the table. 'All right, sunshine?' He ruffled Toby's hair. How could he be this casual, after yesterday's bombshell?

'I'll put kettle on,' Bill said awkwardly, turning and promptly knocking into the coffee table. 'Ouch.' He darted off rubbing his calf, while Toby watched Sandy lift the baby from the carrycot. He wished he could escape to the kitchen too.

Jasper put his hands on Toby's shoulders and looked into his eyes. 'I'm so sorry, Toby. It was wrong to keep it from you. We can't change what happened.' He took his hands away and glanced at Sandy.

'I didn't lie to you, Toby. I didn't know. Not till last night.' Sandy's face was sad and as she spoke, her gaze fell to his arms. He saw it then—a wall of guilt behind her watery eyes. His life was the result of her actions. She'd swallowed the pills.

She wasn't to blame. He felt compelled to reach out, tell her this, but she'd always been cold towards him, he'd always been aware that she'd resented all the times he'd spent with Jasper. There was a barrier between them. An air of unreality about the situation. This sexy woman who always had the effect of making him blush—she'd given birth to him. His mother. A flush of adrenaline tingled through his body. He felt hot. Sick. This—it wasn't right. He was cringing inside, just wanted to hide in his bedroom.

'We had to keep it a secret,' Jasper said. 'But we love you, Toby, we all do.'

Toby stood rigid. Didn't know how to respond. Out of the corner of his eye, he saw Bill making tea, whistling to himself like he did every day of the week. Toby realised it was all too much for his dad; he couldn't handle it and it was easier to keep out of the way. The only way he could cope. What did he imagine would happen? He wasn't about to move in with them, start a new life. That was never going to happen, he wouldn't want that.

'Are you *really* my parents?' He looked at each of them in turn. Felt wobbly on his feet. Sandy had settled herself on the sofa, the baby in her arms. Jasper was still standing.

'Yes, yes we are,' Jasper said with a broad smile, his eyes shining.

The lights blinked on in Toby's head. This was real but it was freaking him out. 'I don't know who I am anymore.' His voice broke and unable to hold the tears back he flopped on the chair opposite Sandy, looking down at the carpet through misty eyes.

Jasper went over and knelt beside him. 'It's okay. It's a massive shock for you.'

Choked up, he looked across at the baby and gulped. 'I've got a sister.'

'Yes.' Sandy smiled at him. 'Yes, you have. Do you want to hold her?'

'I don't know how to hold a baby.'

'It's okay,' Sandy said, getting up and bringing Angela to him. 'Sit right back, take your shoes off and put your feet up on the settee. I'll put her in your lap for a few moments so that you can have a good look at her.' Sandy lowered the baby onto his lap and knelt close by, her hand ready to stop Angela from rolling off. She looked so cute, wrapped in a shawl and underneath, it looked as if she was dressed in a nightie. She gurgled, white foam frothing around her mouth, and opened her eyes. 'I think she looks like you, Toby.'

'Does she?'

Toby glanced at Jasper, who wasn't passing comment.

'She's so tiny. Little hands.' He wished he could touch them, play with her fingers. But for him, that wasn't easy.

Bill had crept into the room and was standing quietly against the wall. He wondered what had happened to the tea.

'All babies look like Winston Churchill,' Bill laughed.

'Where's the tea?' Toby asked. He wished his dad would stay out of the way. He didn't want him to hear the questions Toby intended to fire at Jasper and Sandy.

Bill went back into the kitchen and there was a clink of crockery and the clatter of a tray. Toby couldn't find the right words, had to be quick before he returned.

He glanced at Sandy, uncomfortably. 'You didn't want me. You were going to give me away.' As soon as the words were out, they felt wrong. He'd overstepped an invisible border. But it had to be said.

Jasper lifted Angela from his lap and gave her back to Sandy before he sat down himself.

'I was young, Toby.' Her voice was gentle.

'How old were you?'

'Nineteen.'

'That's not young.'

'Jasper and I weren't together. I couldn't bring you up on my own.'

'Why not?' Such feeble answers.

Sandy stood up to jiggle the baby. She frowned, shrugged. 'I did what I had to do. It's hard for you to understand. You're still young.'

'Imagine giving Angela away,' he blurted in a sarcastic tone. He glared at Sandy, then at Jasper. Looking shocked, Sandy sat down again.

Bill came in with the tea tray setting cups on the table, making a fuss of asking who had milk, sugar, who wanted a biscuit, cake. Toby wanted him to shut up. He hated this about his dad. Always loud. Tactless. Interrupting conversations at critical moments with questions about food or drink. He preferred it when he'd kept out of the way in the kitchen, but now he was part of this agonising discussion.

'Different circumstances,' Bill said.

'Wasn't asking you.' Toby scowled at his dad. His emotions were flip-flopping all over the place. He couldn't control how he felt, towards any of them. Love, anger, bitterness, annoyance.

'It's a fair point, Toby,' Jasper said, rubbing his chin. 'You're an intelligent boy. It's natural you're angry. This *is* a really big deal.'

Jasper had no right to tell him how he felt. 'Not angry. You didn't want me. You won't admit it. None of you will. It's just a load of excuses. I'm not stupid. I'm not a little kid that you can fob off.'

'We know you're not,' Sandy said, taking a sip of the cup of tea that Bill had handed her.

'My mum and dad wanted me.' Toby's voice was ragged. 'My mum was the best. You never met her; you wouldn't know.' A tear trickled down his face. 'I miss her.' His bottom lip wobbled. If only his mum was here now, she'd know what to do. Her arm would be around him. She'd make it all right.

'And you're a credit to her,' Sandy said, putting her tea down and retrieving a bottle from her bag for the baby's feed. 'When I was pregnant with you, I had no idea you were handicapped. That wasn't the reason I was planning your adoption.'

Toby shrugged, looked over at Jasper. 'You lied to me. When that bloke from work thought I was your son, you should have told me then. You denied having photos of yourself when you were young. I found a photo of you, that day you asked me to look after the dog.'

Jasper looked surprised. 'I didn't enjoy lying to you.'

'Grown-ups are always telling kids they mustn't lie, but they do it themselves. You're supposed to set an example.' Toby sniffed. It was the truth. He felt better for having said it.

Sandy raised her eyebrows in Jasper's direction. He'd lied to her too. The tension between them, it looked as if they'd argued.

'It's my fault.' His dad, leaning against the wall, put his hands to his face and let out a big sigh before stepping forward and resting his hands on the back of the settee. 'All of this, it's my bloody fault.'

'I'm to blame too,' Jasper said. 'The lad's right. We should have been honest.'

'Yes, well, hindsight's a great thing isn't it, Jasper?' Sandy said, straightening her back.

'I begged Jasper to keep it a secret.' Bill's face was flushed as he looked at Sandy.

'And he was too weak to stand up to you. To tell you it wasn't right to keep it from me.'

'And me,' Toby said in a quiet voice. This was his life they were discussing. He was a child and all they were bothered about was protecting each other.

'We've been over all this, Sandy. I know I should have told you.'

'Is it just me, Toby, how could we have been so stupid not to see?' She put her hands out.

'See what?' Jasper replied.

'He's a copy of you.'

'People see what they want to see. Strangers were always commenting that Toby looked like Rona. They weren't to know. Something to do with the shape of their eyes. Couldn't see it myself but it made Rona happy.'

'Who was it you said I looked like?' Toby laughed. This was like sitting through a bad village play if it wasn't so painful. 'Aunt Maud?' He glanced at his dad who was just about holding himself together with considerable effort.

'I'm sorry, it was a stupid thing to say.'

'You must have really laughed behind my back, coming out with that corker.'

'I didn't know what to say. You caught me off guard and I would never laugh behind your back.'

Toby fidgeted in his chair. 'How can I believe anything after this?'

Jasper looked at him. 'There's no such thing as a perfect parent, Toby. Or a perfect adult. We try our best. It's not only children who grow and learn. Parents do too. We're all damaged goods. Products of our own messed up childhoods.'

'I don't know what you're on about,' Toby said dismissively. 'Adults are always telling kids not to lie. You should practise what you preach.'

'I agree, Toby,' Sandy said, glancing at Jasper. 'How difficult can it be?' Her face looked pained. Did she want the chance to get to know him better, did she feel anything for him?

'What else don't I know about?' He looked at each of them in turn but all three had blank expressions on their faces.

There was more to this. They were about to tell him something much worse, as if this wasn't bad enough. Breathless, he couldn't take any more, had to get out of the house, be on his own. He rose, made a dash for the front door and out into the fresh air. There was no way back from this. His life, it felt as if it was collapsing.

'Toby, come back, it's going to rain soon,' Bill shouted after him, but he didn't glance back. What harm could a drop of rain do when he had three grown-ups lying to him? Feet pounding the lane, he was powered by the twin engines of resentment and bitterness. He veered off the lane and into the wood, crashing through the bracken and nettles. He didn't stop running until he found a clearing and collapsed beside a tree. Broken, lost, he stared up at the bruised sky, catching his breath. It looked as if the heavens would split. To be in a wood, wet, alone, what did it matter? His nausea ripened into a darkness he dared not consider.

At least out here there was a sense of peace, silence, apart from the sounds of nature. Space in his head to think. No adults, no voices. No more of their excuses.

The sky trembled with thunder. His body vibrated with it. Sporadic drops of rain hit his shoulders, then harder and faster until he was soaked through, his denim jeans clinging to him.

Amidst the twisted foliage and silver birches, he could've sworn he heard his name on the wind. It was a strange sensation, as if the branches were calling out to him. But it was just his overactive imagination.

He rose and started running again, adrenaline spiking his veins and on towards the school, seeking shelter from the deluge. Damp seeped into his canvas shoes, deep cuts of sorrow inflaming his chest. In this baptism of rain, he thought: *God is angry too. God hates liars.*

He found shelter under the canopy of the school's entrance. The water poured off his shoulders, trickled down his neck. *The past will define me forever. I am my past. And whatever I do, it will keep pushing its way in, ugly and unwelcome.*

The purr of an engine cutting through his thoughts made him look up.

Jasper got out of the driver's seat and rushed over. 'Come on, Toby, get in the car. Being out in the rain isn't going to help.'

He lingered in the porch for a couple of minutes. To think he'd trusted Jasper. Admired him. Just because he had a good job, earned lots of money, didn't make him a clever man or better than Bill, and yet that was what he'd come to think. Toby felt ashamed of himself. He didn't want to get in Jasper's car. Ever again.

'No. I'll walk back in a minute, it's not far.'

'Suit yourself.' Jasper lingered, his head dipped against the rain. Brushing water from his head, he dived back into the car and was off.

A few moments later, the car was back. This time Sandy was

driving. From inside the car she beckoned him to get in. He couldn't stay out forever; at some point he'd have to return. He caved in, dashed over, and got in the car.

'I don't want to go home. No yet.'

'I know, pet.'

He cringed beneath the weight of her words. Since when had she started calling him pet? What was she hoping—to cosy up to him, pretend to be Mummy? They were nothing to each other.

'But you need to get into some dry clothes.' The rain had stopped, and the sun was peeking through the clouds. 'Bill's taking Jasper and Angela home. The cottage will be empty. How about you run in, get changed and I'll take you for a milkshake in the Wimpy?'

39

Was this how it was going to be? Sandy going the extra mile to try to get to know him. It was a bit late now. And they had nothing in common. This was awkward. How would he drink his favourite milkshake sitting opposite her, their conversation strained and stilted? But he found himself agreeing to the idea and half an hour later they were sitting on red seats facing one another, the pandemonium of breakfast over, the waiters looking frazzled, hot oil hissing from behind the counter. He knew enough about Sandy to know that out of preference she would have chosen the Lyons Corner House or a sedate café in a department store to the Wimpy. It seemed a bit downmarket for the likes of her.

'Look at you,' she beamed. 'This is surreal. So hard to believe you're alive.' Her eyes were watering.

'Yep, I'm alive, last time I looked in the mirror.'

'I thought we should talk alone, away from them,' she said after her first sip of tea. Strands of loose hair were falling around her face and she pushed them behind her ears with smooth fingers in that sexy way of hers. He looked away, frightened in case his face gave his thoughts away. It was obscene. She was his mother. He'd have to stop thinking about her in that way.

'I just wanted to explain, help you to understand better what I was going through.' Her voice was softer than her usual tone. 'It was hard to accept I was pregnant. I tried to convince myself I wasn't.'

Toby stared at his strawberry milkshake then looked up at her. 'You didn't want me,' he muttered after his first sip.

'Pregnancy was the worst thing I could have done as a teen, short of killing someone. My parents were appalled.'

The word *appalled* hit him as if he'd been struck, and he felt himself begin to well up.

'I'd let them down and this needed dealing with. If I agreed to give you up, I could stay at home. Either that or be thrown out. Simple as. Things were different back then.'

Toby felt sick. 'I needed *dealing* with?' Something inside him collapsed. This was awful.

'No.' He saw a shadow move across her face. 'Poor choice of words, I'm sorry.' She reached out and stroked his face.

It was as if a bolt of electricity had jolted through him. Shocked, he quickly sat further back in his seat so that she couldn't touch him again. He didn't want her touching him. Not now, not ever.

He saw the panic in her eyes. 'Don't shut me down, Toby. I'm not heartless.' She made a despairing gesture with her hands.

'Did anyone other than your parents know you were pregnant?'

She shook her head and frowned. 'God, no. Unmarried mothers were shamed into hiding their pregnancy.'

'Why?'

'That's how it was. I was made to feel guilty. They wanted it kept a secret. So that they could get on with their lives.'

'What happened?' he asked, nudging his glass away from him.

'They shunted me off to a hotel in Brighton, then a mother and baby home. And after I'd had you there was no time to grieve, or dwell. I was expected to pretend it never happened.' She stared, unseeing, into the distance as if he wasn't in the room, caught in her private thoughts.

He wanted to ask what she was thinking, but it wasn't his place. It was way too awkward. He tried to speak but was finding it hard to swallow and all that came out was a little gasping sound.

'I'm sorry if I come across as cold, but there was no time to be sentimental. Life moved on. I was back at work within weeks.'

'You took the easy way out, planning to have me adopted.' He sniffed.

'Adoption doesn't mean you don't love your baby.' She reached out again and tried to touch him, but he was too far away. 'I wanted to give you the best chance. The best life.'

'I could have been adopted by horrible parents.'

'It was the right decision. Life would have been very stressful.'

Stung by her words, he said, 'All babies are stressful. Angela included. You had a life growing inside you.'

'You're a wise kid, Toby.'

He couldn't look at her. Her patronising comment grated on him.

'I couldn't think like that. I was being practical,' she added. 'Do you know what the worse thing was?'

He wasn't sure he wanted to know. Just wanted to escape, be alone.

'I was told you'd died, but never got to hold you. I always wondered what that would have been like, felt like. I wondered how heavy you would have been in my arms. What you looked like, smelt like.'

'Powder and puke, I expect.' Toby smiled for the first time, even though he still didn't feel relaxed. 'I can't believe Jasper didn't tell you the truth. What are you going to do?' Toby was curious.

She picked up her spoon and absentmindedly stirred her remaining tea, as if needing to do this to think.

'I suppose I have a choice,' she said wearily and unconvincingly. 'To focus on what's tearing us apart, or what's holding us together. There's a lot to work through.' She smiled at him, but it was a strained smile with the weight of worry behind it.

'I don't want to ever get married.' And he meant it.

'You're young, you'll change your mind.' Her smile was softer this time.

'I'll never replace your mum, I wouldn't try to, but our door is always open. Come round whenever you want to. Nothing changes, Toby.'

He didn't doubt it, but for now it all felt too weird. He kept thinking he'd wake up and find it had all been a bad dream.

40

Several days later Jasper arranged a meeting with Vince at his Fleet Street office. Greeting him in reception, Jasper ushered him into a lift which carried them to the fifth floor.

The offices had recently been renovated to give them a modern, stylish feel. The brick walls adjoining the corridor had been replaced with half wood, half glass panelling. Although there was complete privacy for phone calls, anybody could glance in and see who Jasper was interviewing. This hadn't presented a problem—until now. Sod's law, Ronny would wander by and spot his brother. Jasper deliberately offered Vince the orange bucket chair so that he would be seated with his back to the corridor. For now, it was best that Ronny didn't know what was going on. He could have taken this scoop himself, written a great report but his pig-headed attitude had stopped him. Jasper dreaded to think what had happened in their childhood to make the two brothers hate each other so much, but it was clear they weren't on good terms.

After making a phone call to his secretary for coffee, Jasper took out a notebook and pen and began firing questions.

'Let's start at the beginning. How long did you work at the hospital?'

'Fifteen years.' Vince crossed his legs and adjusted himself in the chair.

'If it was so awful, why didn't you just leave?'

'Jobs aren't always easy to come by. It was convenient, I guess. Why is this relevant?'

Jasper ignored him and carried on. It was completely relevant. If it was so bad there, surely, he would have left? 'What you told me the other night was deeply disturbing. The bodies of hundreds of aborted, miscarried and deformed foetuses were incinerated with clinical waste?'

'That's right. And some of that waste was used to heat the hospital. Keep the lights on.'

'It's totally unacceptable.'

'A gross disrespect for life.' Vince shook his head. 'The main point is that the parents weren't consulted. They weren't asked what they wanted to happen to the remains. Mothers were told they were being cremated, but in fact they were incinerated. I know.' He banged his chest. 'Because it was my job to deal with the waste. Human waste mixed in with medical crap—scrubs, needles, plastic gloves, masks, contaminated bedding. You name it, it all went in.'

'It sounds like a total lack of transparency. The parents were misled.'

'It was horrific, on a genocidal level.'

'Good words.' Jasper saw the headlines. 'You mentioned thalidomide babies.'

'I assume you know the figures. Around forty percent of thalidomide-damaged babies died at birth or before birth. Many were seriously deformed. Work it out. Their remains were incinerated too. As if the mothers hadn't suffered enough.'

'I'm going to have to run this past my editor. He's the

commander-in-chief charged with controlling the entire war effort here.'

'Of course, but Ronny told me that Sam, your editor, is big muckers with the hospital chief, so is he going to want this story buried?'

'We'll see. It depends on what other stories he wants to prioritise. Sometimes it can take years for the full story to emerge on important matters, so don't expect anything immediately. But with my editor's agreement I'll investigate any leads you give me, gather the facts, speak to eyewitnesses.'

Jasper was about to ask him the names of people to contact when Ronny burst into the office.

'You.' He snarled at his brother. 'Might have known you'd come sniffing round Cooper, begging him to take your story on. He doesn't hold the power round here, I know you seem to think he does. It's up to Sam, he's the editor.'

Vince ignored him. Rising from his seat, he reached out and shook Jasper's hand. 'Good to talk to you, I'll leave you to ponder over everything.' He left the office and they watched him head towards the lift.

'I'd appreciate it if you knocked in future, Steadman.' Jasper glared at Ronny. 'If you don't mind, I'm a busy man.' He held open the door for him to leave.

JASPER BOOKED an appointment to meet with Sam, to discuss the scandal Vince had highlighted.

'Vince had to handle the remains of thalidomide-affected babies. As you know this is an area of interest to me.'

Sam sat back in his chair smoking, having listened to everything Jasper had to tell him. He didn't speak for several moments, appearing to be in deep thought, frowning and rubbing his chin.

'The thalidomide scandal was campaign journalism at its

finest, we were fearless taking on a huge corporation and after a long and bitter battle we won some pretty decent compensation for the families. But sometimes I ask myself, did we do it right, would it have been better to have kept out of the whole affair? Some of the parents found the exposure a painful experience. If we run this story, it will only cause further distress to families. Is that really what we want to do?'

'Surely you still believe in justice? Without the thalidomide campaign there might not have been compensation.'

'Vince Steadman needs to write to his MP, the Health Minister, and the hospital chief. Find out what they have to say.' He was thoughtful for a few moments. 'Prepare the groundwork, poke around a bit, but hold fire.' Another long pause. 'I'm not sure about this one. It's maybe too much for the public to stomach.'

'Okay,' Jasper said.

'In the meantime, I've been thinking of another story. It would involve more interviews. Compensation can attract gold-diggers. People look on the thalidomide children as though they're football-pool winners. The first thalidomide children were born in the late 1950s. They'll be coming of age soon, getting into relationships. Some will even be thinking of marriage. Get out there, Jasper. Find the disturbing stories of greed and envy. The children who've been attacked and kicked in the school playground. And in a few years' time, there'll be more stories. Girls marrying money-grabbing bastards who'll do a runner when the money dries up. Greedy parents stealing money from their children. It's all out there. The world is a horrible place.'

'I thought you just said we should have kept out of the whole thalidomide affair.'

Sam leaned back and looked thoughtful. 'It's something I've asked myself, but I don't know.' He rubbed his head. 'It's what we journalists do. We expose and hopefully we improve lives.'

They discussed ideas for several moments, then, fired-up and invigorated, Jasper left Sam's office to draw up a list of families to contact. It had been several years since he'd spoken to some of them, and it would be good to hear what had been happening in their lives.

As he sat at his desk, he thought about the story he wanted to write. His mind drifted and he found himself thinking about the struggles in his marriage and his relationship with Toby. One day that struggle would become a story too. But not for the public domain. It would either be a story about why he divorced or a story about how he and Sandy worked together to build a stronger marriage. He hoped it would be the latter. It was within his power to make that happen. But most of all, his story would be about his relationship with his precious son.

THE END

Thank you for reading *Every Son's Fear*. If you enjoyed the story, I would really appreciate a short review on Amazon.

Follow Joanna Warrington on Amazon: https://www.amazon.co.uk/Joanna-Warrington/e/B00RH4XPI6/

Every Son's Fear is book 3 in a series which was inspired by the thalidomide crisis of the 1960s. You will find book 1: *Every Mother's Fear* and book 2: *Every Father's Fear* on Amazon. Just follow this link: https://www.amazon.co.uk/gp/kindle/series/B084KZ8NCB?

OTHER BOOKS BY JOANNA WARRINGTON:

Don't Blame Me

My Book

When tragedy struck twenty-five years ago, Dee's world fell apart. With painful reminders all around her she flew to Australia to start a new life. Now, with her dad dying, she's needed back in England. But these are unprecedented times. It's the spring of 2020 and as Dee returns to the beautiful medieval house in rural Kent where she grew up among apple orchards and hop fields, England goes into lockdown, trapping her in the village. The person she least wanted to see has also returned, forcing her to confront the painful past and resolve matters between them.

Weaving between past and present, this emotional and absorbing family saga is about hope, resilience, and the healing power of forgiveness.

Holiday

My Book

Determined to change her sad trajectory Lyn books a surprise road trip for herself and her three children through the American Southwest and Yellowstone. Before they even get on the plane, the trip hits a major snag. An uninvited guest joins them at the airport turning their dream trip into a nightmare.

Amid the mountain vistas, secrets will be revealed and a hurtful betrayal confronted.

This book is more than an amusing family saga. It will also appeal to those interested in American scenery, history and culture. This is part of a loosely related family drama collection. Book 2 is *A Time To Reflect*

A Time To Reflect

My Book

When an aunt and her niece take an epic road trip through Massachusetts, their relationship is changed forever.

It's a trip with an eclectic mix of history, culture and scenery. Seafood shacks. Postcard-perfect lighthouses. Weather-boarded buildings. Stacks of pancakes dripping in syrup. Quaint boutiques. A living history museum showing how America's early settlers lived. Walks along the cobblestone streets of Boston, America's oldest city—the city of revolution.

Everything is going well, until a shocking family secret is revealed. In a dramatic turn of events, Ellie's father joins them and is forced to explain why he has been such an inadequate parent.

An entertaining but heartfelt journey through Massachusetts from Cape Cod to Plymouth, Salem, Marblehead, Boston and Rhode Island.

Every Family Has One

My Book

Imagine the trauma of being raped at age fourteen by the trusted parish priest in a strong 1970s Catholic community.

Then imagine the shame when you can't even tell the truth to those you love, and they banish you to Ireland to have your baby in secret.

How will poor Kathleen ever recover from her ordeal?

This is a dramatic and heartbreaking story about the joys and tests of motherhood and the power of love, friendship and family ties spanning several decades.

The Catholic Woman's Dying Wish

My Book

A dying wish. A shocking secret. A dark, destructive, and abusive relationship.

Forget hearts and flowers and happy ever afters in this quirky unconventional love story! Readers say: "A little bit Ben Elton" "a monstrous car crash of a saga."

Middle-aged Darius can't seem to hold on to the good relationships in his life. Now, he discovers a devastating truth about his family that blows away his future and forces him to revisit his painful past. Distracting himself from family problems he goes online and meets Faye, a single mum. Faye and her children are about to find out the horrors and demons lurking behind the man Faye thinks she loves.

Printed in Great Britain
by Amazon